Prai
Seneca Surrender

Seneca Surrender is a tale with true-fold characters that open up their heart, emitting real emotions. Sarah and White Thunder live up to the happenings around them and try to accept things while enduring hardships. I enjoyed their conversation, their cultures, even though separate, and how they reached out to each other. With tormented souls, they do everything to find a way to become one. The secondary characters enhance the story making it even more realistic. Karen Kay writes a story enabling the reader to feel the pain, agony, anguish, peril, and racism that goes much deeper, within the characters, of some of the people, in the story, to make this read remarkably good. She pens an outstanding extraordinary story beyond words.

Cherokee
Reviewer for Coffee Time Romance & More

Look for these titles by Karen Kay

Now Available:

Lakota Series
Lakota Surrender
Lakota Princess
Proud Wolf's Woman

Blackfoot Warriors
Gray Hawk's Lady
White Eagle's Touch
Night Thunder's Bride

Legendary Warriors
War Cloud's Passion
Lone Arrow's Pride
Soaring Eagle's Embrace
Wolf Shadow's Promise

The Warriors of the Iroquois
Black Eagle
Seneca Surrender

The Lost Clan
The Angel and the Warrior
The Spirit of the Wolf
Red Hawk's Woman
The Last Warrior

The Clan of the Wolf
The Princess and the Wolf
Brave Wolf and the Lady

Seneca Surrender

THE WARRIORS OF THE IROQUOIS

Karen Kay

PK&J Publishing
1Lakeview Trail
Danbury, CT 06811

Seneca Surrender

Print ISBN: 978-1-09079-0-439

Cover by Angela Waters

Dedication

For Michael Badnarik, author of the book *Good to be King* and stepfather of the Constitution; Mellanie K. DeLisle, for her help and assistance; and for my husband, Paul Bailey, who holds my heart.

Acknowledgements

A special thanks goes out to the following who are Karen Kay/Gen Bailey's Warriorettes. You have not only my appreciation, but my utmost respect.

Frances Miller, Cathie Morton, Janet Hughes, Diana Tidlund, Jane Squires, Sheila Lawson, Sharon Crumper, Katherine M. Kakegamic, Dena Walton, Beth Reimer, Terry Stuart, Emma L. Metz, Kristy Centeno, Catherine Abernathy, Denell Wieczorek, Melissa Keith, Amy Lytle, Raeann Williams, Arlene Jones, Marilyn Wigglesworth, Jenny Cooper, Kimberly Roulean, Katherine Edgar, Debra Guyette, Lori Barnes, June Phyllis Baker, Rebekah Elrod, Heather Bennet, Diane Dicke, Tami Bates, Melinda Elmore, Jennifer Johnson, Deanna Fullbright, Sonja Dimitrovski, Dianne Westbrook, Malana Whited, Linda Barnes, Monica M. Carter, Kathy Lynn Reed, Jean Paquin, Robin Priddy, Debbie Mercer, Tressa Thorp, Donna Bratton, Deidre Durance, Carla Corless, Lillian Gilliers, Pepper Cash, Vickie Batten, Michele Rose Sonnenberg, Kristen Waxler, Debbie Cosentino, Sarah Wendt, Tamara Miranda, Heather Wentz, Charlotte Everhart, Paula Willhoite. Recent Warriorettes: Starr Miller, Yvette Poulin, Carolyn Benton, Christine Martin

Author's Note

I would like to acknowledge the following sources of reference:

The book *White Savage* by Fintan O'Toole. It was in this book where I first learned the story of how the white race came to America, and learned more of the Condolence Ceremony.

And the book *The Code of Handsome Lake, the Seneca Prophet* by Arthur C. Parker, 1913.

Both of these books reference the story of how the white race came to America.

Also, the book *Roots of the Iroquois* by Tehanetorens. It was in this book where I learned the early history of the Iroquois.

Prologue...

The year is 1755. It is a time of unrest. Both the English and the French are battling for control of the North American continent. Both seek the support of the united and strong Iroquois Confederation. Deprivations are extant on both sides of the quarrel, the French and Indians of Canada against the English, the Mohawk and Seneca of the Americas.

As always, in any time of dissension, there are those who seek to profit from the ruin of others.

Chapter One

The Territory of the Iroquois Indians
Lake George area in upstate New York State By the Lake-That-Turns-to-Rapids
Saskekowa Moon, September 1755

There were eight enemy warriors paddling their two canoes on the lake. One canoe held four of the Ottawa warriors. The other carried two Frenchmen and two more of the Ottawa. At the sight, Sarah's stomach twisted. They were all heavily armed with guns, tomahawks, hatchets and knives, some carrying two muskets. Sarah's guide, on the other hand, possessed only one musket, a hatchet, a tomahawk and several knives. And he was only one against eight.

Sarah bit her lip and placed her arm around Marisa, a younger woman who was under Sarah's charge. Although Marisa was now full-grown, Sarah, at twenty-and-nine, was the elder by ten years. Plus, Sarah was Marisa's confidante and companion, as well as her maid. She was also Marisa's tutor, and, as far as Sarah understood it, they were best friends. So it had been for most of Marisa's life, and fourteen years of Sarah's.

"They have seen it," whispered Black Eagle.

"What?" muttered Marisa.

"The silver dish. They will come here. And when they discover it, they will find us. Go to the horses now, mount them and ride away from here. Go now! Go fast! Ride to Albany. That will be safest."

"And leave you?" Marisa said.

Black Eagle stared long and hard at Marisa, his look emanating a love so deep, it caused Sarah to sigh. In truth, for a moment she wondered if she might ever be on the receiving end of such attention from a man—one who was so deeply in love with you that he was willing to give his life to protect you.

Sarah shook her head and gazed away. She might never know. Indeed, if circumstances continued in the same vein as they had begun this day, this might very well be her last day upon this earth.

At last, Black Eagle yanked his focus away from Marisa. "Yes, you are to leave me, and at once. I will hold the enemy off for as long as I can." As he spoke, he turned his attention to his weapons, whereupon he proceeded to load his musket with powder and lead.

"Go! Now!" He waved them away.

Marisa hesitated. Then, as though compelled, she inched toward Black Eagle and laid her hand on his arm. "I cannot leave you."

Sarah would have spoken up in denial, for it was her duty to protect her charge. But she was spared the opportunity.

"You must," responded Black Eagle gently. "If you stay, you might be killed accidentally. Now, go! Both of you. Go!"

Grabbing a handful of the material of Marisa's dress, Sarah urged the woman to crawl backward with her. But Marisa broke free of Sarah's hold and again scooted close to Black Eagle. Placing her fingers over Black Eagle's hand, she massaged it tenderly before she said, "I want you to know that I love you."

He replied simply, "I know. Now, go!"

Unfortunately for Marisa, there was little more to be said. Sarah knew this, and although Sarah watched the two lovers exchange a look, she backed away, knowing that this time, Marisa followed.

The horses were already saddled. Both women were good riders, and, though Sarah offered a hand to help Marisa into her seat, Marisa waved her away. Sarah wasted no time and ran to the other mount, but had no more than placed her foot into the stirrup when Thompson appeared out of the woods, running toward them. He was a big man and unclean. Plus, despite the fact he was supposed to be their real guide, in Sarah's opinion, he was little more than a bully. Lucklessly for them, he had his sights set on Marisa and was racing toward her like a well-aimed bullet.

"Yaw!" he shouted as he ran. "Where do ye think ye are a- goin'?"

Neither Sarah nor Marisa had a chance to utter a word. In an instant, Thompson had laid siege upon them, attacking Marisa first, pulling her off her seat. Instinctively a scream formed in Sarah's throat, but more than aware of the enemy about them, she contained it. After whisking her foot out of the stirrup, she came down, landing on both feet. Immediately, she pulled two pistols from their cases on her mount, pushing the guns into the pockets of her dress, and rushed toward Marisa. Thompson held Marisa in his grip, but by sheer willpower alone, Sarah snatched her out of their tormentor's clutches.

Thompson was a persistent opponent, and, bringing up his flintlock, he focused its deadly barrel on Marisa. However, luck was on their side. His gun wasn't primed.

Both Sarah and Marisa ran for cover. After extracting one of the weapons from her pocket, Sarah handed it to Marisa, keeping the other gun for herself.

Fortunately, Thompson's shot never materialized. Perhaps the brute was well aware of the threesome's precarious situation. Mayhap he was cognizant that Black Eagle and the two women might never escape.

Whatever the reason, instead of loading the weapon and finishing his purpose, Thompson merely grinned toward the spot where the women had disappeared. Then, clutching hold of both the horses, Thompson fled back into the woods, but not before he said, "I leave ye to yer fate."

"Pray," Marisa mumbled softly. "Black Eagle was right. It was Thompson who has been the cause of our troubles."

"Yes," agreed Sarah, "so it is."

"Well, there's little we can do now. Let us return to the shore and help Black Eagle as best we can."

"Yes." But exactly what help they could be to him remained to be seen. They needed Black Eagle's protection much more than he required theirs. Still, both women bent down to hands and knees, and, pushing their skirts out of the way, they scooted back toward Black Eagle.

They found Black Eagle in the same spot where they had left him, and Sarah was quick to note that one of the canoes, the one carrying the two Frenchmen, was continuing forward on the lake. However, the enemy's other canoe—the one transporting the four Ottawa warriors—had turned to shore. Sarah glanced at Black Eagle. This was it. It was only she, Marisa and he against a well-armed enemy. What was Black Eagle thinking? Was he preparing himself mentally and physically for what was to come?

But what if the confrontation never came? After all, it was possible that the enemy might examine the silver cup that she and Marisa had mistakenly left next to the shore, the one that had obviously caught their attention, and do no more than be happy with the treasure.

Even as she thought it, Sarah knew it would not be so. These seasoned warriors were Indian. They would take witness of the tracks both she and Marisa had made when they had been washing up after their noonday meal. Indeed, with all the impressions she and Marisa had left on the shoreline, their prints would lead the Ottawa warriors to them, and neither she, Black Eagle, nor Marisa would be spared.

Meanwhile, Black Eagle was tense, alert.

"Sir Eagle," Marisa said.

Briefly, Black Eagle swung around to look at her. Obviously he had not been expecting this turn of events. He looked incredulous. "Why are you not gone?" he asked in a whisper. "I told you to leave."

"I'm sorry, sir, but we cannot do so," Marisa whispered. "I fear that Mr. Thompson overpowered us before we had even attained our seats on the horses."

"Where is Thompson now?"

"He rode away, taking the horses with him. But before he left, Sarah was able to secure these." She held up her pistol. Sarah did the same.

"Do you know how to use those weapons?" he asked her.

Sarah nodded, and Marisa whispered, "Yes."

Black Eagle ordered beneath his breath, "Both of you, move back behind me. Stay down. Fire only if you get a good shot, otherwise do no more than watch. If I go down, do not fight the enemy. Yield to them. It is doubtful that they will kill you. Do you understand? Do nothing."

Sarah and Marisa both nodded, and, following Black Eagle's orders, they each backed away.

Panic was mounting within Sarah, but oddly, now that the moment of confrontation had arrived, a strange calm came over her. She positioned herself for the best possible advantage, checked her powder, and took aim.

Meanwhile, the canoe slid silently to the shore. The warriors disembarked in the water, keeping themselves low. Slowly, quietly, they brought their canoe farther inland, anchoring it on the rocks lining the sandy bank.

Stepping onto the ground, one of the warriors bent down, examining the tracks over the rocks. Another warrior crept forward toward the bushes, where Black Eagle, Sarah and Marisa were hiding. The two other warriors were sneaking toward the item that had gained their attention—the silver dish. Black Eagle waited with what appeared to be great patience, until the warrior who was stealing in the direction of the bushes was almost upon him. Then, crying out, he jumped up, the savage attack and the element of surprise in his favor. The ploy worked, but only for a fraction of a second. Still, it was enough. Black Eagle thrust his tomahawk into the warrior's neck.

However, with the first war cry, the three other Ottawa warriors went into action. Black Eagle was ready for them. With musket in his left hand, he fired a shot toward one of them. An almost instant scream followed, and another warrior hit the ground.

Without pause, Black Eagle tore forward, launching himself toward the other two warriors. They were prepared, muskets ready.

Sarah had taken steady aim toward them. She dare not miss. She fired. It was a good shot. Another one of the warriors fell.

Unfortunately, Black Eagle hadn't waited to see if the shot made its mark. Instead, he hurled himself toward the remaining warrior. The Ottawa was ready for him and thrust out at Black Eagle with his tomahawk.

Marisa gasped, for it was a deadly joust, but Black Eagle was agile and quick. He threw himself down, turning a somersault underneath the man's arm. Coming up on the other side of the man, and with a backhand, Black Eagle rammed his tomahawk into the back of his opponent. The warrior was thrown off balance. Regaining his feet, Black Eagle finished the job. Using his hatchet, he landed a disabling blow into the warrior's arm.

Still, the Ottawa was standing. Taking hold of his tomahawk, Black Eagle dealt the man a clean blow to his chest. That finished it. The Ottawa went down.

But it seemed the ordeal wasn't over. Black Eagle was calling to the women. "Come!" He pointed toward the lake. "Do you see? Their friends have come back to investigate. Hurry to the canoe. We'll take our chances on the water."

Sarah and Marisa jumped to their feet. Springing out of the bushes, they made a line to the canoe. Luckily, the enemy had left their paddles in the dugout, and Black Eagle had set the boat out into the lake. Both women hurriedly splashed toward it.

By this time, Black Eagle was waist deep in the water and shouting, "Get in. Pick up a paddle."

Already, shots from the oncoming canoe were hitting the water around them, the barrage a deadly reminder of what was to be if they didn't escape. Sarah plopped herself into a seat and reached out to help Marisa, but her young charge needed little assistance. Marisa was more than able and ready to seat herself. Quickly, they each picked up a paddle, and, adding their assistance to Black Eagle, they set out in the water.

Without warning Thompson reappeared, splashing his way toward them. Sarah lunged toward Marisa, her fingers coming into contact with Marisa's weapon, since Sarah's pistol was useless, having just been fired.

Marisa stayed her hand. "Maybe he has come to his senses and will help us."

"I fear your heart is too kind," exclaimed Sarah over the noise of the water and the oncoming enemy. However, Sarah hesitated.

Thompson pulled himself up alongside the canoe and plopped himself into it. He even picked up a paddle. Maybe she was wrong. Amidst all the adversity, perhaps the man had changed the color of his stripes.

"Let's get out of here!" Thompson yelled, and Black Eagle didn't argue. After hoisting himself into the boat and settling his paddle into the water, Black Eagle guided the boat out into the deepest part of the lake, heading west, away from the enemy, but in the direction of a sound that had Sarah's heartbeat picking up such speed she could feel it in her throat.

It was a waterfall, and, from the noise of it, a large one. Was this their only advantage?

Perhaps it was so, for they were outnumbered. In a fight, it would be the two men against four of the enemy, two French, two Ottawa. Worse, Thompson was an obvious traitor whose actions could not be trusted. Still, now that he was back among them, it was Thompson's neck as well as their own.

"Faster!" yelled Black Eagle.

Arrows, aimed at their speeding canoe, hit the water beside them with deadly force. Marisa's paddle made contact with the lake's surface at an angle, causing her to tip dangerously out of their craft. Sarah threw down her paddle and pulled Marisa back against her with one arm while she gripped the side of the wet canoe with her other. Though her fingers slipped, Sarah held fast.

As Sarah nestled Marisa into her arms, the two women sat silently, riding out the jerks and sways of the boat.

The scent of Thompson's unwashed body assailed Sarah, causing her to wonder that a human being could emit such odor. Why was Mr. Thompson back? Though she feared it was for no good, Sarah held her tongue.

"Faster!" Black Eagle yelled again.

Behind them, the French and Ottawa kept up a steady stream of fire, the arrows landing dangerously close. The odds were against Black Eagle. It was impossible. And yet, he must escape. They all must. If they didn't get away...

How had they gotten themselves into this? Suddenly the scheme of journeying to New Hampshire to visit friends seemed a bad idea, indeed. Was it only minutes ago—perhaps no more than thirty—when Sarah and her ward had been seated beside the lake, calmly washing up after their noonday meal?

But that was when they had first caught a glimpse of the enemy. Had it not been for the silver dish they had left at the water's edge, the enemy might have passed them by. But it was not to be.

The Ottawa *had* spotted the dish. They *had* investigated. And now, because of her own error, she had taken another's life.

The killing of a human being was not an action to be entered into lightly. But, it had been kill or be killed. Ultimately for her, there was no going back now.

The sound of rushing water, of the pounding roar of the waterfall, drowned out her thoughts. She could now see the deadliness of their position. Rapids. Surely, Black Eagle wasn't thinking of braving those?

Instinctively, Sarah leaned toward the shoreline, as though by sheer inclination alone she might steer the boat in that direction. An arrow hit the water, scraping her hand. Close, much too close. Perhaps the rapids were their only means of escape, after all. Black Eagle must be thinking so, for he was steering their canoe directly toward the source of that turbulence.

Again, Sarah's heart jumped into her throat.

Meanwhile, the canoe had picked up speed, heading toward the waterfall at a deadly pace. Marisa was still leaning back into Sarah's arms, and Sarah instinctively tightened her hold on her friend. There was no changing course now. The speed of the water had them within its grip.

Sarah threw a look over her shoulder. Even now, the enemy was almost upon them.

Truly it was a test. Which would come first, the watery death on the rapids, or at the sure hand of the Ottawa's?

The velocity of the current pushed at them and thrust them one way and then the other, taking them into an ever-faster speed toward the noise that signified the end: the waterfall.

Another well-aimed arrow knocked against the canoe's lining, barely missing Sarah's shoulder. Was the enemy, too, chancing the rapids? Sarah glanced back hurriedly. No, the French and Ottawa were turning back, paddling their boat toward the southern shore of the lake. Sarah inhaled deeply, but her relief was short-lived.

Before them lay a greater danger and surely as deadly a hazard as the Ottawa.

Black Eagle struggled to turn their canoe toward the northern shoreline, away from the enemy, but the currents pulled him back.

"Damn!" Black Eagle muttered. The curse word seemed unusual coming from his lips. In all their adventures so far on the trail, Sarah had never heard him utter anything but more formal speech. She watched helplessly as Black Eagle set his paddle into the water once again, pressing to gain the opposite shoreline from their enemy. He had no more than set his course when a hidden eddy took hold of their canoe and swung it around and around.

The canoe rocked back and forth unnaturally, and Sarah, looking back over her shoulder, was startled that Thompson had come up onto his knees and was crawling forward. Reaching down, he grabbed Marisa out of Sarah's grasp.

Instinctively, Sarah tugged at Marisa, trying to keep hold of her. When that failed, she used all her strength to pummel Thompson with her fists, but he was much too big and strong, and he kept a grasp on Marisa despite all of Sarah's attempts to thwart him. It looked bad. He raised Marisa to his shoulder level and would have thrown her from the canoe, into the lethal undercurrents of the eddy, had Sarah not bitten his arm.

Thompson and Marisa screamed at the same time, but Sarah clutched at Marisa, and she fell back into the canoe, guided by Sarah's hand. But Thompson didn't give up. He grabbed hold of Marisa again.

At last, Black Eagle, who had been centering his effort in the act of saving their canoe, became aware of the fight. Throwing down his paddle, he surged back toward the skirmish to confront Thompson.

Thompson had no choice now but to let Marisa go, and the two men, fighting in an upright position, sent the boat rocking so greatly Sarah feared it would tip over and throw them all into the tumultuous water.

By the good luck of the Lord, it didn't happen. However, their fate appeared to hang on the ability of a single man, Black Eagle, to best a man who was both bigger and stronger than he. Thompson raised a knife. Black Eagle blocked Thompson's hand, thrusting the man's arm high in the air. Each struggled for supremacy. The canoe lurched precariously against the currents, and Sarah and Marisa used their energy to keep the boat afloat.

The struggle pitched the canoe out of the eddy. The forceful motion hurled the boat more furiously than ever into the rushing current, setting the canoe steadily toward the thundering sound of the rapids. Just how high was this waterfall?

The two men didn't notice, locked as they were in their own mortal struggle. Thompson launched out at Black Eagle, socking him in the jaw. The blow knocked Black Eagle backward, but he recovered easily and shot forward, catching hold of Thompson's arm and raising it again high in the air.

Both men fell down into the canoe. Thompson looked up, and Sarah was witness to the horror that came instantly onto his face. Without further pretense at the fight, Thompson let go of Black Eagle and dived over the edge of the canoe, disappearing into swirling streams of water.

Black Eagle, who was still in the throes of battle, must have briefly felt the urge to do the same—to take the conflict into the water's fatal depths. But with a quick look about him, his gaze turned to one of love as his eyes sought out Marisa.

Then, a flash of dread fell over Black Eagle's features. It was indisputable. Their boat was on a one-way path to the falls.

They were doomed.

Black Eagle knelt beside Marisa. Within his gaze was so much love and admiration that Sarah felt as though she were an intruder in something utterly private. It was as if Black Eagle were saying to Marisa, by intention alone, that were this to be his last moment on earth, he would shower her with adoration.

Marisa appeared to be of a similar frame of mind. Her stare at him matched his. Sarah glanced away, feeling again as if she were trespassing.

It couldn't last, however. Time wouldn't allow it. Black Eagle at last jerked his gaze away, and Sarah watched as he scanned the scene in front of them. Instantly, he sat up, alert.

"Take Sarah's arm," he yelled to Marisa. "Don't let go!" He got to his feet.

Marisa and Sarah exchanged a gaze and took hold of each other.

Black Eagle grasped Marisa's arm. "Don't let go of me," he ordered. "Use all your strength, both of you. Use the power within you, but don't break your grip on each other."

Marisa and Sarah nodded as their boat, caught in the currents, tipped over the edge of the falls. Both Marisa and Sarah screamed. But it wasn't over, not yet.

There was a branch Sarah hadn't noticed, a strong and sturdy part of a mighty oak tree that was extended over the falls. If Black Eagle could but reach it with his arm...

He did it. Black Eagle seized the tree limb at the same moment their canoe would have carried them past it.

The force of the motion jerked all three from the canoe, and there they hung, each one dangling from the other's grasp. Were they saved? Sarah couldn't say with certainty. She was clenching with all her might onto Marisa, who was, in turn, grasping Black Eagle's arm. But the force of the movement out of the canoe swung both the women back and forth, causing Sarah's grip to slacken.

Thank goodness Indians were conditioned to carry heavy loads, for Black Eagle kept them both close, using only one arm to do so. Then, taking advantage of their natural momentum, Black Eagle began to swing them both toward the shore. It wasn't that far away.

"Hold on!" Black Eagle shouted. "I'm going to sweep you both to shore."

Sarah slipped.

"I can't," she hollered, crying, bringing up her other hand to obtain a better grip. "I can't keep hold. It's too slippery!"

"*Nyoh*, you can. You must!"

"I'm trying to, but—"

"She's slipping away from me!" Marisa yelled.

"I've got you," Black Eagle called to her. "Keep hold. Keep hold!"

But Sarah's hands were too wet, as were Marisa's. Though Sarah tried with all her might, her grip was loosening. Black Eagle was pitching them toward shore with all due haste, but Sarah's strength was failing.

Marisa wouldn't let go. "Sarah! Keep hold!"

With a deafening scream, Sarah's grip broke, and she fell, her screams echoing over the rushing water, drowning out the sounds of the pounding weight of the falls.

The last thought she had as she swooped down into the water was that she had failed in her duty—she would not be there to chaperone Marisa and Black Eagle. Indeed, her fate now lay elsewhere.

Chapter Two

White Thunder rested his weight upon his flintlock, looking west, toward the sky, where the sun was a low, half pinkish-orange orb on the horizon, announcing its departure from the day in glorious streaks of sunlight. Shafts of light, streaming from the clouds, beamed down to the earth, looking as though heaven itself smiled kindly upon the land. And what a magnificent land it was. The birch trees were yellow, the maples red, and the oaks announced their descent into a long winter's sleep with browns, oranges and golds. The hills were alive with autumn hues, while the air was filled with the rich, musky scent of falling leaves.

It was a beautiful time of year, when the days were still warm, but the nights were cool. But it wasn't the beauty that was set off before him that had drawn him toward the lake this day. He'd been hunting, when something had called to him upon the breeze. Perhaps it was the rustle of the water that had announced that there was a subtle difference between the lake environment of yesterday and how it was today. But what?

Stepping quietly toward the lake, he squatted and set his musket onto his lap as he bent over to partake of a drink from the water's cool depths.

Instantly he sat up, alert. From out the corner of his eye he caught the movement of something, and, glancing toward it, he recognized a piece of clothing. A woman's skirt? Rising, he stepped toward it to get a better look at the thing, if only to satisfy his curiosity.

That's when he saw her. She was a white woman, blonde-haired and slim.

Was she alive?

After hauling himself onto the rock where she lay, he stepped toward her and bent to look at her. He placed his fingers against her neck, feeling for a pulse. Her body was so very cold, and he was more than a little surprised when he felt the sure sign of life within her. The pulse was weak, but it was still there.

Turning her slightly, he was intrigued by her pale beauty. Of course, being Seneca and from the Ohio Valley, he'd had opportunity to witness the unusual skin color of the white people. But it wasn't as familiar a sight to him as one might reckon.

Who was she? How had she gotten here? And what had happened to her?

Glancing in all directions, he took in the spectacular sights of the forest. Where did she belong? Who did she belong to?

There was nothing here to answer him, nothing to be seen, no other human presence to be felt. Nothing but the ever expansive rhythm of nature.

Using his right hand to brush her hair back from her face, he noted again how cold she was. However, he couldn't help but be aware of how soft her skin was, as well. Putting his fingers against her nostrils, he felt the weak intake and outflow of breath. She was alive, barely.

Did he dare take her away from here? A white woman?

He hesitated and waited. He watched. *Nyoh*, he was the only one here, the only one to settle her fate.

That decided him. If she were to live through the night, he had best take care of her. She needed warmth, nourishment and a chance to heal.

Bending at the waist, he laid his hands over her torso. Depending on the type of injury he might discover, he would either nurse her here or take her to a more protected spot. He ran his fingers gently over each of her arms, including her hands and fingers. He felt for anything broken.

He could detect nothing. Widening his range, he sent his graze over the sides of her ribs, ignoring her ample breasts. Though his scrutiny was fast, it was thorough. Were there any bruises? Was anything broken? Amazingly, he found nothing.

He continued his search down each of her legs. Surely, there must be some clue that would tell of her recent history. Perhaps she had broken her neck, or back? With an easy touch, he tested the theory, sending his fingertips down over the muscles and bone structure of her neck. Nothing. Nothing substantial to indicate a problem that would claim her life. Turning her lightly onto her side, he felt along her spinal column. Several bones were out of place, but nothing was broken. Her body seemed intact.

He frowned. Again, he wondered what had happened to her.

Was it the spirits of the water? The falls? This was a dangerous area. Had the force of the rapids claimed another victim?

But why would she have been near the falls? A white woman in the woods alone? His jaw clenched. There had to be someone close by. Glancing up and looking around again, he realized that the puzzle of her appearance would not be solved here. His examination of her had at least established one fact. She was fit to travel.

Taking her into his arms, he was more than aware that she felt light in his grasp. He stepped down off the rock. Not knowing exactly how she had come to be here, he kept his attention attuned to the environment, listening for a sign of other life, anything to indicate the presence of another in the surroundings. She was a beautiful woman. Whomever she belonged to would miss her.

Again, he could sense nothing unusual in the environment around him—not anything that would give him any idea as to what had happened.

Enough. She required care.

Gathering her in his arms, he rushed toward the security of the woods. If someone were here watching, the trees and bushes offered sanctuary. At least there he could hide himself and her, as they fled deeper into the woods. But where would he take her? He hadn't yet constructed his own shelter for the night, and it was already late in the day.

If his memory served him correctly, there was a cave nearby that might lend itself well for their purposes, provided that a bear or other animal hadn't laid claim to it. It was a quiet place, if he remembered rightly, away from the all-seeing eyes of the forest. Plus, it was little known by his own and other tribes. Long ago, his grandfather had shown it to him, indicating it might serve well if ever he were in trouble.

As White Thunder hurried toward that spot, he gazed down into the pleasing features of the woman, realizing that his curiosity about her hadn't abated. However, there would be time enough to discover who she was once they were safely sheltered. For now, he had best make haste to see if the cave were occupied or vacant.

Balancing her weight and his musket into more secure positions, he darted through the forest, disappearing into it.

***

"Wah-ha, young beauty, sleep well into the night.
The Creator shall take pity, so fear thee not.
Wah-ha, young beauty, sleep well into the night.
The Creator shall take pity, so fear thee not."

White Thunder's deep voice echoed off the walls of the cave, giving the song an eerie quality, as though it might have been a ghost instead of a man repeating the lyrics. Carefully, he sprinkled water over the woman's forehead, enough to keep her fever low but not so much as to kill it altogether.

He could almost hear his grandmother speaking to him, as if she were standing at his shoulder now, telling him what to do. What was it she had once said to him? That a fever was not always an object of fear. If kept to a minimum, a fever had the power to drive away the evil spirits from within the body.

White Thunder laid his hands on the woman's forehead, then he moved down slowly to her cheeks, on down to her neck, then one hand down each arm. He repeated the action, once, again, over and over, gently singing the song he had composed.

"Marisa!" The cry of the woman's voice was choked, barely a sob.

He placed a finger over her lips.

She squirmed beneath his touch and rocked her head back and forth. "Marisa! Beware!"

He understood her words well. Having lived among the white people for three years, White Thunder had grown used to the strange language and ways of the missionaries who had come to bring their beliefs and their God to the Seneca.

He didn't regret the time he'd spent with them, for they had taught him much about a people who seemed to be swarming the countryside. But not all the English and the French were as honest and intent as those missionaries had been. Indeed, strange were these English and French who were invading the territory of the Seneca, and, as they came, they brought their conflicts and wars with each other into Seneca country.

"Always they want something," his grandmother, Evening Song, had said to the council of sachems. White Thunder had been present, listening. "Always they ask for Seneca boys and men to fight their wars. 'Come and die for us,' they say. 'Come and die for us, and we will ensure you keep the land you have always owned.' Beware, I say. He who gives a man what is already his is not to be trusted."

Silence had followed her speech.

At last, a chief of the third party of the sachems rose to speak. "Your words are wise, Grandmother. Have you said all that you wish to say?"

Evening Song had nodded.

"*Oyendere*, good. But I will say this. Do you forget that a council was held on this matter and that the outcome has already been decided? We, of the Seneca Nation objected to siding with the English in this fight, but as is the law of the Confederate Council, the matter was referred to the Firekeepers, the Onondagas. As you well know, their decision is final.

"Let me repeat in my own words their resolution: Long it is that we have been tied to the English, even before William Johnson, who represents them, came to be a member of our Nation. As you might well know, at the time of the Firekeepers' decision, the Mohawk were already fighting the war alongside William Johnson, and, as we have been cautioned by the Peacemaker, if we of the League are to remain strong, we must be united. Besides, when have either the English or the League broken the Covenant Chain, a silver chain that was forged long ago, and which binds us to the English? Never have they broken that chain. Never have we. It ties us to them, and they to us.

"Has not William Johnson shown us how the English will debate and discuss our problems as though they were their own? And if he is our brother, are we to ignore him in his time of need?"

There was silence in the hall as the wise sachems listened and nodded their approval.

Yet, Evening Song rose again to address the council. "Have you spoken all that you wish to say?"

"I have."

"*Oyendere*, very good. Your words are true. William Johnson has done much for the Mohawk. But beware. He is English, though he presents himself as Mohawk. Now, he attempts to speak for all the people of the Six Nations and place himself as one of our wisest sachems. But William Johnson is not Seneca. He does not know our sons and daughters, and thus, not knowing, how can he provide for their needs?

"But do not think, because I say this about William Johnson, that the French are any better. Have you not noticed that whenever the French trader, Joncaire, comes to our country that he talks a crooked talk? And the English are the same. With their words, they each try to incite our people to hatred for one or the other of them. Do you not recall how, last summer, Joncaire spread stories of fear and hatred of the English? Did he not say that the English desired to kill us and take our lands? That both the French and the English were planning to attack the Six Nations and drive us from the face of this land, Turtle Island? Yet, we found these tales to be lies.

"Save for William Johnson, have not the English done the same? Overstating a half-truth so as to incite our men and women to hatred of the French? And what is it that they want, that they all say? 'Fight for us,' 'Send your best into battle for us.' I ask this about that: What is wrong with the English and the French that they cannot fight their own wars?

"Harken, ye wise sachems. He who would once lie to you about a matter will do so again. As a lion cannot change his ways of stealth, so, too, this sort of man cannot change habits. Have not our wise fathers told us that he who lies even once will always in the end revert to telling false truths? I say to you, by the truth or not of his words, we can know him, and so knowing, can disgrace him for the rest of his life.

"This is how it should be. Are we then to send our sons and husbands to fight the wars of liars? I say no. I am against this."

Strong words. True words. Words that had influenced White Thunder—though, as a youth, he had sought the ways of war.

But long ago, he had determined to ignore the French and English war and all its influence on his people. He had to. Indeed, he would go about his life as he always had. Besides, it was his opinion that it mattered little who won this conflict, since both the English and the French had their eye on the same objective: taking control of the country…Indian country.

Though once a warrior of repute, White Thunder knew he would never again go to war. There was the matter of his oath to consider, his duty and pledge to Wild Mint, she who had been his wife. It had happened so long ago…yet, in many ways, it might as well have occurred yesterday….

***

White Thunder knelt next to Wild Mint. Her breathing was strained, coming in short gasps. Tears streamed down White Thunder's face as he watched her, wished it were he, not she, who had been in the village to confront the enemy. He had faced death many times—it was an expected trait of a Seneca warrior—but never had he thought he would bear witness to Wild Mint's death. Picking up her bloodied hand and bringing it to his face, he cried into it.

"Who did this to you?" White Thunder had been away from the village when the raid had happened. He had been hunting.

"An evil man." She coughed, the action bringing up blood that spilled down over her chin. Gently, he wiped it from her face.

She was dying. He knew it. She knew it. Worse, there was nothing to be done. Their baby had been cut from her body, leaving their child, in its eighth month, dead…and Wild Mint would soon cross over, as well.

Who would commit a murder so wicked?

It was not that he was unaware of torture. Many tribes—his own included—persecuted prisoners who had been caught in war.

But this rarely extended to women, and never to an unborn child. Most tribes prized the gift of a woman prisoner, particularly one with child. Didn't they desire the prisoners as replacements for those loved ones lost in war? Didn't his people usually treat the prisoners well, making them so much a part of the tribe that often, even when a former prisoner had the chance to return, he or she didn't?

"Find him," Wild Mint managed to say. "Do not spare him."

"I will find him and I will kill him," promised White Thunder, and he meant every word. If need be, he would spend his life fulfilling that oath.

"I cannot rest 'til it is done," she choked out. "My blood, the blood of our child, is on his hands. Find him. Seek revenge, but kill no other in his place. He, alone, must pay. I will wait...." She coughed again and took a deep breath, which rattled deeply in her throat. In an instant, she was gone.

"I will kill him," vowed White Thunder. "I will."

Tears fell down White Thunder's face as he cried openly, unashamed of the emotion. He loved Wild Mint, had loved her since they were children. In truth, it seemed as though he had loved her all his life, for he could not remember a time when had hadn't admired her. He would find this man who had done this to her and to his unborn child. He would find him, and he would exact his revenge, as was his right.

Yet, this matter, sworn to so easily, had not proved a simple task. Though White Thunder had spent fifteen long years searching for this man, his duty to Wild Mint remained unfulfilled.

It should have been easy, since there had been survivors who could bear witness. He knew for instance that the attacking party had been Huron. He knew also that little more than fifty men had made that raid. Under normal circumstances, he would have found the murderer and quickly brought about the well-deserved justice.

But it was not to be.

No one fit the description of this man as given to him by the survivors; no Huron seemed to know who this man was, even when the deed was described in detail. And although the Huron might lie to him about this thing, it had proved to be true. Worse, White Thunder had no other option but to find and execute this exact man. He could not kill another Huron in the murderer's place, a remedy often sought by the Seneca. By his oath, only this one person must pay for the crimes committed. Wild Mint would not rest until this was accomplished.

And so he searched. It had proved to be a lonely business. So many villages scrutinized, even those that were not Huron. So many people questioned, so many disappointments. Yet, in all this time, with so much investigation, White Thunder was no closer to finding the culprit than he had been at the beginning of his quest, except for one fact. Recently, he had discovered that the raiders had been Huron *and French.*

Was the murderer a Frenchman? To satisfy this new discovery, White Thunder had journeyed to the north, seeking out the villages of Quebec and Montreal. It had been a long trip, an intense search. But it had ended in the same way as all the others, with nothing to show for his efforts but the passage of time.

He was only now returning from that quest.

"No, do not leave me. Do not go in there!" The delicate woman with soft ringlets of yellow hair sat up all at once. Her eyes were wide, yet unseeing. "Mother! Stay with me! Do not leave me!"

White Thunder enfolded the woman in his arms and simply held her. Bending his head toward her, he endeavored to take her pain upon himself. But it was not possible. Her misery came from something he knew not of. Still, he tried.

"Mother! No! Don't go! Stay with me!"

Her tears fell to his shoulder, and, in reaction, his stomach fell. Empathy for her flowed through him, and yet another thing was happening to him. Though he knew he shouldn't feel as he did, he gloried in the warmth of having a woman in his arms. She was soft, she was sweet, and her scent was delicately feminine, a heady perfume for an unattached male. He had forgotten the pleasure of holding a woman so closely. Her hair was fragrant now with the aroma of the smoke from their fire and the herbs he had used to rub into her scalp. The one injury had been the only scrape he could find upon her. Luckily, the abrasion was little more than a finger-long scratch.

Its discovery had caused him to wonder again what had happened to bring this woman to the brink of death.

One fact was certain: Duty to his beloved, which was keeping him celibate, was not a sound frame of mind for a healthy male.

"No! Not my mother, not my father! No, it cannot be!"

Her pain sent shivers up and down his spine. This woman had known real torment. It was in her voice, in her words. The knowledge drew him closer to her, and, as her tears became more profound, he rocked back and forth, his arms wrapped firmly around her.

There was nothing for him to say. Instead, he held her until the last of her tears became a mere hiccup. Even then, he didn't release her.

Tentatively, he massaged her spine. It wasn't until her breathing was free and her eyes were once again closed that he laid her back against his blanket. Beneath it were fragrant, cushy boughs of pine branches, enough so that her body did not repose upon the hard floor of the cave.

Quietly, he exhaled. He didn't want to admit it, but he was drawn to her. Or, perhaps it was simply that he hadn't held a flesh-and-blood woman in his arms for too many years.

With a deep sigh, he realized there was yet work to be done. The fire needed stoking, and, if he were to nurse this woman back to complete health, additional sustenance had to be found at once. While his meager diet of dried meat, corn and berries might satisfy him, she would require the healing properties of fresh meat to restore her vigor, and it had best be in a liquid form since she was not conscious enough to eat on her own.

Dutifully, he rose to begin the work that must be done, though he couldn't help but wish for his grandmother's presence beside him, speaking words of wisdom to him. An herbalist, she would have known the exact plants and foods that would bring this woman back to health. Unfortunately, White Thunder's skills in this realm were rudimentary, for he had never harbored an interest in learning the craft.

"No! Do not ever touch me again! My body is my own! Get back away from me!"

White Thunder fell to his knees beside the woman, taking her in his arms to give comfort.

"I will repay my parents' debt to you, but I swear it shall not be in this manner!"

Her words made White Thunder want to weep, for he did not misunderstand. Did the Englishmen misuse their own kind?

As the woman's tears fell, White Thunder found that his grief, though of fifteen years in length, mingled with hers.

"No! No!"

Gently, he rocked her, until at last her fears quieted.

Even though White Thunder would never act on such an impulse, his body was ready and willing for the ultimate action between a man and a woman. The reaction surprised him. It also caused him to consider a truth: Man lives best with a flesh-and-blood woman, not her mere image. And when absent...

He breathed in deeply, loving the fragrance of the English woman's hair. He had best not like it too readily, however. Until Wild Mint's murderer was found and justice served at last, there could be no other woman in his life.

Perhaps, like the white man's double-edged knife, this was a test of him, of his strength and devotion, for, no matter which way the knife was thrust, it cut.

But enough. The woman in his arms needed special sustenance and attention. He would give her both.

Chapter Three

The delicious aroma of meat and vegetables awakened her.

Was that a soup she smelled?

She opened her eyes and looked up at the dark ceiling of… Were those stalactites hanging from the ceiling above her?

She narrowed her eyes so as to obtain a better look at them. And if these massive columns were stalactites, what were they doing here in a bedroom? Weren't these icicle-like projections of rock normally found in caves and caverns? She was in a bedroom—wasn't she?

Carefully, slowly, she took in the dark terrain of her surroundings. Except for the dim light of a flickering fire at her feet, she was surrounded by a murkiness so dense it was like staring into the starless black of night. There was a chill in the air, though luckily, the warmth from the fire presented her with a means to keep in her body heat. Was it raining outside? If so, that would explain the sound of dripping water that seemed to come from somewhere close by to her. Was she in a cave?

And if she were in a cave, *why* was she here? She searched her memory. Unfortunately she could recall only rudimentary details, but that didn't include her name….

Closing her eyes, she endeavored to remember what had happened. But there was nothing there to present itself to her, no memory, nothing to answer her questions.

Returning her attention to the environment, she discovered a feeling of warmth beneath her, like the flannel of a blanket, and there was some indefinable softness wrapped around her. Miserably, she became aware of her situation. She was naked beneath this blanket.

Where was this place? Why was she naked? What had happened to her?

A tantalizing scent of pine added its fragrance to the aroma of food, and she wondered at its source until she moved slightly and discovered she was sleeping atop pine boughs. She was definitely not in a bedroom.

She exhaled and slowly moved her head so as to take in more of the features of her surroundings. Perhaps if she could see a little bit of it, she might recall what had happened to her and why she was here. Her name would be a good place to start.

Turning to the right, there was little for her to see except the blackness penetrating this place. However, in the flickering light off the cave wall, she made out the silhouette of a man. Firelight seemed to paint his shadowy image in glimmering flashes of light and dark.

She could tell very little about him, save that he appeared to be as big as a bear. If she shifted just so—not so much as to draw his attention, but enough to look toward the fire—she could see him in the flesh.

For a long moment, she studied him. Then, she lay back.

He wasn't so big after all, although he did look to be tall— perhaps six foot or more. Only a side image of him was turned toward her, but it was enough for her to realize that he was an Indian. Odd that she should know that detail about him, but not remember her own name.

Except for a section of longer hair styled atop his head, he wore his hair clipped close to the head, much like the Mohawk did. However, a section of his mane was allowed to grow to great lengths in back, and tied to this longish hair were what appeared to be eagle feathers.

Her gaze ranged down over his body, and she noted that, excluding several tattoos covering his arm, his chest and that arm were bare. He wore necklaces of stones and beads, and the ever-present breechcloth that the Indian male seemed to favor was tied around his waist. A red cloth sash was fashioned around his slim waist, and leggings that came up high on his legs outlined the muscles of his thighs. Undecorated moccasins covered his feet.

Was the man a Mohawk warrior? Perhaps. But she knew there were six tribes that made up the Iroquois Nation, though how she knew this when she couldn't recall who she was, was not quite clear. However, she decided this man might originate from a different one of the tribes that made up the Iroquois Nation, since his hairstyle mimicked the Mohawk, but was not exactly the same.

Hopefully, he was not Ottawa.

She frowned. Why would she hope he was not Ottawa?

Again, she tried to concentrate. But her mind drew nothing but blanks.

The man was handsome, and she allowed herself several more glimpses, admiring the clean look of bare chest and that strange mixture of short and long hair. Odd, too, that she wasn't afraid of him.

Shouldn't she be?

It did strike her as peculiar that a man so muscular, so incredibly male and so obviously fit for manly tasks was at work over a fire, doing chores considered feminine. He was cooking a meal. Despite herself, his image made her smile.

But why should she smile? She was naked beneath this blanket and couldn't remember the most elementary things about her life. Logic, alone, would dictate she should be afraid.

But she wasn't.

Did she know this man? Was that why she wasn't frightened? Frustrated, she let out a soft moan and returned to her assessment.

He was young, perhaps younger than she. There was also something about him that stirred her curiosity. His demeanor was very sexual, although why she should think so, she didn't understand, unless...perhaps he was her husband? Or maybe it was his attire—or lack thereof—that caused the consideration.

Unfortunately, that thought had the effect of reminding her that she was scantily dressed. Had this man taken advantage of her? Now came the fear, and a sensation of vulnerability swept over her.

Who was this man? Who was she?

Wretchedly, she realized there was nothing else for it but to find out what was going on. After chasing the knot that had collected in her throat, she asked, "Excuse me, sir, but have I had an accident?"

The man looked up from his work, and, turning his head, he glanced at her. "You are awake, at last."

He spoke English. She frowned at the thought, marveling again at how much she knew without knowing. However, he hadn't answered her question, and she tried again. "Yes, sir, I am. But please, I beg you to tell me, have I had an accident?"

"You have," he said simply.

"Do you know what happened? And if you do, sir, could you please relate it to me?"

"I do not know exactly what happened to you. I was hoping you might be able to explain the story to me."

"Oh." Gazing quietly toward her hands, she found them nervously clutching her blanket. Their color was pale, at least when compared to the sight of this man's hands, which were brown. Perhaps her next question wasn't the right query to ask, given their circumstances, but she couldn't help herself as she probed, "Sir, are you my husband?"

He hesitated as he scanned her features. "I am not," he said at length.

She took in his reply with some bit of shock, more than aware of her state of undress beneath the blanket. She said without thinking, "I am deeply unhappy to hear that, sir."

He frowned.

Seeing his reaction, she asked, "Sir, please excuse my coming directly to the point, but I would know immediately, if you please, if it is your intention to torture or rape me." She stopped and cleared her throat, realizing she was more than a little afraid of his reply.

He answered her readily. "That is not my intention."

She paused as she let out a breath. "I am very happy to hear that."

He nodded and returned to his work next to the fire, but positioning himself in such a way as to present her with his back.

"Pardon me again, sir, but I feel I must bring your attention to the fact that I am in quite an ill state of dress beneath this blanket, and I was wondering—"

"It was necessary to remove your things after I brought you here," he explained, interrupting her. Gazing at her from over his shoulder, he continued, "Your clothes were wet, and you were very warm with fever. It was done to tend to you, and for no other reason."

"Ah." She paused while she sought to test her failed memory. There was nothing there to steer her in any direction. It was as though her memory had been wiped clean.

He continued. "I little understand the English woman's style of dressing, nor did I recall which piece of cloth went where, and so I did not attempt to re-dress you once your fever had abated."

"Oh, yes, of course."

The man shifted position again, scooting around until he faced her. It was the first time she had looked upon his features in full. It would have been most reassuring had a memory of recognition stirred to tell her something about him, or about herself. But it was not to be.

Again, not able to help herself, she asked, "Do I know you well, sir?"

"*Neh*, no."

She took in this fact well enough, then questioned, "Do I know you at all?"

"We have never met." So saying, he presented his back to her once again.

She remained silent, unsure of how next to proceed. If this man didn't know who she was, how then, was she to discover it herself?

In the end, she decided to change the subject. "That smells

delicious." She came up onto her elbows to see if she could discover what it was he was cooking. "I think I'm hungry."

"That is to be expected."

He didn't turn around or say anything further, not even to indicate when she might eat, and so after a while, she lay back against the soft bed of blankets and pine boughs that cradled her. Somehow, she didn't feel strong enough to make a point of it. If he didn't desire to share his meal with her, it was beyond her to do anything about it.

But she had reckoned too soon. Within moments, he had moved to kneel beside her. She shivered. Up close, he looked formidable, dangerous, alien, and alas, handsome.

It seemed, however, that he had nothing more in mind than feeding her. In his hands, he held a large shell. Its contents were steaming, and smelled like heaven.

"I will require you to sit up if you can," he said. "Since it is soup, it is best eaten in an upright position."

She gazed up at him, noting several things she had missed when he'd been sitting next to the fire: the proud tilt of his head; the healthy look of his skin tone, even though its color was a few shades darker than her own; the long fingers that looked capable enough to snap her in half, if he desired. As she stared into his eyes, she beheld a gentle look about him as well, and it was toward that spark of kindness she responded. "I think I can sit up. Shall I try?"

He nodded and waited.

She struggled to do it. To her chagrin, she was too weak to accomplish more than coming up onto her elbows. Moreover, even that small movement sent her heart to beating heavily. Her breathing quickened as a result, which caused her some anxiety. Not knowing him, fearing he might be untruthful about his intentions toward her, she was afraid the movement of her chest might attract his attention toward her bosom, a thing she wished to avoid.

But it didn't. He focused on her facial features alone. However, he made no move to help her sit into a better position, either.

At last, casting him what was probably an irritated glance, she said, "I fear 'tis as far as I can come."

Again, he nodded, and setting the shell carefully to the side, he placed an arm around her back, bringing her up into a full sitting position. "It is good that you tried to rise on your own. There is no other way to regain your strength."

His voice was low and pleasant, a deep baritone, and his face was so close to hers, the intake and exhalation of his mint-scented breath was soft upon her. It caused her to wonder at the odor of her own mouth, and she closed her lips, as if that might keep any offending smell at length.

Keeping one arm wrapped firmly around her, he picked up the shell containing the delicious-smelling liquid and brought the concoction to her lips.

"It is hot," he warned. "Beware. Do not drink too much at first."

Eyes wide, taking in his image, she obeyed, for there was no reason not to. She welcomed a tentative sip of the brew and decided at once that it was good. Indeed, in her state of mind, it tasted as if it might be the nectar of the gods.

"Hmm..." Briefly she closed her eyes. "'Tis an excellent cook you are, sir."

A simple nod acknowledged her compliment. "I'd like some more, if you please," she said.

He accommodated her, bringing the shell once more to her lips. He said very little to her, making her wonder if there were a reason why he was niggardly with his words. She raised up her hands to his, helping him guide the shell toward her, and every now and again she gazed up at him. His features remained handsome even so close up, though she was amazed to discover not even a hint of a beard on his countenance. Did he shave it, or did he honestly not have one?

She tried to recall what she might know of the Indians, but unless her mind volunteered the information, there was little for her to gain from her memory.

As she stared directly at him, she noticed his eyes were dark, almost black in hue. As he stared back at her, she recognized a strength of spirit that was at odds with her impression of what the Indians were about.

But what impression was this? Was it a memory?

She concentrated, doing all she could to bring the recollection back to mind, though it was impossible to keep it from fleeing.

"Do not worry." He reached out to smooth the lines between her brows. "You will regain your strength. Here, eat more. If you are to recover, you will need to nourish your body."

"Yes, of course you are right. Thank you for helping me, and for this meal. It must be vexing for you to have to prepare it."

"It is nothing. A man learns enough about cooking to do it a little, since he is often away from his home." He offered her more of the soup, which she was quick to accept, and it wasn't long before the entire amount of liquid in the shell was gone. "Would you like some more?"

She nodded.

"Good." He set the shell to the side, then laying her back on her bed, he rose gracefully and stepped back to the fire.

She continued to study him. His was a tall figure, slim and well-built. He was young, good-looking and probably had a dozen young maidens awaiting a proposal from him.

As he gathered up more of the food into the shell, he asked matter-of-factly, "Do you remember who you are?" He returned to her as soon as the shell was filled, and, although he didn't look at her directly, he took her again into the warmth of his arms, as he brought her once more into a sitting position.

Although he had probably already guessed what her answer might be, she didn't reply instantly. In fact, she was afraid to. Even though his mild manner was allaying her fears, she was wary—perhaps she had been taught to be so. After all, she didn't know him. If he thought she had no one looking out for her, would it change his intentions toward her?

"If you will tell me where you are from and who is your family, I will return you to them." As though he were aware of her thoughts, he added, "It is the only reason I ask."

Something about the look in his eyes caused her to believe him. "I…I recall nothing."

"Nothing?"

"Yes, sir." Nervously, she waited. What was going to be his response? When he didn't answer at once, she went on to say, "What I do know, or what I can recall, seems to come to me in odd ways, for I remember much, but the details I recall are all unimportant." She cast him an anxious glance, and fearful, pulled away from him.

If he were affected by her reaction, he didn't show it. He simply nodded. "Perhaps it is to be expected, since you have witnessed much trauma. Do not be afraid, however. Your memory will return in time. More rest and nourishment will aid in your recovery."

"I hope you are right. But I have another question I must ask you, sir. Do you know how I came to be here?"

"I brought you to this cave to provide a place where you could recover, although why you were in the forest alone and unconscious remains a mystery to me."

"Oh." She frowned. "I was unconscious? How did you find me, then?"

"You were lying atop a large, flat rock. I assume you had been washed ashore by the waves of the Lake-That-Turns-to-Rapids. You were alive, but barely."

"Oh, I see." She bit her lip. "The Lake-That-Turns-to-Rapids. I don't recall it. But if what you say is true, then you have most probably saved my life." She had meant it to be a question, but it came out as a statement of fact. Suddenly, she was struck more forcefully by fear. Did this man want something in return for his kindness? Something she might be unwilling to give?

The enormity of her vulnerability and dependence on her rescuer became too real for her. He could do almost anything to her, for she would be unable to rebuff any slight whim that might take hold of him.

She swallowed noisily, and, as panic coiled like a serpent within her, she was more than aware of the state of her nudity. Under the possibility of threat, her femininity reacted in an age- old, womanly fashion, and she felt a wetness in a place most private—perhaps in preparation for the worst. It was not a pleasant feeling, however. Far from it.

Nervously, she swallowed, and, with wide eyes stared up into the dark gaze of her "protector".

Chapter Four

They looked at one another, as though both were taking in the measure of the other. At length, she roused her courage, and queried, "May I ask, sir, if it is you who has been nursing me back to health?"

"It is. It was not my desire to see you die if I could do something about it."

She paused. "Again, I admit I must give you my solemn thanks."

He nodded.

"But, sir, I fear I have another concern that I would voice, if I may."

"I am listening."

The muscles in her neck convulsed as she tried to gather her nerve. She was already much too aware of this man's touch upon her. The fact that he was very close—so close she could breathe in his scent—was not helping to ease her mind. Oddly, though her anxiety was almost palpable, she found his fragrance pleasant. Manly and musky, but pleasant.

She didn't know how to ask the next question. But because her alarm would not abate, there was nothing else for it but to blurt it out. "Have we...Have I...In my stupor, did we engage in...I mean to say—"

"On this day, you are as intact and whole as you were before I found you. You have asked for nothing from me, and we are still strangers to each other in all ways except one. I have been feeding you each day and caring for you in your fever, hoping it would soon reduce and that you would awaken. I believe there is a fairy tale in your world about a princess who was awakened by a kiss." There was a hint of a smile within his words and upon his lips.

"Did we kiss, then?"

"*Neh*, we did not, though I was tempted to test the fairy tale to see if it be true."

She settled back with a sigh as her apprehension began to ebb. But it was her recognition that he was trying to soothe her disquiet, not heighten it, that calmed her. Innately, she realized this was the action of a good man, and it drew her to him, if only minutely.

However, she was curious. "How is it, sir, that you are familiar with European fairy tales?"

"I spent more than three years with missionaries."

"Yes, of course. That accounts for your command of the English language, also, does it not?"

"I believe that it does." He smiled, but it was brief, a half-smile at best.

Shyly, she returned the gesture, then blushed and turned away. "I can see I have been a burden to you, and for that, I apologize."

"You are no burden," he assured her.

"Am I not? I thank you for trying to ease my mind, yet if it be true that you saved me, I am certain you are not pleased with my many questions."

He shrugged. "Your questions are natural, since you have awakened to find yourself in the hands of a man you do not know. It is not a bad trait to be wary of a stranger. Trust is an honor to be earned, not given without cause."

"But perhaps there is cause."

"Maybe. You will have to determine that yourself. But if I can put your mind at ease, I will try."

"Do you know how far away we are from a white man's town?"

"Many days' ride by the white man's horse, or longer by foot and canoe."

"Much too far for us to go."

"I fear it is true."

"Then if I recover, or *when*, I will owe much to you."

He shrugged.

"And...what is it you would like from me in return?"

"Perhaps the recovery of your memory."

"Is that all?" Even she could hear the doubt in her voice. "There are some men who would ask for much more from a woman."

"Not a Seneca man." He squared his shoulders.

"Oh?"

"Only a beast, who is more decayed flesh than human being, would ask for more from a woman than she is willing to give. Furthermore, only a fool, tied to nothing but the physical, would take what *Hawenio* has brought to him, and destroy it." He paused. "I hope I am neither kind of those men."

"Yes, I hope so too," she agreed. "Tell me, what does *Hawenio* mean?"

"The Creator. He who made this world and who placed us here in it."

"Ah. That is a beautiful word."

He nodded. "So it is. Now, when you are able to sit up and can do the deed for yourself, your clothes are dry, and you will be able to dress yourself. I have placed them in a stack by the fire."

She glanced toward the place where he indicated. "I...yes, I see them."

She started to return her gaze to him, but then, she became more than unusually aware of this man's arms wrapped tightly around her. Suddenly, her skin felt heated by his touch, and she averted her gaze. To her shame, she realized she liked the feel of his hands upon her.

The recognition startled her, because a fleeting memory reminded her that she didn't like to be touched. Not usually. She hadn't liked it since...

On that note the recollection ended, leaving her feeling more than a little frustrated. How on earth was she to ever remember who she was or where she was from if memories came and went with such speed?

As though he, too, were aware of her disappointment, he said, "Let me help you to lie back. You should rest now, and you should seek to sleep often. Gradually, you will remember more and more periods of your life. Until then, do not worry."

"Yes, thank you. I will try to keep from worrying. But it is hard to hold back my discouragement. What if no recollections ever return?"

"They will."

She sighed. "Oh, if only I had your certainty. Before I lie down to rest, I would like to ask if you might be so kind as to bring my clothes close to me so I might dress myself as soon as I am able. Though you have been the utmost in gentleman-like conduct, I am nervous about my state of undress."

"At once." He placed her back against the blanket and set down the shell holding the soup. Speedily, he retrieved her clothing and returned to her side.

"Thank you, sir," she said as he again took her in his arms, and, bringing her up, offered her more of the broth. Before partaking of the soup, she added, "You have greatly aided me. And I believe there is no human being alive who would doubt you are a man of ethical quality."

"*Nyah-weh.*" He nodded. "Thank you for the compliment, but do not give me your trust so easily. Be skeptical, doubt me, test me, before you pass judgment."

"Sir, are you saying in a more covert way that you might, after all, be inclined to force me to…to…"

"*Neh*, no. Were that the case, I believe we would not be discussing it. But since you are obviously nervous and question whether or not you will remain a maiden under my care, let me try to reassure you. Though words are often hollow, I tell you this. I give you my promise that I will not take from you that which you are unwilling to give. The fact that we are alone, that I am physically stronger than you, will not move me to change my mind.

"I pledge my word of honor that your feminine beauty and privacy are safe with me so long as you wish them to be. Honor alone will keep you safe, for in my society, a decent man takes his pleasure only from the one he aims to make his own. At least, a man who is my age does."

Again, she detected humor in his voice as he continued. "In a man's youth, it is not unusual for him to accept whatever a woman is willing to give, even if there is no intent to marry."

"Sir!"

"But time and age can work on a man to make him wiser, I think."

An uncomfortable silence followed this declaration. Though she realized it was kind of him to do his best to settle her mind, in truth, she had no idea how to respond to him. Thus far in her life, she'd had little experience in confronting such brutal honesty from someone, especially a person of the opposite sex. The world in which she moved never discussed such concepts—at least, not in social settings.

There it was again—a reference to her past. How did she know these details? More to the point, were there other memories attached to this one that she might recall?

Frowning, she touched her forehead, as though that action alone might release the floodgates.

"Did you remember something?"

She shook her head. "No, I thought that perhaps I had, but, pray, I am still as unaware of my past as you are."

"Do not alarm yourself," he said reassuringly. "In time, your memory will return."

"I do hope you are right. I sincerely pray it will be so. But tell me, you said something a moment ago that caught my attention, and I fear I must ask you about it. You said, 'a man of my age.' Surely, sir, you are not so very old."

"I am thirty-and-five summers."

So he was older than she was, after all. Why, she was only… Dear Lord, even the knowledge of her age escaped her. She sighed hard. "And are you married, sir?"

"*Nyoh. Neh.*"

"What does that mean?"

"Yes and no."

"I fear I do not understand. Yes and no?"

"My wife is dead. But she still lives on, deep within my heart."

"Ah. Now, I think I understand." And so she did, although why she shared such empathy with him was not completely clear to her. "How long ago did she die?"

"It has been fifteen summers since she walked this earth in the flesh."

"Fifteen summers," she repeated. "I am sorry for your loss. 'Twas fifteen years ago? She must have been little more than a woman in her teens. May I ask what took her away from you at so young an age? Was it childbirth?"

He shook his head. "*Neh*, no. And I mean no offense to you, so please do not take one. I do not speak of her death."

She gazed away from him. "I understand."

"I know you do."

"Do you?"

He said merely, "You spoke often of people you love."

She frowned.

"In your sleep," he explained. "In some ways, we are alike, you and I. We both love people who can no longer be with us in the flesh."

"Yes," she replied, but she was embarrassed. Though she couldn't bring back to mind the memories she'd told him, apparently in her stupor she had related her deepest thoughts—and perhaps, her most intimate secrets. Alas, the fact was disconcerting. "I am very sorry to hear that I spoke out as I did. Had I been awake and in my senses I would have never burdened you with my memories."

"Do not be sorry. Your pain has endeared you to me."

"Oh? Endeared?" Again, she was caught off-guard. She simply didn't know what to expect of a man who was so utterly forthright in his words. Indeed, it seemed to be out of her realm of experience.

So as to steer the subject back toward a topic more easily spoken about in a polite society, she said, "I am frustrated. I have awakened only to find that I do not know who I am, where I am from, or even who are my friends."

"It is true, and what you feel is to be understood—but with time, it will come to you," he assured her. "You have only awakened this very first day. Do not expect too much too soon. One begins a long journey by first taking a single step. Yet, if he keeps onward, placing one footfall after another, he will eventually arrive at his destination. Rest, sleep, eat well. You will remember. And, when you at last recall the details most important to you, upon your request, I will return you to those who are your people."

"Yes, I would like that."

But did she really like the idea of that? Some innate warning caused her to doubt the sincerity of those words even as she spoke them. If that were true, why did she not feel more elation at the prospect of returning home?

"Come," he said, "we have talked enough. It is time for you to rest again. We will have time aplenty for talk later."

She might have remarked on his presumption, for she was uncertain she could go back to sleep simply because he required it of her, but she held back any criticism. When he gently lowered her back against her bed, she murmured, "Thank you again, sir. You have been most kind. May I ask the name of my benefactor, please?"

He didn't utter a sound. Instead, as though she had grown hot to his touch, he laid her down and ended their embrace suddenly, albeit too quickly. In truth, the action was so hastily done that it drew Sarah's attention away from herself and on to him. Odd. He acted as though he couldn't get away from her fast enough.

He got to his feet. Only then did he say, "A man does not speak his own name. To do so is dishonorable."

"Oh?" As she settled in against the cushion of pine boughs and soft blanket, she studied this man before her. "Then, what shall I call you, sir?"

He smiled, and she thought the very atmosphere around her might have turned brighter. If it were true that some people's smiles graced the world around them, and, that a single grin might be sufficient to cause others to smile too, then this man certainly possessed that gift. The impulse was more than she could resist, and the corners of her mouth twitched upward.

She gave him her full attention as he said, "You state a good point, and so I think I might make an exception with you since there is no other way for you to discover who I am."

"Yes, it would be most kind of you to tell me, sir."

"*He-noh*, White Thunder. I am known as White Thunder."

She breathed in deeply. "*He-noh.* It is a good name, Mr. Thunder. A good name, indeed. Is there a reason?"

White Thunder didn't pretend to misunderstand her question and came down to kneel at her side. "It is well known among my people that the thunder is a kind god, for he accompanies the rain, which nourishes the earth. But he is also a lonely god, for his wife, the earth, is ever separate from him. Sometimes, he cannot contain his loneliness, and we oftentimes witness what happens when this is so, for the lightning kisses the ground. You have seen this?"

"Yes."

"Because my wife is ever separate from me, I am called Thunder. Because she is amongst the Sky People, I am named White for the clouds."

She was quiet for the beat of a moment while she registered all he had said. Then, softly, she uttered, "You must miss your wife very much."

He didn't respond to her by word. Instead, he drew away from her, as though she had trampled upon forbidden territory. "Sleep now," he said. "Food to nourish you and uninterrupted rest will see that you regain your strength."

Thus spoken, he rose, and, before she could say another word, he turned his back on her and stepped away, leaving her alone to watch his retreating backside.

He was gone so quickly that his reaction might have seemed strange to another, but not so to her. She well understood the ill effect that a great loss could hold over a person.

She might not remember exactly why she knew this, or how she had come to know it—she realized only that it was. Perhaps, when it involved matters of the heart, instinct alone was all one needed.

Chapter Five

Gradually, the darkness that accompanied the return of dawn became the shadowy silver of early morning. Dew clung to every leaf and blade of grass as the world around White Thunder awakened. The trees, the shrubs, the bushes were bursting with the colors of gold, red and orange as the life in the forest announced its departure from this world into a wintery sleep. Even without the sun, the landscape's brightness lit up the land as though each living thing contained the mystical powers of the light.

Interestingly, here and there, White Thunder spotted the pigment of yellow, placed in amongst the greens, reds and golds of the forest. The color reminded him of the hue of the English woman's hair. Little Autumn, he thought. It was a good name.

White Thunder shook his head. He was beginning to think he was besotted with this woman who had literally been dumped into his life. In truth, if he were honest, he would admit he was drawn to her. But there was not a thing he would do about it. Not only were the two of them from different worlds—giving him no reason to flirt with her—his heart, his very life, belonged to another, to Wild Mint.

Spreading out his arms toward the eternity of the skies above him, he prayed as he sang:

"Howenio, Creator, I greet the morning with the happiness of a new day.
"Howenio, Creator, I thank you for what you have brought me.
"But, Howenio, Creator, I do not understand.
"Is there a reason this gift has come into my life?
"Howenio, Creator, my heart belongs to another, will always belong to

another.

"Howenio, Creator, though I thank you for what you have brought to me, I wonder.

"Do you test me?

"Howenio, Creator, I will do all within my power to remain faithful to the one who will always hold my heart.

"But, Howenio, Creator, a man is but a man, and this woman you have brought to me is beautiful.

"Howenio, Creator, I do not understand.

"Howenio, Creator, thank you for your gift."

"Howenio, Creator, I greet the morning with the happiness of a new day."

White Thunder lowered his arms to his sides and turned away from the east, where the sun was only now beginning its artistry, painting the skies with pinks, blues and golds. Soon, the world would be bright with the radiance of autumn and sunlight.

As White Thunder stepped away from the large rock where he had recited his morning prayer, he felt a cold touch upon his shoulder. There was no one there, and no reason to turn around, save one. It was Wild Mint.

He smiled. Wild Mint was here with him. Hadn't she vowed she would be—at least until his task was completed?

Alas, so heinous had the crime been against her, he understood that she could not, she must not, pass into the realm of the Sky People, even though a ceremony had been performed to release her. Not until true justice had been served, regardless of how long that took, would she be able to travel into the next realm of existence.

On a brighter note, he was happy she was here with him. Her touch was always welcome. It was her way of reassuring him that she was here, at his side, keeping him firmly grounded in his purpose.

But he did wonder, was it her voice or was it the wind that

whispered to him? *"Do not forget your duty."*

"Never!" he cried.

Oh, to hold her in his arms again, to hear her laughter, to touch her, to make love to her.

No sooner had these thoughts begun, when, unbidden, the image of another woman filled his vision. She was delicate, with a small bone structure and a short stature, a woman who would probably come no higher than his shoulders were she to stand upright. With natural ringlets of blonde hair and deep, trusting blue eyes, she had managed to become a part of his musings.

Little Autumn, the English woman. What was he to do with her?

His life held no place for her, although he admitted that if he were free to woo her, he might try to persuade her into his arms. He might even attempt to coax her into his life. In truth, the mere idea of wedding her and bedding her encouraged such instant changes to his body that his mind spun with the possibilities.

It was a shock. He'd thought such cravings were long dead within him.

Staring down, he was not happy to witness the effects mere thoughts about her had on him. Although his body's reaction affirmed he was still a healthy male, this state was a complication he could ill afford.

White Thunder sighed. Were cold-water swims, taken during any part of the day, to become a regular habit with him?

He hoped it would not be. Unfortunately for him, he feared many a cold bath might lurk in his future. For days and days now, he had held Little Autumn in his arms as he'd nursed her and fed her and coaxed life back into her. If he were honest, he would admit to experiencing more than one moment when he had wished she were his.

Even then, his body hadn't reacted like this.

What would it feel like to experience her surrender? If he were to kiss her, what would she taste like? If he were to enfold her body within his in a most natural and elemental way, what would be her response?

He sighed as he fantasized, for he knew it could never be. He was not free. He might never be, if these last fifteen years were to serve as an example. For so long he had lived with a mission, which was as yet unfulfilled. He had also lived his life as though there would never be another woman but Wild Mint for him.

Perhaps it was true. Maybe there never would be someone to take that hallowed spot.

But maybe there was still love to be found in this oft-times broken-hearted world. Mayhap, if he reached out...

No. It could not be. Not with a woman who was English.

Still, he was not dead. Not yet. Could it be that when he reached his village again, he might find a pleasing face who might wish to spend her life with him?

But not until his duty to Wild Mint was fulfilled. He must never forget.

Pivoting, he retraced his steps toward the Lake-That-Turns-to-Rapids, astonished that, with nothing but the mere thought of Little Autumn, his body was still firm, alert, ready....

***

A few days turned into a week. Aided by a diet of nourishing soups and fresh meat, her strength gradually improved until she was able to sit up on her own.

As the need for sleep became less and she was awake more often, one of the first details she noted was that White Thunder was frequently gone from the early hours of the morning 'til dusk. At first, she had done little more than sleep while he was away from her, but as she grew better physically, she began to realize she desired his company.

Certainly Mr. Thunder took pains to ensure her comfort before he left and when he returned, but she was becoming aware that she had an emotional need for the company of others. She desired conversation. She wanted to laugh and exchange confidences. What she desired most, she realized, was a friend.

She had even broached the subject with White Thunder once, and he had listened very intently to her. But in the end, nothing had changed between them, and she was beginning to wonder what it was that an Indian gentleman did all day.

She was not left long in pondering the puzzle. Every day, he returned to the cave with some form of nourishment. Often, he brought a deer or other meat to the cave. Other times, he returned with his bags crammed full of wild vegetables, berries, and fruit.

She helped him sort through the vegetables from the comfort of her bed whenever she could. However, that was often strained due to her inability to walk about freely. Although her strength was returning, she had yet to take any of her weight upon her feet.

Still she found that she could crawl. That first day when she had discovered her hands and knees as a means of movement had been a joy. The first deed she had accomplished—after dressing herself in at least her chemise, corset and underskirt— was to inch forward toward the fire and prepare herself a drink.

That had been several days ago, and it had become an everyday habit. She still refrained from dressing herself fully, since crawling wreaked havoc on her clothes. Thus, she would save her open gown for the day when she returned to her people.

But who *were* her people? She lowered her head into her hands as if the action might cause the memories to return. Straining her mind, as she was doing now more times than not, brought about nothing but a headache.

She heard a rummaging in the corner. Raising her head, she saw it was Mr. Squirrel, an animal that had taken an interest in the goings-on in the cave. Mr. Squirrel had become a daily visitor, and she had taken to talking to him, if only to ease her need for conversation.

"Well, there you are," she said to the squirrel "You know that you could come even closer to me, and I would feed you without trying to make a soup out of you."

The squirrel looked at her as if to say, *I don't believe you.*

"It's true," she ventured. "You've become my friend, and I wouldn't make a meal out of a friend."

The squirrel picked up a plum, which she had deliberately left in a corner of the cave, and the animal stared back at her as he began to munch.

"It's good, isn't it?"

When the squirrel didn't answer, she sighed. "Do you know that seven days have passed since I awoke here, and still I can't remember my name, or who I am, or where I come from?"

The squirrel chomped happily on the plum, staring at what must seem to him to be an odd human being. Yet, the animal acted as though he were a friend to her, and that he would happily listen to her troubles.

"Nor can I recall why I am here, or why I was in the woods, or if I were with someone or alone. But if I were alone, how had I come to be there?"

The squirrel threw down the plum and looked at her as though he might answer. But instead of speaking, he picked up one of the berries that she had also left, and began to chew on it.

"And what am I to do about Mr. Thunder?"

The squirrel stared pleasantly, as if saying he had no idea what she was talking about.

"Who is this man? Can I trust him? I certainly want to. Without him, I am doubtful that I would now be alive. So, of course, I want to like him. He is alien to me, though I must admit I find him handsome. Do you know, Mr. Squirrel, that if you promise to keep a secret, I'll tell you that I find my gaze drawn to the look of the man's chest more times than I ought." She smiled. "Indeed, so much is this so, that had I the cloth, I would make the man a shirt simply to keep myself from wondering what it would be like if…" She paused. "Well, never mind."

The squirrel finished the berries and picked up another plum.

"Dear Mr. Squirrel," she said, "speaking of Mr. Thunder, I do believe I have come to the decision that he is trustworthy. He certainly is kind and is helpful to me. Nor does he offer criticism as a means to assist me. He is the utmost in decorum and gentlemanlike behavior. Pray, I fear that from a woman's perspective, her heart might be in danger with this man, for these qualities are said to be rare, indeed."

The squirrel shifted his head to the side, as if to get a better image of this person who spoke. "But," she went on to say, "there are problems…. He's Indian. I'm not. But this, I can understand and appreciate. What I don't comprehend is why he appears to be cold toward me. There are times when I fear he must be made of snow, and I of fire, for he is always cautious when he touches me, even when he must do so in order to help me."

The squirrel sat on his haunches, looking for all the world like he were more than mildly interested in the conversation. He even offered some advice, chattering to her in squirrel.

"What was that you said?" she asked. "That perhaps I make more of this than I should because he is the only human being in my vicinity? Maybe you're right, because it does seem to me he is faithful to the image of his deceased wife…perhaps to a fault. Truthfully, I am left with the impression that Mr. Thunder might never be unfettered of his former wife's hold over him until…well, I don't know until what. Perhaps he might never be free of her influence over him at all. But this speculation could be the frivolous wonderings of a feminine mind. After all, I am in a position where he—and you, of course—are my whole world. I know more about him than I know of myself. I have wondered, what if I am married? I could be."

"Do you speak to a ghost?"

She jumped, and her heart leaped into her throat. She turned quickly toward the cave's entrance.

In a moment, the racing of her heart settled back to its normal pace. How much had he heard?

"Oh, Mr. Thunder," she gulped. "I didn't know that you were here. I'm afraid you startled me."

She placed her hand on her chest, not for theatrics, but because she had been truly startled. "I fear that you so rarely return before evening that I had let down my guard. I was not expecting you."

"Forgive me. It was not my intention to startle you. I heard talking and was wondering if someone had come to visit."

"And so someone has," she replied. "'Tis Mr. Squirrel, who visits with me most every day. However, Mr. Squirrel is no longer here. I fear he ran away when you entered."

"As well Mr. Squirrel should. Otherwise, I might take it into my mind to have him for a meal."

"Oh, no. I specifically told Mr. Squirrel that I am his friend and I would not eat him."

White Thunder crossed the room to the campfire where she was reposing, and she couldn't help but wish that Indian men wore more clothing. His deerskin leggings fit like a glove and came only to mid-thigh, leaving almost nothing to the imagination. Additionally, his breechcloth, which was blue and made of cloth, emphasized the fact that he was so obviously male. And although he wore necklaces, his chest was always bare, and, the dear Lord help her, it was a magnificent sight.

She still held a shell full of pine-needle tea, and, to her embarrassment, her hand shook. Thankfully, he seemed not to notice.

"...Then I shall not place an arrow in Mr. Squirrel's side." He knelt on one knee beside her, and she became aware that he had been speaking to her all this time. She swallowed, hard. He had come down so close to her that she would have been able to reach out and touch him, had she the nerve. But she didn't, and she gave him her full attention, as he said, "Usually when I return, you are asleep, but I see you have managed to make your way to the fire."

"Yes."

"This is good. Did you walk?"

"No. I am crawling. I fear my legs will not hold me, yet."

"You are gaining back your strength, and soon you will be walking about. I have been thinking about what we might do when you come to remember your former life. And I concluded it would be best that I should take you back to your family, who will be happy to know you are still alive, I think."

She bit her lip. "And if I don't remember anything? 'Tis hard for me, for I recall nothing."

He placed a hand on her shoulder, and she closed her eyes as a jolt of pure desire raced over her nerves. What was wrong with her that he affected her so? But he was speaking, and she gave him her attention as he said, "You will remember, given time. Be at your ease. It will come."

She gazed toward his hand, where it lay so close to her breast. He meant it as comfort, but it did not impart a feeling of relaxation, since every part of her being was responding to him as though she and this man were long-acquainted lovers. She could hardly speak, but after a moment, she was finally able to say, "And, if my memory *doesn't* return?"

"Then I will take you to my home, where you will be welcomed as a guest until a new home can be found for you. My mother will be happy to have you."

And you? Would you be happy to have me? She wanted to ask the question, but knew she dare not. True, she might react to him physically, as though they were on an intimate footing, but the truth was that she barely knew him, and she was uncertain of him, and of herself, as well.

"I have brought you something," he said.

She lit up. "Have you, now?"

"It is not much." He presented her with a stick. But to call it merely *a stick* was to do it a disservice. Truthfully, it was a work of art, for the rod had been carefully carved into the shape of a cane, perfectly polished. At the hand hold at the top of the cane were images of leaves, gently carved so intricately that even the veins in each leave were distinct. "It is to aid you in walking, Little Autumn. You must try to stand, and take a few steps every day, for it may require some time for your leg muscles to remember again that their duty is to take you from one place to another."

She smiled up at him. "It is a beautiful present, and I will cherish it and use it, indeed. Did you make it yourself?"

He nodded. "I did."

She was moved. Very moved. "Thank you," she whispered. "I will prize it forever. Excuse me, but what was that you called me?"

"Little Autumn?" He looked at her sheepishly. "It is what I have decided to call you. It is a good name, for your golden curls remind me of the falling leaves, and, after all, you came to me in the fall, and so the name is appropriate, because it describes your beauty and the time of year that we met."

Had he just told her, in an off-hand way, that she was beautiful? All at once, tears filled her eyes, and, as the wetness fell over her cheeks, she hiccupped.

He seemed at once concerned. "I mean no offense. It is the Seneca way to rename those who become…"

"Become?"

He shook his head.

"My tears are because of happiness. You are so kind to me that…forgive me…."

"Forgive you?"

"I…I…" Words escaped her. She wanted to tell him she liked him—very much liked him. But she knew she shouldn't, for he was still committed to his wife. She sighed, deciding to change the subject. "How did you know that I needed a cane? It might help those times when the muscle spasms in my legs are so painful that they cripple me."

He frowned at her. "This should not be." His voice was so firm that she sent him a wide-eyed stare. "I will have to sit and contemplate and try to call back to mind the knowledge that my grandmother endeavored to teach me when I was a child. If I recall correctly, she used to say that most physical problems come from something missing in the food a person eats. Though she tried to instruct me in specific cures, I fear I do not remember them."

"Is your grandmother still living?"

"*Neh*, no, she passed into the next world many years ago, and unluckily for me, the knowledge she possessed died with her. I was not apt at learning the wisdom of her years. At the time, I thought of little more than the glory of the war path."

"The war path? That seems unreal," she observed. "For you are very kind."

"And yet, it is so, for only as a warrior could I win the hand of Wild Mint, she, who had hold of my heart from the first moment I ever beheld her."

Sarah was silent. Yes. Wild Mint. The woman whom, for all appearances, he still loved. After a slight pause, she offered, "Again, I am sorry for your loss."

"*Nyah-weh.* We grew up together and we were always in love. We married as soon as we were of age to do so. Had I been able, I would have gladly perished with her. But I could not.... It is my place to seek the revenge in this world that is rightfully hers and mine to take."

Sarah reached out to place her hand over his. Instantly, she wished she hadn't, for a fiery sensation raced over her being. She shouldn't have chosen that moment to look up into his eyes, either, for what she saw there made her wish to have his arms encircle her, perhaps even to have him kiss her. She drew her hand away, and whispered, "I am truly sorry."

"I would like to kiss you," he murmured, as though he had read her mind, "but I must not. Know, however, that I wish it."

She swallowed, and looked away from him. Faintly, almost under her breath, she muttered, "I wish it, too."

He must have heard her, for he placed a finger under her chin and brought her face around to his own. Gradually, he closed the distance between them, and, when his lips touched hers, it was as though a bolt of lightning surged through her body. Her stomach dropped, and she felt as though she melted beneath the flood of sensation drenching her.

His lips clung to hers for so long, and the feeling was so pleasant yet awe-inspiring, she began to wish she could stay in this position forever.

But it could not be. At last, he ended the kiss. As he did so, he whispered, "I would like to kiss you forever, I think."

His breath was minty and fresh and she could only wonder at her own, and hope that hers smelled as good as his. Her concern kept her from responding, and when she remained silent, he went on to say, "And now, I have frightened you."

"No!" she said at once. "I...I liked that very much."

He groaned. "You should not tell me that if you do not wish me to do it again."

She shut her eyes momentarily, as though to savor the fire racing through her body. "I wish it very much, but—"

"You worry you are not well enough to do more than share a mere kiss with me? That is to be expected. I only wish now that I had listened more intently to my grandmother."

Actually, she had been about to say that she liked the kiss very much, but she realized it would be in appropriate, for his heart remained with Wild Mint.

"I believe that Grandmother told me that the broth I brew should contain foodstuffs found only in the bones of animals. Perhaps I am not boiling the bones long enough to ensure the marrow's healing ingredients are in the broth."

She sighed. He was already embracing another subject, and she was too shy to bring the matter of discussion back to kissing. And, perhaps that was best. He was, after all, still in love with Wild Mint.

Swallowing her desire, she nodded and commented. "It could be the problem. At home, we often boil the broth for one or more days. It takes that long for the nourishment to leak out of the bones and into the liquid."

"*Nyoh,*" he agreed. "I will try that, and we shall see if the cramps in your legs become less. But for now, if you would seek your bed and lie down, I feel I should rub your legs since that often takes away the pain."

She shut her eyes at the suggestion, being that desire, pure and simple, rushed over her. "Do you think that is wise?"

"Probably not," he replied truthfully. "But I would not have you in pain, even if it means my own."

"What do you mean?"

"Is it not evident? I desire you. And for a man, that can be painful."

The rush of excitement, which spread over every nerve ending of her being, startled her with its intensity. She breathed, "I would not have you in pain."

He gulped, and his Adam's apple bobbed a little as he swallowed hard. "I know you do not mean that in the way I am taking it, and so I am thinking that what you are saying is that I should not rub your legs?"

"Yes," she agreed simply. It didn't help that she noticed that he seemed almost as relieved at her refusal as she was to give it.

He said, "Do not fear me, for even though I desire you and all that a woman and man can experience with each other, I will take no advantage of you. I wish only to help take away the pain. At least, that is all I want for this moment."

"I thank you, and I understand that well, but I grasp, too, your hesitation. After all, we are alone, and—"

"You are safe with me, for I swear that I will do nothing that you do not desire me to do."

She brought up her gaze to stare at him. "But don't you understand? It is myself I fear. You are kind, you are gentle with me, and I deeply enjoyed that kiss, and I fear that—"

"I, too, feel concern for what might happen between us. But my love for Wild Mint runs deep within me, and I think that I can control these physical urges."

There it was again, that fire that sparked and burned as it rushed over her system. She tried to remain calm, reminding herself again that he was in love with Wild Mint, and that any man, if left alone with a woman long enough, would start to find that woman desirable. Still, she couldn't help but wonder what it would feel like if this man's passions were directed toward her, instead of Wild Mint?

She should do nothing, drop the subject entirely, and so it was barely creditable what she did next. Perhaps his words triggered a challenge, or maybe it was because this man aroused her so. Whatever the cause—although she was unable to look him directly in the eye as she said it, she whispered, "But, Mr. Thunder, what would you do if I were willing to…to…experience the wonders of—"

He groaned, and she felt that groan to the very depths of her being.

At last, he appeared to come to grips with himself, and he whispered, "Let us be clear. Are you considering testing the pleasures that can be found between a man and a woman? Because if you are, and yet are unwilling to make love to me, then no, I should not touch you, not even to dispel the pain, for I fear it would bring us both pain of a different sort."

"I—I…" What should she say? The truth?

"Do you? Is that where your thoughts are tending?"

"I… No." There it was. She couldn't quite bring herself to utter what she was really thinking.

"Then, there is no danger." His manner and his voice appeared to be practically normal again. "Come, lie down. I will rub your legs so that the pain goes away. And as I do so, I will tell you a story to take our attention away from the pleasures that men and women can experience with one another. Do you think that might help to make you feel more at your ease?"

"I..." She couldn't quite lift her eyes to look at him, and so she simply said, "Yes, please. I believe I would enjoy your touch upon me very much."

His response was a stunned silence, then an involuntary growl—low, soft, and utterly masculine. Unwittingly, her very femininity responded to him, but she was quick to say, "I'm sorry, that didn't come out correctly. I meant that—"

"I understood your intent," he said, and they stared at one another for so many moments, she was left almost breathless.

What was happening to her?

She wasn't certain, but whatever it was, it felt wonderful. She warned herself, however, that she dare not like the feeling too greatly. There was pain in that direction, for he made no secret that he still loved Wild Mint.

Besides, for all her knowledge, she might be pledged to another, too. Unfortunately, the thought did not comfort her.

Chapter Six

"This is a story often told by the old men of our Nation," he began.

"I am honored to hear it," she said.

"Very well. Once, not so long ago, a great Seneca sachem was visited by three spirits." White Thunder's words were low, almost a whisper. "These spirits showed themselves to this great man so that they might tell him the story of how the white man came to this land that we Seneca call Turtle Island." White Thunder, who was kneeling beside her, paused as he shifted his massage from one of her legs to the other. "Is it the lower muscles of your legs alone that spasm when you try to walk?"

"Yes, it is. And they convulse even when I am resting." She was lying face down on her fragrant bed of blanket and pine boughs. Interestingly, though it would never do to possess such a berth in a stately home, this makeshift bed was unusually comfortable. "Sometimes," she continued, "that is when it is the worst."

White Thunder frowned, looking as though his thoughts might be weighty. He continued to knead the painful muscles in her legs absentmindedly. Meanwhile, she settled down to enjoy the simple pleasure of being cared for. There was a risk, of course. They were both more than aware of it.

Still, the massage did ease the pain in her body; so much so that it seemed to her that this man's touch was a little like stumbling onto a bit of heaven. Perhaps it was worth whatever risk they both took in allowing it. Besides, having dressed herself in her chemise, stays, and underskirt, she felt secure that there were enough layers of clothing beneath this thin covering of blanket to provide adequate propriety.

Besides, she trusted him. Even though beneath her skirt she was quite bare—as was the fashion of the day—she trusted him with what was probably her most precious gift.

She had never given the form of feminine clothing much consideration, since it was the general mode by which all women of quality dressed. But when White Thunder's touch ventured up toward her knee—a scant few inches away from an area of her body that was most private—she was dismayed to discover that she wanted his touch so much that...she was afraid to finish the thought.

"I fear that I must find a way to present more foodstuffs in your diet," he said, "if you are suffering from this pain even when at rest."

"Yes, that would be most beneficial." She gasped silently, for his fingers had ventured over her knees. Her body's instant response was carnal, deep and exotic. Indeed, at the moment, were he to venture even farther upward, toward her femininity, she might likely let him. She gasped, for it was a sobering realization. To hide her response, she said, "Were you not going to tell me a story?"

"*Nyoh*, yes, I was. Forgive me, for I was considering how best to obtain the nourishment you need."

"The bone broths might help."

"*Nyoh.* That they might."

"And I should like to hear that story, very much, I think."

"I will begin. This is the tale that the spirits told one of our wise sachems, and it has been repeated often since then." White Thunder's voice was deep and soothing. When combined with his gentle touch, it was more than any feminine heart could easily reject, and she couldn't help responding to him.

"Long ago," he continued, "at a place across the great salt water, was a land that was ruled by a queen. There was trouble in this land, for the people there had hunted out most of the game, and they were hungry. It happened that the queen had a servant who was a preacher, who was told to dust some old books. When no one was looking, this servant boy read one of these books, and he learned many things that prior to this, he hadn't known. He began to dream."

"Hmm..." She winced beneath his massage. One of her muscles convulsed.

"Did I hurt you?"

"No, you did not. 'Tis only the contraction of my muscles. Sometimes it feels as if the muscle is pulling away from the bone, for the pain is that intense."

He said nothing, but his touch softened. "Is that better?"

"Indeed, 'tis so. But please, do continue the story. What did the boy dream?"

"Before I tell you, I would like to ask you a question."

She nodded.

"Are you aware that, to the Indian, some dreams are sacred? That some dreams are a communication from the Creator?"

"No, I didn't realize that."

"I thought it might be so. It is important to understand this fact. Otherwise, the story might not be grasped in its magnitude."

"Yes, I believe I understand."

"Very well, then. In the servant's dream, he beheld an island he'd never seen before, and on this island was a castle made of gold. There was also a bridge leading from where he was to the island. This young servant could not contain his curiosity, and so he crossed that bridge. There, he met a handsome young man who was brown-skinned and dark-headed. The handsome man complimented the servant, and told him that since he had ventured across the bridge, he was a fearless man. Because of this, he told the servant that he would divulge a secret that would make the young man rich.

"This was pleasing to the servant, and the handsome stranger went on to say that across the great salt water was a land where a whole people was virtuous, where honesty and integrity to oneself—to one's family and to one's tribe and to his Creator—was without fault. 'They have no evil inclinations,' said this handsome man, 'and because of this, you can become a rich man if you do as I say.'"

As he spoke, White Thunder's hands ranged up to her knee and again, a little higher. She shivered under the titillating sensation, for mere inches separated his kneading from her most private place. Yet, she wouldn't have stopped him had she desired to do so, which she didn't.

White Thunder carried on with his tale. "The servant listened intently to what this strange man had to say, which was this: 'There are five things that all men and all women take pleasure in, and I will give you a bundle that contains what these five things are. But before I give them to you, you must promise me that you will do all you can to ensure that these things are taken across the great water to the people there.'

"The boy hesitated, but when the handsome stranger reinforced his demand by stating that the boy would be amply repaid for his efforts, the servant agreed."

"What were the five items?" she interrupted, then sighed. White Thunder had removed her slippers and had set to work rubbing each of her feet. Softly, she moaned. "That feels...quite heavenly."

"I am happy to hear it. And the muscle spasms? Have they ceased?"

"They are less."

"Good. I will continue to massage you until they stop altogether."

"Do you think they will go away completely?"

"I think they might."

"That would be most pleasant." She breathed in deeply, and relaxed. At length, she asked, "But tell me, for you have piqued my curiosity. What were the five things that all men and women desire?"

"*Ah, nyoh,* the five things that all men and women desire. I will tell you soon, but you must be patient, for I have not yet come to that part of the story."

"Hmm. 'Tis a shame, for I am quite inquisitive."

"I had hoped that you would be. Now, to the young servant, the handsome man said, 'Take this bundle and study it well, and ensure that these things are transported across the water. If you do this, much wealth will be yours.'

"Suddenly the young servant awoke, and when he did, he discovered that he held a bundle in his hands. Had it been only a dream? It is hard to say this was so, for the items were real. At first, the boy was frightened, because it appeared that whatever this was held magic. But soon, his desire to see what was inside overcame his fear, and he opened the bundle. There were playing cards, a bottle of rum, a few of the white man's gold coins, a fiddle, and a leg bone that was so old it barely held together without breaking in two."

"That's odd. Such strange articles."

"*Nyoh*, it is so. When the boy saw what was inside, he felt much as you, for these were unusual items to give to a person, and he couldn't conceive of bringing them to a people across a great body of salt water. Yet, the boy remembered his promise to the stranger, as well as the vision of the riches he would acquire, if he did exactly as he was told to do. And so the servant boy sought out another man and told his story to this man, who was an adventurer. From that moment on, this man and all the other people who followed him carried these five things with them when they came to Turtle Island."

"And what were those objects again?" she asked.

"Be patient, for I have not finished the story yet. Now, these gifts soon spread throughout this new land, Turtle Island, for these items were very much the entities that all people take pleasure in. Now, do you remember what I told you about dreams and about the Creator?"

"Yes."

"Good, because this handsome stranger was a man we, of the Iroquois Nation, call *Hanisse'ono*, the evil twin of the Creator of this world. *Hanisse'ono* laughed at the mischief he had caused and said to himself, 'The cards will cause the people to gamble away all their property and will make them fight amongst themselves; the bottle of rum, when drunk, will make the people indulge in the evils of their bad mind until they will fight and kill each other and become fools who will sign away their country; the coins will bring about dishonesty amongst the people and will make them lustful of others' property, and they will forget the teachings of the Peacemaker and Hiawatha; the fiddle will cause the men to dance with women of easy virtue and cause gossip and the tattling of tongues, tearing down the reputations of good people; all of these things will bring about the ruin of the people, and they will lose all sense of who they are, thus the gift of the bone that withers away."

"But your Nation has *not* withered away," she objected. "I may not remember much of my past, but I do know that the Iroquois Nation still exists. It is strong, united, invincible."

"So it is. Now. But if my people do not hearken to these warnings from our great sachem, we might become a people who were only once mighty. Think of what has happened in a mere few years. My people have become reliant on English trade goods, the blanket, the iron pots and pans, the gun. Where, before we were the creators of all things that we needed, we now make almost none of those goods that keep our society together."

"But isn't that the way of all great civilizations? For instance, I have no desire to weave the cloth that I use to make my dresses, but someone else does, so I buy it from him, but he might not be able to make the style of dress that I create, and so he then buys a dress from me."

"True. But you are English. You will still find cloth even if your governor argues with the French. It will still be there because there are those among you who know how to weave the cloth and sell it to you. But imagine if no one among your nation knew how to weave this cloth, nor even desired to do so, and that only the French knew this skill. Imagine now that *if* your governor argued with the French, so that the

French became upset and stopped trading with you, what would you do? Go naked?"

"We would probably take war into their country."

"You might if you were united and strong. But now let's observe that others come into your camp and try to divide you. Some want you to fight the French and take their cloth from them, but others want you to trade only with the Dutch, who also have a cloth, though perhaps of lower quality. You cannot muster a force of arms, because you are not united in your cause, but have become scattered, like seeds to the winds. Indeed, you have sold the soul of your nation for want of being able to make the things you now need amongst yourselves."

"But," she interrupted, rising onto her forearms and casting him a speculative glance, "you carry a gun, and your shirt is made of cloth. Even this blanket that has become my bed is European made. How can you be honestly critical of something, when you engage in buying those things from the people you criticize?"

"A man must purchase from whatever source he can garner the objects he needs to clothe himself, and since the Seneca no longer make these things, we are left with no choice but to buy what we can where we can. In the past, we used the skins of animals to make and sew our clothing; even this skill is disappearing. Consider, also, that in the not-too-distant past, these commodities were free to the man who could trap and kill the animal. Now, we must buy the cloth from the English, if we are to clothe ourselves. And with what exchange do we purchase it?"

"With gold or with silver?"

"It could be, or the skins of animals that we little value, but that the English seem to esteem beyond even gold. And when the animals are gone, what will we use as an exchange then? Gold? Silver? And where shall we obtain those metals?"

"From the English?"

"Perhaps. But recall that these things were once free to us before the

English invaded our country."

"But isn't your society better for all this?"

"Better? How do you mean better?"

"I little know, since I have never been among your people. But I think that perhaps your women might not have to work so hard. That would be an advantage. Maybe these pots and pans and cloth make their lives a little easier so that they have more time to spend with their family?"

"Ah, but do they spend more time with their families, or do they spend the time they save by arguing over the iron pot that their neighbor has?"

As he spoke, his touch quickened over her, and she winced under the accidental pressure. Seeing her reaction, he gentled his massage, and she again relaxed, putting herself willingly into his care.

"Our lives were not so bad in the past," he went on to say. "While we did not have the guns or steel of the English or French, we had one valuable the Englishman has want of."

"Oh? What is that?"

"Harmony in our villages and between each other, and an independent spirit. What need did a mother have to spend more time with her children when her children were beside her in the fields?"

"But if a person had more conveniences and life wasn't so hard—she had more leisure—then she could spend that time thinking, considering ways to make life even better, couldn't she? After all, as human beings, aren't we always striving to better conditions for ourselves and our children?"

"True. What you say is so, and in a perfect world, it would be this way. But what if these comforts were used, not to better a person or his family, but rather to chain them to another? And what if those chains were forged, not to fashion a tie of goodwill toward one another, but rather to hold one back?"

"Then that is not progress."

"No, it is not, and so it is not for the Indian, I think. We have these new things, but what has been the result of having them?"

"I don't know."

"War. We have constant war in a land that was set into motion to be a nation of peace. Since the English and French have been among us, we have war among ourselves over mere triflings of pots and pans and cloth for clothing. Then, we are persuaded to go to war for the English against the French, or for the French against the English. Since the English and French and Dutch have come to our shores, bringing with them their many and varied things, we have been involved in more war than is within the living minds of our elders."

She lay still in silence, not knowing what to say, for she recognized some truth to his words. White Thunder had made a rather convincing point.

When it appeared that he had little more to say on the matter, she asked, "Then you're saying that these items of worth that the Europeans bring are evil?"

"Perhaps these 'conveniences' are not themselves evil, but they bring an evil with them that is unparalleled to the Indian mind. If we could make these things ourselves, if we weren't dependent on the English or French, we would have a chance, I think, to remain united and be a force to be reckoned with. Without this, it is only a matter of time before we are run over by the English or the French for want of their iron and beads."

"But, sir, if you were to have your way, you would remain living in poverty."

"Poverty? We had no poverty before the Englishman came to our shores. There are four requirements that a human being needs in order live: food and water, shelter, and clothing. All were free to us before the coming of the English and French. All that we wanted was made from the earth by our own hands. If a man were ambitious enough, he might hunt better than another and make a name for himself. A woman, too. Poverty was unknown because all that the earth produced was free to take, to harvest, to make, to produce. Only since the coming of the English and French have we had to pay for the necessities that a human being needs to simply live. Is that the action of a friend?"

"No," she was quick to say, "but by the same argument, in order for all to be free, all people then would have to engage in the same occupation—all would need to be farmers or hunters or workers. And there are careers beyond these to which a human being also aspires, those occupations that if a man is without, or if they are withheld, he will deteriorate."

"Such as?"

"The arts. Music, literature, painting, creativity."

He nodded.

"If one had to till the soil and work the fields, when would he have the time to write a great work of music, or paint the great pictures, or build the awe-inspiring architecture?"

"And within your society, there is room for this?"

"There is. It took a bit of leisure time to think of and invent the gun, to make the iron pots, to put together the little trinkets that make life tolerable."

"And these people who do this, how do they pay for their necessities?"

"From the profits they make by selling their works."

"And do they live easily and free?"

"I..." She stopped. No, they rarely did. Unless they were taken under the wing of some monarch, they usually experienced poverty and hardship.

"If the English had come here and let us remain free to make our own goods and harvest our own food and build our houses, and brought us goods that would make our lives easier within our own idea of how life should be lived, that is the action of a friend. We, too, could have expanded our society to include music and much, much more. But to bring with him a means to exact a payment to him for items needed to do nothing more than live, is to enslave a man. For who, then, can be free but he who holds the most wealth?"

She didn't know what to say to this piece of logic, and so she simply asked, "Was your grandmother happy, then?"

"It was so. If she were alive and you were to ask my grandmother if she lived a hard life filled with poverty, she would have laughed at you, for her life was happy. Yes, she worked the fields, she made the meals, she clothed the children, but she did so with the help of her mothers, her sisters, her aunts and grandmothers. A day that was spent sewing was a day spent socializing. A day when she worked the fields was a day she played games with her children, chased off crows, climbed high posts, looked for faraway enemies."

"It does sound almost...ideal."

"I think it was. Now, with these new inventions of the English, we need each other less, and so our socializing is less. We even go to war and act on our own, instead of staying together as a united whole."

She paused while she contemplated what he said. "Although I understand what you say and can appreciate it, you must realize that one cannot live forever in the past. New inventions are a part of life, if only for the reason that the young will always try to find new ways to do old things. There must be a happy medium."

He nodded. "And so there must be. For my part, I believe we Seneca should learn to make those items that the trader brings us. Either that, or do without them."

"Perhaps you are right." Changing the subject, she uttered, "Hmm...after this massage, I am thinking that I might obtain a good night's sleep."

"Have the cramps awakened you from your sleep at night?"

"They have, indeed."

"I was unaware of that. Usually, I awaken easily, but I have not heard your plight."

"That is because I have not given one. I have done all I can to remain quiet."

"But if you are in pain, then you should tell me so that I may help. It is not in my mind that you should grieve."

"I will remember that."

"And now, if your pain is less, I think that I might bring in the fresh meat that I hunted this day. I believe we can make dry meat with it and some soup to help you on the path back to health. If you can, try rolling over and standing."

She did as he asked and came onto her back, so that she lay face up. "I fear I might still be too weak to stand. When I am on my own and have tried it before, I seem to do nothing but collapse."

"But I am here now, and if your legs cannot hold you, I will catch you."

"Very well, then. I will try. Perhaps you could assist me to stand?"

She sat up, and as she did so, his arms came around her. It was nothing unusual, since he had been helping her in this manner every day since her awakening. But at this particular time, there was a difference about him, about her. Perhaps it was due to her body's wayward reactions to him. Whatever the cause, this time, when he helped her to rise, and when they stood chest to chest within each other's embrace, there was a seductive pull that caused her to see-saw. She swooned toward him.

It was a tense moment as he caught her, made more acute by his gentle breath upon her hair.

She looked up at the same time he glanced down at her, and they stared at one another until at last, he said, "You are most beautiful."

There. He'd said it again. "I?" she questioned. "Beautiful? After being almost drowned and lying here with a raging fever?"

"Yes, I think you are beautiful."

Then, he kissed her on the cheek. Perhaps it was meant to be no more than a light peck, a gesture given to bring comfort. But after having conversed already about their physical desire for one another, it seemed to further accentuate the problem.

When she turned her face into his so that all he had to do was move his head ever so slightly, he seized the opportunity, and kissed her on the lips, fully, completely and without restraint.

Although she seemed to be acting on instinct, rather than reason, this she did understand. She wanted more. She wanted to be held closer, loved and cherished. Unable to stop herself, she drew in even nearer to him. It was a mistake. She knew it at once. Yet, the good Lord help her, it felt so incredibly good, she sensed she might be drowning all over again.

Chapter Seven

It was a moment of rapture. It was a moment set out of time, reminiscent of the Englishman's heaven.

But it was wrong—the wrong time, the wrong place, the wrong woman. Yet contradictorily, something about her was *right*, and White Thunder surrendered to the softness of her curves, her scent, her taste.

It had to end. It should have never begun. After all, he had his duty, and she...she couldn't even remember who she was. Might she not belong to another?

Common sense demanded he withdraw. Gut reaction saw him reaching down and pulling her buttocks in closer to his body.

She didn't object. This was his downfall.

He thought he might go mad with desire. He deepened the kiss, opening his lips so he might explore the warm inner recess of her mouth.

He groaned. She sighed and fell in toward him. So close was she, he could feel every feminine hill and valley of her form. The knowledge sent his mind spinning, and his body reacted with all the pent-up frustration of an aroused male. His heartbeat raced, and he could barely catch his breath.

In the end, he had to breathe, and he ended the kiss, but not the embrace. In fact, he shortened the distance between them, memorizing her every feminine curve. They both gasped for air.

He should say something. But what? At last, all he could think to utter was, "I am sorry."

She didn't respond, not by word or by action. Instead, she remained fixed in his arms.

After a brief hesitation, he decided he should explain himself. "I am sorry because I, who have told you that you are safe with me, have yet taken you in my arms." He shook his head against hers, but he didn't release her.

At last she spoke, her voice soft and breathless. "You have nothing to be sorry for. If I remember correctly, you promised that as long as I didn't desire your attention, you would not give it."

He nodded. "That, I did."

"However, I fear I am as much to blame as you are." She paused. "You see, I wanted to be kissed."

He pulled away from her to glance down at her, although his arms remained firmly locked around her. Surveying the look in her eyes, he realized at once the truth of her words—and he recognized another detail…something more profound. Passion, amorous and sensual, peered at him from the depths of her gaze.

His heartbeat leaped into furious action, and blood surged through him with alarming speed. At once, his body was ready for her. Could she feel it? "Do not say these words to me if you do not mean them, for it encourages me very much. I have taken it on myself to care for you, which does not, and must not, include making love to you."

"That's not necessarily true. In this instance—"

"Do you tease me? You must know I am already thinking I will not let you go until we have explored one another as a man and a woman might."

"As a man and a woman might? Please be precise in what you mean, sir."

He didn't answer.

"In my society," she continued, "men do not speak their intentions to a woman unless that man is contemplating marriage, for to do so is unseemly. And yet, I can hardly believe that marriage is your goal."

He gulped. Marriage? His heartbeat stilled. Even his arms loosened from around her. Luckily, with that distance came a ray of sanity.

How could the conversation have progressed so far in only a few minutes? He realized he had to tell her. He had to be truthful.

But how did a man explain the truth of his life to a woman who was as sweet and desirable as this one? How did he tell her what was in his heart without tearing out hers by doing so?

He breathed in deeply, then took the plunge, his voice barely a whisper as he confessed, "Know this. I would make love to you and give you all that I could that is within me to give, but I cannot ever marry again; at least, not until my duty to my deceased wife is fulfilled."

She was silent for so long, he almost wished he hadn't spoken.

"Wild Mint."

"*Nyoh,* yes."

"Oh." It was all she said before she backed away from him, her countenance gradually mirroring her understanding. "I fear this conversation has gone too far, much too quickly."

He agreed, yet he felt bereft without the warmth of her body next to his. In this case, distance was not to be so easily gained. While it might have been a good intention on her part— to restrain herself from him—her legs wouldn't hold her up, and, almost as soon as she stood on her own, she collapsed. He caught her and enfolded her in his arms momentarily until she again struggled against his embrace.

"Do not fear," he said. "I will take you back to your sleeping robes, where you can invoke your need to be away from me if you choose."

"That would be most kind."

He picked her up in his arms and stepped toward her bed. No sooner had he started, when she said, "Sir, I fear there are further problems. If I do not recover my memory, there will be no option for me but to remain close to you. This would be difficult for us both, I think."

He dipped his head in agreement. "True, but if we have to do it, we will. I cannot leave you here on your own. To do so would be as to commit murder, for I do not think you could easily forage for yourself."

"Yes, you are right, I fear." She stared away from him. "But let us pray that my memory does return; the sooner the better. For the well-being of us both, I think."

"*Nyah-weh.* I will pray that it will be so."

He set her on the softness of the pine boughs and blanket, and, as soon as he did so, she lay back and took several deep breaths. He watched as she gazed up at the ceiling of the cave. She was silent. He was the same.

At some length, she said, "'Tis quite a dark place that you have chosen for our shelter, is it not?"

"That is the way in which caves and other passages underground are formed, for they do not have the warmth of the sun to light them."

"Yes. I have wondered. When I first awoke, I heard water running here in the cave, but I have not been able to find the source, since my legs will not hold me. Tell me, is there water near here?"

"There is an underground stream that flows not more than a hundred or so feet from us. It is farther into the cave, and so there is no light there. It would be hard to find on one's own."

"Ah, that accounts for it." She sighed as she turned her face away from him.

Watching her, he felt helpless. He realized his words might have seemed harsh to her after he had held her in his arms and kissed her, but there was little he could do about what he'd admitted to her. He had spoken the truth.

After some deliberation, he decided to converse about trivial things, much as she was doing. "I have brought us fresh meat. It is a deer, and should provide a good source of food for days. We can make dry meat, and from the bones, we can boil a broth that should supply you with the necessary nourishment to keep your muscles from becoming painful."

"I...Thank you, sir."

He hesitated. "I will bring the carcass near the fire, where we will be able to skin it at our ease. Would you like to help me?"

"Yes, very much, I think." But she didn't sound as if her heart were in it.

Feeling utterly powerless, White Thunder rose to his feet and stepped to the front of the cave. Retrieving the game, he placed it around his shoulders and brought it toward the fire, where he set it down. "Would you like me to pick you up and bring you to the fire?"

She didn't reply at once. At last she said, "I think I would like you to prop me up so that I am in a sitting position and can watch you from here."

He did as she suggested, being careful not to touch her overly much. But it was difficult when he was aware that they both would like so much more. Still, he managed it. "Are you comfortable?"

"Yes, I am, and thank you."

He nodded and returned to the fire, where he set to work over the deer.

To ease the undercurrents awash between them, he continued to talk. "Have you ever skinned a deer?"

"No, I have not."

"It is not a hard task to accomplish if you know how to do it. If you will come here, I will show you the way of it." Almost sheepishly, he asked, "Will you?"

"Yes, though I fear you must again help me to the fireside, for I cannot make it there on my own."

So quickly did he jump to his feet to come to her aid, he wondered if he'd startled her. Reaching down to take her in his arms, he said, "Know that if I were able, I would—"

"Please, there is no need to belabor the point. You are committed, and I...I don't remember my past. I could very well be committed, also. We are both doing the best we can in a very poor situation, so do not feel there is a need to explain."

He nodded, and placing his arms beneath her, he carried her to the fireside. But it was like magic. It took no more than a mere touch to send his body into readiness.

Were he not sworn to his obligation, were he not consumed with duty, he might like to come to know this woman better. But these ideas were useless to consider, for they could not be.
Why, he wondered, didn't that feel right?

***

"You make a slit here in the belly of the animal from the rump to the throat, and when you pull the skin away, it comes off whole with little trouble." He showed her how to do it.

She nodded, but at the first sight of blood, she realized this was a skill she might never use. Propped up so she was in a sitting position, she watched him work, her attention on his hands. There was danger in letting her thoughts drift in that direction. Was it only minutes ago that those hands had held her?

To keep her focus on other matters, she looked away. Truth be told, she was upset, but not with him. Her hurt lay with…circumstances.

How could she have encouraged him to kiss her? Hold her? How could she have practically begged him for his embrace— only to be turned down?

It was a sobering realization.

"You are quiet," he observed after a while.

"Yes. That, I am." She didn't offer further communication, and he didn't seem inclined to press her.

After some moments, she decided to confront this tiger, stripes and all, and she uttered, "I don't blame you for what happened."

He paused. "I am glad."

"However, I would like to say that, although I have been aware that you are committed to your former wife, I didn't realize the extent of your devotion, and I think you should have been honest with me about how far your dedication took you before you kissed me. Perhaps before you massaged my legs also, for I believe that is what started this."

"I agree. I am sorry. But massaging your legs is not what started it, I fear."

"Is it not?" She spared him a glance.

"*Neh*, it is not."

"If not that, then what? When?"

He exhaled before he threw her a sharp glance. "I will tell you, but in doing so, I do not wish you to think I am trying to change the conditions between us."

She nodded briefly.

"I have been watching you and admiring you since I first found you, for you are fair of face and figure. My feelings have been building up to this from the beginning, awaiting only an outlet."

She swallowed noisily. "You compliment me, sir, but I hardly think that would cause you to want to make love to me."

"Then, let me say it to you this way. Had I been massaging my grandmother's legs, I would not have felt the need to kiss her and leave my imprint upon her."

"Oh, yes, of course." She paused. "I...I should have realized that you are, after all, male, and..." She frowned and turned her head away, rubbing her forehead. It was as though her thoughts hurt.

"Did you remember something?"

"No, but I do seem to be possessed of numerous opinions—which require no memory a'tall. 'Tis strange."

He nodded. "It is. What opinions are these that worry you?"

"I fear I cannot say them."

"Why can you not?"

"Because they are hurtful opinions, and perhaps not based on fact."

"Hurtful to whom?"

"If I were to tell you that—"

"Tell me."

She breathed out on a sigh and glanced down at her hands. "Then it would be toward you."

He nodded. "I had assumed that, and I thank you are sparing me."

"You are most welcome."

"But I think," he went on to say, "that I would know the worst of it."

"I cannot say it, sir. I should never have brought it up, for I simply cannot bring myself to use my lips to say the things that have been told to me."

Laying down his knife and ripping open the carcass of the deer, he commented, "Someone has said that the Indian man is a beast and will rape women and children, hasn't he?"

She hesitated, though she was hardly surprised that he was so astute. "I cannot recall," she lied.

"And you believed it?"

"Until I met you and one other...." She scowled, and grabbed her head. Suddenly, it hurt.

"Another memory?"

"Almost." She cast her gaze upward. "After all you have done for me, I fear I now believe that the opinions I have been told are based on nothing but terrible gossip. And, yes, I have remembered something."

He glanced up at her, eyebrows raised in surprise, but he didn't push her to relate her memory.

"I recall a man," she began, "...an older gentleman, who was well-to-do, I believe. He had...some business with the Indians, I recall. It was he who told me this gossip, and it was, indeed, similar to what you said."

"I thought as much, for it is common for a man to accuse another of those deeds he does himself."

"Is it, now?"

"It is. Have you never observed this for yourself?"

"No, I don't believe I have."

He sighed. "I will tell you the truth, although it is probably useless to do so. But even if you do not believe it—and I fear you won't—you will at least have both sides of the story, and can make up your own mind about what is and isn't true."

"Yes. Please. Go ahead."

"*Nyah-weh.* It is a matter of record," he said, but he didn't look at her. His attention was taken up in preparation of the game. "Long ago, before the French, the English, and the Dutch came into our country, our women and children were safe to travel on their own, even into the woods, often without accompaniment. Certainly, they were safe in their own homes. However, with the arrival of the European into our country, this and many other conditions changed. Disease came with the English and the French, killing many of us. But for this, we did not blame the new invader. If he brought it, it was unintentionally done. No, what we disdained, what we could not understand, were this man's unhealthy desires to seek his pleasure from our women and children."

She gasped. "Surely, Mr. Thunder, you are not suggesting that—"

"It is a matter of fact. It is written in the sacred wampum— it is recorded in the memory of our elders."

She sat gaping at him, unable to muster a response.

"Because of this," he continued, "to this day, when a white man we do not know enters our villages, we hide our women and children until we are certain of his intentions."

She paused, choosing her words. "You are right. I find that hard to believe."

He didn't answer. Rather, with a shrug, he went on quietly with his work.

She wouldn't let it go. *Couldn't* let it go. "Mr. Thunder, are you telling me that good Christian men—"

"I did not say they were either good or Christian."

"But—"

"In the two years I lived with the missionaries, I came to observe that there were two different kinds of people among the English—those who take and those who give. And the two do not mix. Those who take are not good, and they are not Christian. They do not live by the book that they tell the Indian and others to obey. They lie and they cheat. So much is this true, that our wisest men warn that if such people say a thing is so, it is the opposite. These kinds of men or women are few among the English, fortunately, but they give your race a bad name. Someday, all the Indian Nations might blame your people for the injustices they suffer beneath the hand of these few— which would also be untruthful."

"I'm sorry you feel this way."

"It is not a feeling. It is an observation."

"Yes, so you have said. But, are you implying that your society has no stragglers, no men who serve their own ends?"

"No, all societies have such people. Perhaps the difference is in how a tribe treats a man who lies or serves his own ends. It is an Iroquois law that if a man is seen once to lie or to serve only himself or his family, the women of the tribe dismiss him from his seat on the council, or if he is not a council member, he is banished from the tribe. He is considered an object of horror, and no child will even look upon his face. He is a disgrace. But this is not so among the English, who tend to believe the wagging tongue of the man who cannot and will not associate himself with truth."

She became silent, for she realized what this man said was very near true.

"Until the English find a way to show this man up for what he is, until they serve him real justice, he will leave a disgrace upon the graves of the innocent Englishman, who in his heart is a good, God-fearing Christian."

She stared down at her lap. In truth, she was stunned because what this man said was too astute to be readily dismissed. "I hope, sir, that your look into what the future holds for the Englishman is not an exact look."

"I hope this, too. But I fear this will be as it is unless some force comes into the world to change it."

She sat by silently, watching him.

At length, he changed the subject. "Would you like to try to help me take the layer of fat from the skin? I could bring you here beside me and guide you so you could do it again if the need ever arose."

And be that close to him?

She said, "No, I believe not. I am still recovering, and I am happy watching you."

He didn't comment, although he did allow his glance to scan over her features. Silence again commenced between them.

While cutting the meat into strips, he spoke. "We will dry this meat over a smoky fire so we can make a mixture that will nourish us on the trail."

"And where will we be going?"

"Either I will return you to your people, or, if you have not recovered your memory by the time we are ready to leave, I will take you to my village."

"To your village. Ah, yes, I do remember you saying as much to me." Her stomach dropped. The prospect was frightening. However, if her memory didn't return, there would be little option but to follow him. "However, we are not ready to go yet, are we?"

"Not until you are able to walk on your own. And whichever path we take, whether to your village or to mine, we will need food. Since we will be traveling fast, it is best to prepare it now."

She nodded. "Then I will help you do it…tomorrow." She looked down, staring at nothing in particular, wondering if this were yet another fib, for she couldn't imagine cutting meat off the deer.

She sighed. So many lies…

Chapter Eight

It was only a few days later when, with the aid of the cane White Thunder had fashioned for her, she struggled onto her feet and slowly, with one foot placed carefully after another, began to walk. Soon, within a matter of days, she was walking without aid. And though her muscles still spasmed with pain now and again, neither she nor White Thunder had dared to repeat the deep massage.

True to his word, White Thunder had concocted many meals' worth of bone broth soups. As he offered the soup to her, along with the other foods he had in store, gradually the muscle contractions in her legs lessened.

It was liberating to be able to amble about again, and she realized a limited truth. Lack of movement created, to a greater or lesser degree, a sort of enslavement. Certainly it made one dependent on the goodwill of another.

Within days, she could leave the cave on her own, and, although at first she was reluctant to venture too far, eventually she conquered her fear and strolled out farther and farther into the woods. As she became stronger, she realized that she would be able to leave this place soon. Not yet, because her legs wouldn't always obey her every command. But soon.

Where would she go? What would she do? The worry hung over her like a dark cloud, since, to date, her past life remained a mystery to her.

One factor had changed recently, however. It had started to rain, which was causing her to stay close to the cave. Along with the downpours came a coldness that had settled over the land. Even the autumn leaves, so bright only weeks ago, now hung dismally under an often-gray and threatening sky.

It happened late one afternoon, without warning. One moment, she had been safe and warm in the cave; the next, she had ventured out of it to come face-to-face with a bear—a big, fully grown black bear.

She froze.

The bear growled, stood onto its hind legs and pawed at the air. She was dwarfed by it. It howled, the sound terrifying. Adrenaline and fear washed through her.

She remained frozen to the spot. Though the bear made no forward movement, it was close enough that the air around her became scented with the animal.

Then, something changed, and the bear came down on all fours and started toward her.

She screamed.

Stunned at the noise, the bear stopped, and, looking right and left, it pawed at the ground. Bringing its attention back to her, the bear slowly, carefully, closed the distance between them.

"Put your arms up over your head and growl!" It was White Thunder. "Do it. Now!"

She did as White Thunder ordered. Raising her hands over her head, she opened her mouth and snarled at the bear.

As before, the bear stopped, sniffed at the air and gave her a cautious look, but plodded forward.

"Keep growling. Louder! Make your voice more savage," ordered White Thunder, who was crouched atop high ground next to the cave. "He's tired and looking for a place to sleep. He may decide you're too much for him. Keep growling."

Adrenaline pumped through her, as, following White Thunder's orders, she mustered up her loudest voice, as well as what she hoped was her most ferocious-looking face.

Again, the bear hesitated, but hearing White Thunder, the bear finally took notice of him. Sensing he was the greater danger of the two, it came up onto his hind legs and growled at White Thunder, as though warning him away from his find.

When White Thunder did nothing but stare back and snarl at it, the bear came down to all fours, and, ignoring White Thunder for the moment, turned back to continue its path toward her, as though it had decided she was the least likely to give him problems.

Step by step, the bear progressed dangerously close. All at once, it rose to its hind legs and roared at her, this time extending its sharp paws outward. Only one thought surfaced: She was dead. She was dinner. Never had the desire to own and have a gun in her hand been more prevalent than it was at this moment.

White Thunder shot straight in front of her, placing himself directly between her and the bear. The noise was deafening, for White Thunder was roaring and kicking up as much commotion as the bear.

It was either the most courageous act or the most reckless, for what White Thunder did next startled her. He bent forward, sticking his face into the bear's, which was only a few feet away, and he snarled and snapped as though he were the more dangerous creature of the two.

The animal yowled right back at White Thunder, and, so shrill was it, she thought her eardrums might never mend. Then, it changed, and White Thunder was yelling directions at her. "Make noise!"

Without delay, she screamed and clapped her hands.

"Now, we back up," he shouted at her, "so as to tell him we give him the cave. We are no threat. Slowly, we back up, all the while we make as much noise as possible."

Although White Thunder was holding his gun pointed directly at the bear, she knew it wouldn't be protection enough against a head-on attack. After all, the musket had only one shot, the next attempt requiring priming and reloading.

He took a step back. She followed suit.

The bear came down onto all fours. It roared so vehemently, she wanted to run for cover. But it was impossible.

"If he starts toward us," yelled White Thunder, "and paws at me, you are to turn and run—do you understand? Run downhill. Although bear can out-distance you, even downhill, it is not as easy for it to follow if the steep is great. You are to run as fast as you can and don't look back. Try to find a tree or some other place you can climb that is not within the bear's reach."

"I won't leave you!"

"You have no choice. I give you no choice. If I say run, you are to run. If I am to fight him, I cannot worry about you."

Another step back followed these instructions, another and another.

That was when the bear chose to take a leap toward them. "Run!"

She turned to do exactly as told, but her legs refused to move. What was she to do? Even taking painfully slow steps was impossible. It was as if she were crippled.

Then, she spotted it. Fire! Weren't all animals afraid of fire?

The bear was already attacking White Thunder. She could hear their struggle, though, because of the fear gripping her, she didn't dare look back. But her legs responded at once, and rushing back into the cave, she picked up several of the sticks that were burning red-hot at their tips.

Without thinking of what she was about to do, she hurried out of the cave as fast as she was able. Until this moment, she'd never been aware of being particularly brave. She could only thank the good Lord that when valor was necessary, it was lying dormant within her.

White Thunder was on the ground, the bear over him. She rushed at the bear with the fire.

"Shoo! Get out of here!" Her voice was piercing and loud. She waved the weapon at the bear and tried to get close enough to light its fur on fire.

Her attempts did almost nothing to the beast. Its fur was too matted.

Startled, the bear jumped back, allowing White Thunder a moment to bring up his musket and take careful aim.

Boom!

White Thunder shot off a ball aimed straight into the eyeball of the bear.

It hit.

Still animated, the bear struggled forward. Had the shot served no purpose? White Thunder was reloading as fast as was humanly possible, and, as she watched him struggle against time to prime and reload his weapon. She wondered, was this it? Was life suddenly over? This easily?

Memories instantaneously rushed through her mind. They came with no fanfare, no bells. Rather, they swamped her. Moments from her past flickered before her so quickly, she could barely take hold of them.

So overwhelming was it, she rocked back on her feet. Meanwhile, the battle with the bear was coming to a close.

The animal took one final step forward and fell over, dead.

She watched in horror, almost afraid to turn away from it, fearful it might only be catching its breath. Even as she looked at it, she wondered, what damage had it done to White Thunder?

No sooner had the thought formed within her mind than she was struck with another truth. She cared for White Thunder. Sexual tension aside, she honestly cared for this man.

She was breathing hard and fast, and she could hear White Thunder behind her, doing the same. At least, he was still alive.

Though out of breath, he called out to her. "I told you to leave!"

"I could not do it!" she cried. "You forget that my legs do not always obey me."

At last, she turned toward him. He was on the ground, his shirt torn with claw marks. There were several gashes on his chest and arms where the bear's claws had found their target. As she caught her breath, she could only thank the Lord in Heaven that because of the cool weather, White Thunder had worn a shirt this day. But his clothing was blood-soaked and was becoming more so by the minute.

"Look at what he's done to you," she said as she took several steps toward White Thunder, and came down on the ground beside him.

"They are scratches." White Thunder did the unthinkable. He opened his arms to her, and she went into them willingly, both of them uncaring that he was bleeding all over her.

"You saved my life," she whispered.

"As you did mine."

"You came to my defense. You jumped in front of me and confronted the beast head-on."

"Of course I did. Did you expect me to leave you to fight a bear on your own?"

"I didn't expect anything. I…I thank you." Then a little shyly, she added, "I think also that my mistress will thank you as soon as I manage to find her again."

He pushed her back from him and stared at her.

Tears were streaming down Sarah's cheeks. "It's true. I have remembered my past life and who I am. It happened suddenly. I remembered everything."

"This is good." He was smiling.

"Yes, it is very good. I will tell you more about it later. But come, you are hurt. First, I must do something about that."

"I think I will need little attention. They are only scrapes," he reiterated.

Sarah drew back to look at him. "I will be the judge of that. Come."

Placing her arms about him, she helped him to his feet, taking a great deal of his weight upon her. Together, they limped into the cave.

Using a piece of torn-off petticoat that had been soaked in water, Sarah washed the blood from White Thunder's arms and chest wounds. There was something very intimate about sitting with White Thunder as he reclined on his bedding. She tried to ignore the feeling, realizing it was not an easy feat to accomplish.

"Why did the bear not back down?" she asked him. "Did he not understand that we were retreating?"

"He was threatened by me, and a bear's temper is bad even in the best of circumstances. He must have been hungry, too, for he dared much to come after you. So, although we were retreating, he could not pass up the opportunity to place his brand upon me and at the same time, have a tasty dinner."

"Place his brand on you?" She looked up at him in open astonishment. "He was trying to kill you."

"And he might have done so had you not rushed in upon him and startled him into backing away."

"He did not back away—"

"No, but he was frightened enough to pause, giving me time to aim a shot."

"Yes." Sarah resumed her work over him. "Thank Heaven you are a good shot."

"Do not thank Heaven. Thank my uncles and my father, who taught me to shoot."

"Yes, I shall do so. I will send them my praises, and the Lord in Heaven too, thank you very much."

He grinned at her, then winced as she dabbed at a deeper cut on his arm.

She frowned. "You will need stitches there…at least, on this one cut that is deeper than the rest."

He gazed down at the open wound on his arm. "Do you know how to do it?"

She shrugged. "I saw a doctor do it once. I think I might be able to sew it together, if I can find the right material to use as thread."

"Sinew from the deer can be used once my wound is cleaned, and a piece of bone might be made into a point so as to poke holes in the skin to pull the thread through. Did you spit on it?"

"I beg your pardon?"

"Did you spit on the wounds?"

"Of course not, I know better than to—"

Bending over double, he spit onto the wounds himself, leaving Sarah to watch, gaping. She said, "There are germs in your mouth, sir."

He grinned at her. "*Nyoh*, and there are other good things there, too."

Sarah shook her head, but held her tongue.

He was frowning. "I doubt we have the right roots and herbs to put on the wound to prevent infection, but there is water near here, and it can be boiled and placed on the wound to speed its healing. The water is perhaps a hundred to a hundred-and-fifty feet from us here in the cave, but it is downhill from this place, and it is in the complete dark." He looked at her sheepishly. "I fear I may not possess the strength to take the path to the water."

"I can do it."

"Good, but bring a good fire stick with you when you go there. You will need light to find the stream."

"And what shall I collect the water in?"

"I have several bags, there by the fire." He nodded in the direction indicated. "They should do. There is also a large, hollowed-out rock that can be used to gather water, if you need it. Take more than one of the fire sticks with you when you go there, not simply one. Do not let the fire go out. If it looks as if the fire is dying, return here while there is still light by it. Once blackness falls, it is complete, and there is no way to tell where you are. You could get lost. Do you understand?"

"Yes, I do."

He breathed in deeply and settled back on his bedding of pine boughs and blanket. "I will reload the gun while you are gone."

"Yes. Please do."

He smiled at her. "Are you a good cook?"

"Yes, I am—in the right circumstances."

"That is good, for I believe your skills will be needed while I recover."

"I'll do my best."

He stared at her a moment. "If you have any trouble at the stream, signal me by a cry, high-pitched and loud. I will rouse myself and come and help you."

"Very well, but I think I can manage."

"Yes. We will talk when you return. After all, I would like to hear what it is you have remembered."

She stood to her feet. "It is important, I think, although it seems to me there are still pieces of the puzzle I haven't recalled yet."

"Then, we should discuss it. When you return here from the underground stream, I will listen while you talk."

She nodded and made her way to the underground stream. It was not an easy task, considering she was carrying three bags, one heavy hollowed-out stone and three different fire sticks.

Even collecting the water proved to be almost impossible, since she dare not let the fire on the sticks go out. She made several trips from their camp to the stream and back. But her problems were only beginning.

What was she going to use to boil this water? In the end, she discovered the smoked and toughened rawhide bags that White Thunder used to make soup. They were ingenious, actually. When she heated stones and threw them into the liquid, it was as good as boiling the water over a fire.

It was not the easiest way to go about fixing food, but at least the two of them would be able to eat. It could be worse. The important point was that they were alive. Yes, it could be worse.

Straightening her shoulders, she set about locating the sinew that White Thunder had mentioned. With both it and a knife, she would be able to perform the necessary surgery to his arm.

Hopefully, her hand would be steady.

Chapter Nine

"What do you mean there is nothing to numb the pain? Are there no roots I can dig, no plants that will deaden the nerves, even a little?"

"There is nothing."

"But if I'm to cut into you, there should be something to ease the trauma."

White Thunder's look at her was cautious, but surprised. "There are herbs and plants that might do this, but there is not the time to prepare them for use. We will do without them."

Do without them? She didn't think so. "Am I to presume you intend to remain awake while I poke holes in your skin? And also while I sew up this gap in your arm?"

"*Nyoh*, that is exactly what I have in mind."

She scowled at him. "Are you one of those strange people who enjoys pain?"

"I am not that kind of person, I think, but I will withstand the pain." He grinned at her, and she was astonished once more at the appealing effect a simple smile could create upon his countenance.

"No, sir, I beg to differ."

He raised an eyebrow at her, but said nothing.

"You won't have to withstand it," she continued, "because I simply won't do it. There must be another way."

He frowned as he turned his attention inward. After a lengthy pause, he said, "Perhaps you might push the skin together and wrap it tightly enough so that when it heals, the skin will grow together. If you can do this, we may not need the stitches."

"Do you think that will work?"

"I have no reason to believe it wouldn't. If I understand it correctly, the reason for sewing it together is to ensure that the wound heals completely, and will not leave a gash on the skin. I believe that if you push the skin together and wrap it tightly, it might accomplish the same purpose."

"I suppose it might work," she agreed, though her tone was noncommittal. "We could try it."

Given their circumstances, it might be the best she was going to be able to do. She came up to her feet and turned to the fire. "I'll boil the water."

He nodded, and leaning to the rear, flopped back against his bed.

***

She was beautiful. She was sweet. She was incredibly female, and despite his injuries, White Thunder realized that he was nothing if not all male.

At present, she was working over the last of his wounds, and she was so close to him he could smell the clean, tantalizing fragrance of her femininity. It teased him. It baited him. And every now and again, one of her stray blonde curls brushed against him. Involuntarily, he shivered in response.

It wasn't her fault. He was more than aware it wasn't her intention to become the object of his sexual fantasy. That knowledge, however, didn't change the fact she was fast becoming that.

White Thunder rocked against the backrest of the pine branches she had painstakingly placed between him and the wall of the cave. He shut his eyes.

In truth, he wasn't certain which was more difficult to endure: the pain from his injuries, or her soft touch upon him. At present, she had returned to him from the fire, and was washing his chest with a cloth soaked from the cave's freshwater stream.

As she worked over one of the injuries to his chest—a cut that came close to his nipples—he thought he might likely sink into giddiness. How was he supposed to withstand this? Indeed, a man might very well welcome the pain instead of the unwelcome sexual stimulation.

Her fingers dabbed at a cut, and she accidently rubbed over his nipple. He caught hold of her hand. Immediately, she gazed up at him.

"Did you want something?"

You. He wanted to say it. He dare not. Instead, he took a deep breath, and uttered, "A man can bear up under much, even torture, but oft-times, a woman's touch, sweet and soft though it might be, when so close to sensitive areas of a man's body, can produce more agony for him than an enemy carving out his heart."

She stopped, her lips barely open as she stared back at him. He wondered if she were aware of how kissable she looked. At last, she said, "Have I hurt you?"

He sighed yet again. "Oh, that you would."

"If I have hurt you, I apologize—"

"There is no need." He rubbed his fingers over her hand, which he still held within his own. "But there is a problem."

She looked up at him inquiringly.

He didn't know how else to put his thoughts into words, except to admit the truth, and, after some deliberation as to how he might say it, he blurted out, "I am a man. You are a woman. You are beautiful. And you are working on injuries on my chest."

At last, he beheld understanding within her gaze, and he nodded.

But instead of drawing away—as she should have done— she said, "Do you object, then?" She hadn't taken her hand away from his either, nor did she back off from him, as he had thought she might, as he knew she ought.

"It is not that I object. Rather, I am tested almost beyond my endurance. If you mean to tempt me, this is the way you might go about it."

"I'm not trying to tempt you...only endeavoring to clean your wounds. If you please, I have almost finished the task, the worst injury being to your arm. But 'tis wrapped now, and if you will permit me, I think I might attend to the rest of your injuries more easily."

"But those places you are cleaning are dangerously close to parts of my body that are...sensitive."

"I'm sorry. Please know, however, that I cannot help where the injuries lie. If there were another manner by which to ensure your other wounds are clean, I would do it. If it will ease your mind, I will be finished here soon, since I need to stop and prepare our meal."

He swallowed hard. It appeared to him that in this instance he had few choices. Either he must silently endure the cravings she was awakening within him, or he must take her in his arms and make ardent love to her. Here. Now.

Considering who each of them was and the barriers placed upon them by their respective societies, neither option seemed a good choice. After some deliberation, he proceeded with caution and changed the subject to something less personal. "I have not forgotten that something today jogged your memory. You have yet to tell me what you remembered or even how it happened."

She extricated her hand from his and pressed the cloth against another of his wounds. Though he sighed under her care, she seemed not to notice. At length, she said, "Please excuse me for taking so long to tell you of it. It has not been my intention to hide it from you, 'tis only that I'll be done here in a moment, and I had thought we might talk about it over our supper."

"Are these memories bad, then, that you hesitate to tell me?"

"No, not necessarily." A look of consternation came over her features. "'Tis only that I little know how to relate the particulars to you, and, since it is more important that I attend to your injuries, I thought I would first concentrate on mending those, then fix us something to eat, which would free my mind to tell you what I have remembered and what it might mean to us both."

He scowled. Something in her manner didn't seem right. Shouldn't she have been anxious to tell him about her life? Especially since she hadn't recalled any of it previously?

Had she recollected memories that were unpleasant?

That thought brought up another. Was she running away from some wrong done to her, or an injustice she had done to another? Either of those scenarios would explain how she had come to be in these woods, alone. After all, such circumstances were not unheard of. In the past, the Seneca had given shelter to a few of those men his people called the black white men, those who had escaped their English masters' chains.

Staring at her, he realized it was best to put his ponderings into words. Leaning forward, he again took one of her hands in his, but this time he clasped it within both of his own. "Is there a part about your past that you feel you cannot tell me?"

"No," she replied immediately, perhaps too quickly. "It's only that—"

"Are you running away from something?"

She shook her head. "I don't think so."

He nodded. "Are you married to a man who was cruel to you?"

"No, I am not married."

"No?" He made a face. "Did your husband die, leaving you alone?"

"No. In truth, I have never been married."

His scowl deepened as he contemplated what her confession might mean. "I am attempting to understand this, but I am having difficulty. Perhaps you might help me. How can a woman, who is as pretty as you are, have not seen the marriage bed?"

She bit her lip and looked away, and he was afraid she wouldn't answer at all. However, after some moments, she replied, "The truth is that I am not free to marry."

Not free to? How could this be? "But did you not just remark that you are not married?"

"That is true. I am not. What I am is an indentured servant."

His brows drew together in thought. He knew what a servant was, but an *indentured* one? He must have appeared as puzzled as he felt, for she went on to explain. "I have five more years of service to give to the man who owns my papers. Until that time, I cannot marry anyone."

"The man who owns your papers? Are you like the black white man, a slave?"

"No," she managed to say after clearing her throat. "I am a servant, which is different from a slave."

"Is it? How is it different?"

"Well, a slave is owned by his master for his entire life, and he must toil without compensation for himself or his family. A servant, on the other hand, works for another for compensation, or in some cases he or she toils for another in repayment of a debt. At the end of a certain amount of years, which are needed to repay the debt, he or she is free."

White Thunder thought about her words. "By compensation, you mean money?"

"I do."

"And repaying a debt?"

"A debt is money or services owed to another."

He made a wry face, not directed at her, but rather motivated because of the subject matter under discussion. "Do you work for compensation or to repay a debt?"

"I work to compensate an obligation, I believe, although I'm uncertain how that obligation came to be. That part of my memory is still unclear to me."

He nodded. "Now, you say that a man owns you?"

"My services, yes."

"Tell me, how can a human being own another human being?"

She might have had a good explanation to the question, but he didn't await her response. Rather, he went on to say, "Are we not all part of the Creator's plan?" Warming to his subject, he continued. "This is a fact of the Englishman's society that we of the Seneca have not understood. By what authority does one man feel he can own another?"

She shrugged. "I little know, except perhaps in the matter of debt, since a man or a woman cannot produce all he or she requires in order to live. He or she must work, then, for money in order to buy the necessities of life. Sometimes a man lacks the finances needed for basic requirements like food, clothing, and such. In that instance, he might borrow the money from another and become indebted to him. Thus, he works for another to pay for the money loaned to him."

White Thunder's smirk deepened. "Am I to understand, then, that a man exists who does not give what he has to aid another of his own kind? Without expecting labor and servitude in return?"

His confusion must have been easily witnessed on his countenance, for she immediately replied, "I can see how strange it must seem to you, for you have not been brought up by the English and are not aware of their system of culture."

"I spent three years with missionaries."

"That's not the same thing. In English society, there are those who are rich enough to be beholden to none. They are free men and women because they have the necessities of life and don't owe another their work to simply live. Then, there are those who are not rich enough to obtain such needs as food and shelter. These serve those who are free. It is necessary in order to simply live. I am among those who serve others."

Slowly, he nodded. "And who gave these men, who are free, their freedom and the right to rule another's life to the extent of restricting another's free choice?"

She frowned. "I…I don't know. It has always been this way, I believe. It has to do with money, I suppose. Perhaps the king grants their favor?"

"Ah, the English father. And who gave the English father the right to rule over another's life and take away his freedom?"

She pulled a face. "You ask me questions I have never pondered. But I believe the church gives the king his power.... God?"

White Thunder breathed out on a sigh. "If that is so, then I ask you this: According to the Good Book that the missionaries preached to me, does not the Creator make each of us with the same amount of love? I do not remember the missionaries saying that He smiles more favorably on one of his creatures than another."

"That is true. In the eyes of God, we are all equal."

He dipped his head in understanding. "So it is. And now you understand the Iroquois way. A man is subject only to his Creator and to no other. It is in your Good Book, and it is also part of the Iroquois religion. The fact that, according to the Creator, all men and women command their own lives is understood by those who serve the Iroquois government, also. A man rules his own life. No other. Nor is he *allowed* to rule another. Such conditions were unheard of before the English came to this land."

"But, if what you say were true, there would be nothing but confusion in a country. If all are free, how is one to pay for his necessities? How is another to secure the requirements he needs in order to work and to live?"

"This is a false idea. Do you see confusion surrounding the Iroquois? Or do you see unity?"

"I...I don't know. I haven't had the pleasure of being among your people."

"Then, I will tell you. We of the Iroquois are united. We have laws, but our laws are those given to us by the Creator. Only these must a man obey. And I will tell you this: The Creator made no man to be another man's slave. He who would say differently seeks to enslave you for his own benefit."

At some length, she said, "You seem quite ardent about this, I think."

"Should a man not be impassioned about his own soul, about his own freedom?"

"Yes, yes, of course, it is only that in my society, I have considered that I am lucky to have the position I have. I am housed well, I am clothed. I have good food. Though I am not free, without this position, I little know how I would live."

"You would be married to a man who loves you, and who would take care of you and your children. You would be happy. Your aunts, your uncles, your parents and all others of your clan would ensure your health, also. That is how you would live." He stated it emphatically. "What of your parents? Your aunts? Your uncles? Where are they? Were they also servants to this evil man?"

She gasped, causing him to frown.

He said, "You seem startled that I am so frank, yet the practice of owning another human being is unnatural. Any man who would dare to try to own another man's soul is committing one of the most wicked acts a man can accomplish. Even your own Good Book says so."

"It is not that. I, too, believe the custom of slavery is sinful. Why I reacted is not due to that, but rather because I don't remember who my parents are or what happened to them. I know nothing of aunts or uncles. And, sir, in English society, there is no clan to see to my protection."

"Have the English, then, done away with the family, so there is no one to protect you? Without the family, one could fall easily victim to men with deceitful intentions—as it appears you have."

"Of course the English haven't done away with the family. I gasped not because of what you were saying, but rather at the mention of my parents. I cannot say why, but simply speaking about them makes me feel sad."

His gaze narrowed. Her hands were sweating. Her eyes looked fearful. What had happened to this woman that a simple remark would cause her such anxiety?

However, he didn't ask. "I am sorry I have brought up a matter that brings you sadness. Perhaps, in time, you will remember more."

"Perhaps. But it is maddening. At first, it seemed as if my memory returned in full, and yet I can't recall anything about my own parents, nor under what circumstances I became indentured to this man. I even remember his name—the man who holds my papers—John Rathburn. But about my parents, I recollect nothing."

Sitting forward, White Thunder took both of her hands into his, and, as gently as he could put into words, he said, "It will come back to you. It will come."

As he stared into the deep blue of her eyes, he thought he had never witnessed anyone quite so beautiful. Again, desire ravished him. Again, he cautioned himself to do nothing.

Ah, if only he were free to hold her. If only...

Chapter Ten

She sat back on her heels and loosened her hands from White Thunder's. She hadn't expected his outburst concerning a person's liberty—or lack of it.

His reaction worried her, since she could not predict what his response would be to the request she must make. However, since her memory had returned, and, since she had no option but to ask, she spoke up to say softly, "There is a circumstance I've remembered, and a favor I would beg of you."

He nodded, as if to say, *Please continue.*

Warily, she went on. "Recently, before my accident, I was engaged upon the task of accompanying a young woman who was in my charge. We were traveling through these woods on our way to New Hampshire. Obviously, I am now lost from her, and, if you would be so kind as to help me, I would like to find her and ensure her safety. Since I have recalled who I am and the obligations I hold, I find I'm worried about what has become of this young woman to whom I owe my loyalty."

White Thunder hesitated before he said, "Tell me more about this woman. Is this the same person you mentioned earlier? I believe you called her your mistress. And if so, is she one of the people who thinks she owns you?"

"Oh, no, not at all. She's a young woman who was put into my charge long ago. I've been her friend and companion for many, many years. It was her uncle who assigned me into servitude because..." She stopped and rubbed her forehead. "Pardon me, for I still cannot remember why I am indentured to this man. All I can recall is that I've five more years in his service. As for Marisa—"

"That's her name?"

"Yes. She is truly innocent of all her uncle's doings, and she is more like a sister to me than a mere friend. She loves me, and I love her."

"Yet, if she is related by blood to the evil one..."

"No, no, she's not. He's not really her uncle. He's her step-uncle, so they are not related by a true family line. Indeed, she was trying to take me beyond her uncle's influence—and that is how I came to be here.... I think."

"You think?"

"Forgive me, but I don't recall what happened that I became separated from her—at least, not now. Perhaps, in time, I will remember it all."

"*Nyoh*, yes. In time, I am sure you will." Drawing in a deep breath, he reached out for her, and, taking one of her hands into his, he brought it to his lips, whereupon he kissed it. Her senses suddenly jerked into life, and sensation, carnal and erotic, swept along her nerve endings. Furthermore, from deep within her arose a response that was as pleasant as it was a mystery to her.

What was this? Certainly she liked the man, but this? And from a mere touch?

She did her best to ignore the perception, if only because he was doing nothing more than looking at her—perhaps to ascertain her response. Indeed, after a moment, he continued. "But let me tell you this so that you may know my stance about your people."

"Yes, please. Continue." She loosened her hand from his grip.

He seemed not to notice her withdrawal from him. He acknowledged her with a nod, then he said, "Although I told you that when you remembered who you were and who your people were, I would lead you back to them, I little realized at the time that 'your people' might include a man so degraded he would try to own a fellow human being. Let me be clear on this: I will not take you back to this place where a man deems that he owns you. Not while there is breath within my breast would I do this to you, nor to any other person. I will bring you to my home, instead, where you will be free."

She wrinkled her brow. "But...free to do what?"

"Free to be your own person. Free to live your life as you see fit. In my village, there will be many who would admire you, many who would want to spend the rest of their life with you. You would have a full life there."

Well, this was certainly a new problem to face, and she fidgeted as she considered how best to approach it. "You are kind to suggest this, sir. But I think I would be unhappy if I failed to find and assume my obligation for the young woman who was in my charge. There is more to consider, also, since it would only be a matter of time before those who searched for me would discover me in your village, and then...there would be trouble."

"Trouble matters little to us, for we of the Seneca are used to adversity."

She gazed back at him, and gradually her solemn look transformed into a smile. "I appreciate your kindness, and I thank you for your consideration. But I am not Indian and I'm not part of your tribe, and sooner or later, I fear the past would catch up with me. I worry for the life of the young woman who was in my charge, and I don't believe I'll rest easily until I discover her whereabouts and what has happened to her."

"I understand. It is good you feel this way. But before I agree with what you ask, tell me: If I aid you in finding her, will she lead you back to this man who thinks he owns you?"

"Indeed not. Please allow me to correct a false impression you have, sir. That man doesn't own *me*. He owns my indenture papers."

"There is little difference that I see."

"But it is not the same at all. And please understand that Marisa would never take me back to her uncle. She had gone to great pains to secure me away from him. I believe that's why we were traveling in the woods. We were escaping him and his influence over me. Since you have been open with me, telling me your thoughts, let me also speak with clarity. Even if Marisa were to escort me back to her uncle, I would not object."

"I would."

"But don't you see? Better it would be that I serve out my bond now to this man than never to return and spend the rest of my life in hiding. Surely, you can understand this. At the end of my servitude, I would truly be free to be my own person, and I would then be at liberty to live my life without having to leave my society."

She watched as he bobbed his head, his attention turned inward. At last, he said, "I understand you believe this, but I fear you will only become free in your society if this man can find no other reason to detain you. Beware. At the end of five years, there could well be some other reason he concocts to keep you. I say this because any man who would flaunt the ways of the Creator is also a man who would lie. And such a man would do so without thought of consequences."

"But, sir, in order to keep me, he would have to tell untruths in a court of law, and I don't believe he would dare to do it. After all, a court requires a man take an oath."

"Hmph! A man such as he has already sold himself into the ways of darkness. Therefore, an oath would mean nothing to him because there is so little life left within him. What would it matter to him if he were to lose a little more of that life by telling untruths?"

"I fear I am not following your logic. That man is as alive as I am. Isn't he?"

White Thunder scrutinized her features. Speaking slowly, as though choosing his words carefully, he said, "There is a wise old sachem among us who proclaimed that a man or a woman such as this man does not truly live, because living encompasses not only caring for yourself, but caring for others."

"But—"

"Tell me, how can a man who pleases only himself and no other be happy?"

"But aren't there many who do exactly that?

"Perhaps, and for a short time, that person might be happy...though I doubt it, for true happiness of the mind, body and spirit is not possible to such a man. The laws of the Creator forbid it."

"I…I don't understand. What laws?"

He frowned at her before stating, "Let me tell it to you this way. Can a man find bliss and also ignore the child who goes hungry? Can a man be secure in his own needs when he pretends not to hear the cries of those he enslaves?"

She opened her mouth to answer, but he saved her the necessity when he went on to say, "No. Such men, by the laws of God, must shut off their understanding of others. They must have ears that do not hear and eyes that do not see. Thus they understand less and less, not only about others, but about themselves and the nature of creation. Because of this, such a man cannot experience life as you and I know it. He can only eat and sleep and perhaps ruin the lives of others. He does not truly live.

"If it were different, a man would have empathy for his fellow human beings and would not own slaves, not merely because it is wrong—which it is—but because he would understand that all men and women are alive, too. He would respect it. That is why we of the Seneca say that such men merely exist. Happiness cannot be found at the expense of others, and particularly at the expense of those who you could help and do not."

She bit her lip and stirred uneasily. It sounded so good, so enlightened, and she was struck by this man's observation of life. But she'd lived in this world a good many years, and she'd observed otherwise. And so she countered, "While you speak wisely, sir, and these observations that you make could be true, I fear I have witnessed that such men appear to me to be happy. Marisa's step-uncle, for instance, is this kind of man, and he certainly is able to accumulate many things that should make him happy. Plus, he surrounds himself with the finer qualities of life, and these comforts alone give him a life of ease."

"Ah, but is that really living? Do we live out our lives only to gather objects and creature comforts? After all, happiness is not a thing, and it cannot be bought by the Englishman's treasure."

"True."

"Know that he who would seek to own another's soul, through debt or otherwise, is the kind of man who infects the world around him with the unhappiness of his own blackened soul. It is why when we Seneca discover that a man holding office has lied to the people, he is removed from his position and banished from the tribe. He is an object of disgust."

"Banished? Disgust?" She shook her head. "I fear that in my society, if we were to do as the Seneca, there might possibly be no men left." She gave him a brief smile, for she'd meant it in jest.

It appeared White Thunder didn't share her mirth. "Perhaps you speak as you do only because the Englishman is allowed to lie. Whereas, our people know that he who would tell an untruth about one thing will do so again about another. And if this is so, how then is one to ever trust that man again?"

She weighed his words carefully as she sat back. "You could be right. But, as I mentioned before, there are legalities within the English justice system that would prevent the man, John Rathburn, from subjecting me to slavery."

"And you believe this?"

"I do. Our courts are good and just. They will see that justice is done." Bending at the waist, she sat forward. "But I am confused about one matter. You speak of slavery as if it were an evil that your people have never engaged in or ever considered. However, it is my understanding that there are slaves among the Indians. I've heard that when Indians conquer a people, they take captives as slaves."

"Who has told you this?"

"I...I don't remember their names at the moment."

"Perhaps it is the way of societies that some men see one thing but tell another. Or perhaps they seek to blacken the reputation of another, by seeing in another those things they, themselves, do. I say this because what you have heard is not true."

"But the people who said this, and they wrote it also, had lived among the Iroquois."

"I cannot account for these people or their honesty, since I have no knowledge of them. I will tell you what is true and how it really is if you would care to hear of the Seneca's version of the story."

"Indeed, I would."

He rested back against his cushion, and once again reached out to grasp hold of her hand, causing her to follow him down. She lay by his side, and, seeing that she was settled, he began. "When the Seneca conquers a people, those who are alive are often taken as prisoners. But they do not remain so. These people are brought back to the village, where they are either put to death to atone for the anger of one among us who has lost a loved one, or the captive is adopted into a family, where the person takes the place of a relative who was dearly loved. These prisoners are treated the same as the people they replace, and they are no more slaves than I am. They have a voice in their family, they have a say in the government of their new people and of their clan. They are certainly not owned by another. Indeed, they are a free people."

She absorbed his words in silence until, at last, she murmured, "If this be true, then I apologize. It is evident that the information I have been told is biased. This is how it is for all captives?"

"Not all, but most of the time, this is true. In all societies there are men who practice cruelty. The Seneca are no different than other peoples. To say that a man or woman is always adopted would be wrong. But on the whole, what I have told you is true."

"I see," she said as she leaned against his side, "I believe you." Time passed as they lay silently against one another. "Sarah. My name is Sarah."

He grinned down at her. "I am happy to know it. It is a pretty name. Sarah. Miss Sarah. It's almost as pretty as the woman who bears the name."

"You flatter me, sir."

"No flattery. What I say is fact as I see it."

"Thank you. I am honored." She paused for a moment, then asked, "Will you do it? Will you help me find the young woman who was entrusted to my care?"

"*Nyoh*, yes, I could do that. Or perhaps…" he hesitated, as though he were choosing his words with great care, "…you might consider staying with me."

Stay with him? What did he mean?

Sarah sat up on her elbows so she could stare down into his countenance, trying to read his thoughts. But it was impossible. All she witnessed upon his handsome face was his serious intent. So she asked, "Are you referring to marriage between us, sir?"

"*Neh*, no." He shook his head gently. "Forgive me, for I cannot."

Her stomach fell, and she looked away from him, embarrassed. Of course she'd known this had to be his answer. However, this was the second time she'd introduced the subject of marriage in his presence, only to be rejected. It wasn't as if she could marry him, either; even if he asked her. Since her memory had returned, she was now aware of the many reasons this could never be.

Still, his rejection stung.

At length, she said, "If not marriage, then I suppose I don't understand what it is you are proposing."

He didn't speak, at least not straightaway. In truth, minute after minute seemed to crawl by as he appeared to reflect inwardly. Was he searching for the right words to thwart her? The thought had her leaving his embrace, and she sat up.

He followed her up into a sitting position. "Let me speak plainly so there is no doubt in your mind as to my meaning. In a man's life, there are many people who come and go. This is to be expected. However, now and again, a person appears in his life who he would like to keep close to him. You are such a person."

"I… Thank you." She looked down at her lap.

"It is my thought, that rather than you and I going our separate ways, perhaps you might like to stay with me until I fulfill my duty to Wild Mint. And then…"

She didn't speak for several minutes, and when she did, all she said was, "And then?"

He didn't answer.

What could she say? On one hand, what he proposed was appealing. After all, she was more than aware that this man stirred feelings within her—feelings that were best experienced between a man and a wife. But to stay with him while he was committed to another—even if that commitment were to a person who was a mere ghost?

She couldn't do it. Always, she would wonder about herself and about him.

Besides, there were their separate cultures to consider.

Where would they live?

There was also her servitude that might interfere. Five more years…

When she didn't immediately answer, he uttered, "It is a foolish idea, for I have no right to keep you with me until I am free to make you mine."

Sarah knew she should say something, but what?

Perhaps because of her extended silence, he drew back from her. "You are right. Maybe we should find the one you call Miss Marisa. But we can talk more of this later, after I have had a chance to think over what we have discussed so far."

At last, she blurted out, "It's not a foolish idea."

He swallowed, hard, and she was struck by the observation that her response might be important to him. "I would make another inquiry of you, if I might."

He nodded, as though to encourage her to speak. But it wasn't an easy question to put to him, and she hesitated.

In a few seconds, he asked, "You have a query?"

"Yes. Yes, I do." Sarah raised her chin, if only to give herself courage. "I fear my hesitation accounts for my confusion as to how to ask this of you."

He nodded, as if he understood her exactly. "Be at ease. You can ask me most anything, and I will answer and give you my opinion."

"'Tis not that sort of question...." She drew in her breath and looked away from him. But she knew that once begun, she needed to carry this thought to its end. "I thank you for your offer. But you must know I cannot stay with you. We were, the two of us, raised so differently, and I believe this might eventually cause dissension between us. Besides, as I've already mentioned, I fear my servitude would ultimately catch up with me. Therefore, I have no option but to fulfill my debt. However, it's also because of my debt, and my servitude, that I would ask this of you."

He nodded.

At last, she said, "'Tis my consideration that if I am to serve out my next five years before I'm allowed my freedom then I..." She sighed. "Oh, I can't do it. I shouldn't ask. I know I shouldn't. 'Tis silly, really." She made to get to her feet. "Forgive me. I'll go and fix us our supper if I can find..."

He, too, rose along with her, and grabbed for her wrist when she would have left. "I thought my idea was foolish, yet I asked it. Please tell me, what is in your mind?"

She sat down again and looked askance at him. "I…I…would like to know…"

"Is it something to do with my people? Or perhaps a thing you fear to ask about my people? If so, do not hesitate. I will answer as best I can, and I am not easily insulted."

"No, were it a subject commonly spoken about and not personal, I wouldn't be having a hard time putting my thoughts to words."

Again, he nodded.

"I…I would know…" she stuttered. "I would know…"

Both of them were sitting perfectly still. Both of them were staring at one another.

"Love," she blurted.

He frowned, and she wondered if she'd said something wrong.

What was he thinking? "*Nyoh,* yes, many men and women would know more about this, if they could."

She let out a long breath. "Yes, you are right. But I fear you still don't understand me." She gazed away from him, embarrassed. Thus, as she prepared to say what was in her heart, she found herself looking at her hands instead of at him. "If I'm to serve out my next five years—and I feel that I must—then they will be years spent without love. Therefore, it occurs to me that I'd like to come to know love…now."

He didn't move a muscle. In fact, he looked as if he might have been struck by lightning.

"I'm sorry if I have shocked you, but—"

"You have not shocked me." He blew out his breath slowly, softly, as he closed his eyes. Within seconds, he leaned in toward her and once again took her hand in his.

She didn't understand. Why didn't he say something…anything? Was he now the one teasing her?

She tried to remove her hand from his, but he wouldn't let go. Instead, he gathered her into the shelter of his arms, brought her in close, and said, "I thought you were never going to ask."

Chapter Eleven

He turned her head into his and rubbed his cheek over hers. As though she were a sweetened treat he'd long been denied, he buried his face in the crook of her neck. "I have been waiting for these words from you for days," he whispered.

"But you said nothing to me, and not by a single action have I thought that you—"

"Of course not. Did I not promise you?" His hands were massaging her back, moving up and down her spinal column, and everywhere he touched, he sent shivers of delight over her body. Sarah melted against him.

"Please, fear not that I am trying to encourage you to marry me," she whispered against his shoulder, since she felt she owed him an explanation. "Indeed, you have made yourself clearly understood on that account. And although I still believe a man and woman should be married before they commit the act of love, it is only that..." She sighed. "I little know how to explain it. Seeing you with the bear and realizing I could lose you—"

"Shhh," he murmured, putting his forefinger over her lips. "That is all behind us now. I understand." And then, he kissed her.

At first, it was a soft kiss, nothing more than his mouth against hers. But then, it became something far different. Slowly, his tongue traced the outline of her lips before he kissed her eyes, her nose, her cheeks. His actions were prolonged, as though he might memorize every contour.

However, what was happening to her was far from slow. Wave after wave of excitement had taken control of her senses. Even her stomach responded to him, creating a giddy sensation deep within her, making her feel as if she might have jumped off a precipice.

Sarah moaned, trying to fit her body in close enough to his to satisfy the fiery tide of passion that had taken possession of her. It seemed impossible, for she couldn't seem to get close enough. She wanted, she needed, to feel his imprint against her. She wanted all of him.

He moved, bringing her down into a lying position and onto her side, where he settled in next to her. But he didn't end the kiss. Instead, it became more intense.

Where his lips had adored her before, his fingers now smoothed over those same places, gently touching her eyes, her cheeks, her ears. In reaction, Sarah lost track of time and place.

Indeed, his simple kiss might have been working magic, for it seemed to her that the world around her disappeared. As his lips paid homage to her face, her neck, her shoulders, Sarah squirmed in against him, searching for…something.

When he lowered her so she was lying down on her back, not a single thought of objection occurred to her. He came up over her, but he didn't press down with his weight. Rather, he found new places to kiss and caress.

Gradually, his lips found hers once more, but this time, he encouraged her to open to him. As soon as she acquiesced, his tongue invaded the hot recess of her mouth, and he made love to her with nothing more than tongue and gentle persuasion. She answered him back in the age-old rhythm of love.

Their tongues danced with feverish delight while he explored the inner sanctum of her mouth. Was this heaven? She wanted to embrace him, to love him, to give him the essence of all she was. If only he could be hers. For if he were, she would give all that she had, all that she was, to this one man alone.

As his kiss took possession of her, the exterior world vanished. There was nothing but him.

It was a creation of beauty.

Eventually, even he had to break away from her as he gasped for air. Yet, as soon as his lungs were replenished, he groaned, he growled, and when he next kissed her, it was with the most exquisite passion she had ever known.

Gone was the soft, gentle possession. In its place was a sexual appetite so real, it took her breath. As his tongue again claimed ownership of her mouth, his hand trailed down her face and neck to her shoulders.

The erotic feeling was out of proportion to what he was doing, and she rocked back and forth as the hunger for all that this man could give her took over. She'd never wanted anything more in her life.

"It is good between us," he whispered against her lips.

His words were such an understatement that Sarah couldn't help saying, "'Tis a bit of heaven, I think."

"I, too, believe this."

His hand unerringly found her breasts, and she sucked in her breath at the ultra-rich sensation. Again, she squirmed against him, setting back her shoulders, as though only in this way might she better experience the love being made between them.

"What you are doing is beyond my experience," she murmured. "I fear I never knew I had the capability to feel so much pleasure."

"Little Autumn," he murmured against her, "I, too, am overwhelmed with feeling. It is not always this way between two people. What is happening with us is uncommon, I think."

"Is it?"

"I believe so."

He shifted position, bringing his head to her chest, and, with his lips, he made love to her breasts, even through the barrier of the linen of her corset and chemise. First, he adored one mound, then, the other.

For Sarah's part, she had never felt more loved. She swayed, first bringing herself into one position so he had easy access to her, then another. She was still dressed in her underclothes, but it didn't seem to curtail him in any manner. He kissed and caressed her as if she lay naked before him.

When his hand trailed over her belly, massaging and stroking as he explored farther and farther down her form, her hips rose to greet him. Her petticoats might have presented him a barrier, but thank goodness for the English style of dress. There was nothing under those petticoats but her.

His touch unerringly found that most feminine place on her body, and she reacted as if she had taken a steep plunge off a cliff. Her stomach felt as light as a feather, and her hips moved up and down in a rhythm that was as old as time itself.

Of their own accord, her legs opened to him.

"You are wet," he murmured as he rose on an elbow. "Do you know what this means?"

"I...do not...."

Softly, he explained. "Your body tells me it is ready for me. My only question is, are you?"

"Yes. I believe I am. Please."

Her reply seemed to send a flurry of emotion over him, for he shut his eyes momentarily, as though only in that way might he control the passion within him. "It has been very long for me since I made love to a woman. I will try to hold back my seed for as long as possible, so I might give you much pleasure before I seek my own. Know if that doesn't happen this time, if I cannot hold myself back, I will do so next time."

"You could do most anything at this moment, and I believe it would pleasure me."

At her words, he groaned, and, coming up onto his elbows, he settled himself over her. "You realize...it will hurt, at first."

"I know."

"But it won't always hurt."

"Will it not?"

For a moment, his expression showed his confusion over her reply, but it was quickly gone as his gaze became fiery with desire.

"White Thunder," she said, "I do believe you are…beautiful."

"I?" Even as he spoke, he was positioning himself over her. "It has long been my observation that a person sees in another those traits that he or she possesses. Therefore, if you see beauty in me, it is most likely because *you* are beautiful."

She smiled.

"And so you are," he said simply. And then he brought their bodies together in the ancient dance of love.

The moment was charged with pent-up energy, as well as a little fear. Sarah expected the pain of lovemaking, and she braced herself for it.

This was it. She rocked under the torture of first entry. This part of the act, she remembered. She also recalled that it got worse.

She had asked for this?

But, strangely, this time, it *didn't* get worse. White Thunder hadn't thrust any deeper into her. Instead, he waited for her passion to rise again as he leaned down to encourage that ardor by showering one kiss after another upon her lips, her eyes, her cheeks. With his hand, he molded her breasts.

His patience worked the magic of lovemaking. Gradually, the cramping within her subsided, and pure sensation took command over her. She moved her hips. It felt good.

When he thrust a little deeper, she waited for the misery that she knew usually accompanied the maneuver. But there was none. Instead of the pangs of injury, a whole new realm of pleasure opened to her.

He whispered against her ear, "Someone has mistreated you."

It was no question. He knew. Perhaps it was because their thoughts seemed to be as one at the moment.

She didn't answer. She didn't know how to express that part of her very personal history.

He said, "The man who did this to you should be tortured slowly, first by fire, and then by the knife, until he begs for his death."

"No." She bit her lip. "I would not have the miserable torment of anyone on my conscience."

He nodded, and then he kissed her, lingeringly and gently, as though she might break if he dare heap too much passion upon her. "We will talk more of it later."

"Perhaps. But if I might ask, I would beg you to continue your lovemaking as before. I will not break."

For a moment, he came up to gaze into her eyes. At first, she recognized surprise within the depths of his dark irises, but then, gradually, it changed, and he grinned down at her. "No, I don't believe you will."

That was all it took to spur him into action. She raised her hips to his, and, in response, he took possession of her…all of her.

She met him move for move, thrust for thrust, amazed at the incredible measure of emotion building within her. Surely, this was pure grace happening between them, instead of…

She wouldn't allow herself to recall the horror of her past. She would hold that part of her back. Her body was pushing her, driving her for more. A fire had been lit within her, and something alluring and divine was begging for release.

Without warning, it happened. Pleasure consumed her, exploding and cascading throughout her body.

It was perfect, ethereal. And she wanted more of him…deeper, faster.

He knew how to please her, presenting her with exactly what she craved. Like the rush of a moving stream, it was a dance like none other.

The sensation built within her, until all at once, Sarah tipped over the edge with so much rapture, she cried out. Elation swept throughout her, body and soul, until at last, the ache within her was satiated.

Peace settled over her.

Coming up onto his elbows, White Thunder smiled down at her before taking her lips with his own.

"I was unaware," she murmured against him, "that the act of love could be so... I know of no words to adequately describe it."

"I, too, have no words to recount it, except to say that it is good between us. Always, should it be this way. But it is not finished yet."

"Is it not?"

"I have not yet met my pleasure. Come, let us do it all over again."

Perhaps he might have taken her back into the realm of ecstasy once more, but it wasn't to be—at least, not this time. All at once, he burst forth his seed within her. Sarah, wrapping her arms around him securely, felt as though she had never welcomed anything more.

In the aftermath, they lay in each other's arms, he still a welcome part of her.

This was a surprise. A wonderful and welcome surprise, if only because the only detail she could recall from her distant past was one of revulsion and embarrassment.

There was none of that here. There was only beauty. There was only her. There was only him.

And what was between them was a phenomenon of magnificence.

Chapter Twelve

"I have much feeling for you," he admitted after their breathing had returned to normal.

"As I have for you."

"But come, I do not wish to crush you," he whispered, and promptly moved to her side. But he didn't leave her. He held her tightly within his arms, as though afraid if he let go, she might disappear.

"You were not crushing me."

"I am glad." His next question took her by surprise. "Who is this man who has done this to you?"

Sarah bit her lip. There was no point in denying she didn't know exactly what he was asking. Although the assault upon her person had happened long ago, it had left its scar upon her, even if that scar were only emotional. For good or for bad, this man whose arms were around her was now privy to her most intimate secrets.

As she debated what to say and what not to say, she hesitated. In truth, so drawn out were her thoughts, time passed, and, after a while, she wondered if he had perhaps focused his attention elsewhere. Turning her head ever so slightly, she was able to steal a glance at him as he lay by her side, and she was amazed to discover that his eyes were fixed intently on her, and his look had not lost any of its fervor.

She said, "If I tell you who he is, does that mean that you will have to seek him out and kill him?"

"I will."

"But you already are hunting a man for that purpose, are you not?"

He nodded.

"I fear I have little desire to add to your burden."

"It is not a burden. It is a duty."

"Still, I wouldn't make your obligations any worse than what they already are."

He paused, but his expression was as ardent as ever. At length, he sighed deeply and put the same question to her again. "Who is this man?"

She stared away from him. "If I recall it well, it happened when I was young.... 'Tis odd I can remember this, while other parts of my life still remain a mystery to me."

He waited. "Yes? You were young?" he prompted.

"You must first promise me you'll not go looking for him with the design and intent to kill him."

"I cannot give you my assurance on that." He shifted his position so he was lying on his back. "He deserves to be killed. What this man did to you is a crime. Know that, in my society, such a man would be taken before a council and sentenced to a torture so gruesome he would beg for death. And he would beg for it for many days, because we would ensure he was kept alive for as long as possible. All would see what befalls a man who would stoop to so low an act."

Sarah gasped and came up to her elbows, where she leaned over him. "I...I can't let you do that."

He didn't answer. Instead, he glanced at her and asked once more, "Who is this man? Is it the same man who owns you, this John Rathburn?"

"You remember his name?"

His eyes narrowed. "You change the subject. Is it the same man?"

"I...I cannot tell you. In your culture you would be expected to seek him out and kill him. In mine, I must forgive him and move forward with my life."

"It is he, is it not? The one who thinks he owns you?"

She flopped back against his arm, causing him to wince. She'd almost forgotten that this man had only recently been injured. Instantly, she sat up. "I'm sorry. I didn't mean to hurt you."

"It was nothing. Is it he?"

"Please don't ask me about this any further, White Thunder. I cannot tell you, because I cannot meet my Creator knowing the death of a man is on my conscience."

"And I will not meet mine without seeking true justice. Does not your Good Book say an 'eye for an eye'? 'A tooth for a tooth'? In this same book, even a thief is put to death. Tell me, in view of this, what would your Good Book do with a man who steals the innocence of a good woman?"

Her look at him was frustrated. "You are putting questions to me I can't answer, but I can say there's another Book contained in that Good Book—the one you so nobly quote— and that Book teaches a person to forgive."

"I will forgive this man," he stressed, "*after* he is dead."

Sarah inhaled deeply. "Please, let us not speak of him any further. Can we not talk of us, of what we are doing and how we can go about solving our own problems? You must see that there are many problems between us."

"You will not tell me his name?"

"No, I won't."

He sighed. "You are a beautiful woman. You are a good woman. But you are not following this to its conclusion. What will happen if you do not accuse this man and see that justice is done? Do you wish to have *that* on your conscience?"

"I...I don't understand."

"Do you think this man has the moral fiber to withhold himself from doing the same act again? If no one stops this, and he thinks he can abuse you with no consequence, how many more people will be harmed by him? Have you considered this?"

"I... No, I haven't. But I fear I'm not in a position to bring this man to justice. I'm an indentured servant. I have no legal sway over what this man does. Besides, even if I did, if I were to go to the authorities, what court is going to believe me over a man of wealth and influence?"

"*Nyah-weh.*"

"What does that word mean?"

"Thank you."

She gave him a puzzled look. "Thank you? What are you thanking me for?"

"I now know who this man is. I will find him."

Sarah sighed.

"Since I know who he is, tell me how it happened."

She tore herself away from the look in his eyes before she said, "I don't know if I can. I've never spoken of what happened to anyone except to my friend, Marisa, and then only in a most general way."

"Come here." He opened his arms to her, and, when she fell into them, he brought her body in close to his. It was an odd, yet erotic, feeling. She was still clothed in chemise, corset and petticoats, but he was naked, and in her heightened state, the touch of his body next to hers was as enticing as if he were beginning his kisses all over again.

He nestled her head into the crook of his arm. "You should tell someone about it, and since I am here, I will be that person. Besides, what happened to you is important to me. There was pain. I saw that when we were making love. Tell me, how old were you?"

"I was fourteen. I had come to live in his household as a servant because…well, in truth, I still can't recall why I was there." She bit her lip. "I do remember I wasn't always a servant, though. Once, like you, I was free."

"Did he force himself on you?"

"Yes, he did."

"How many times?"

"Perhaps as many as ten. It did stop, after a while. Within months after my arrival, another came to live under his roof. That was Marisa. Her parents had died at sea, and her only living relative was John Rathburn. Because she was barely four years old, he required a companion for her, which became my duty. When that happened, the assaults stopped. I don't know why. I am profoundly glad they ceased."

White Thunder pulled her even closer into his embrace and simply held her. "Together, we will take away the pain so that in the future when you think of the act of love, you will only remember how good it is."

"Yes, I would like that. But, White Thunder, are you going to kill him?"

"I am," he said without the least hesitation.

"You mustn't."

"I must. But that time is in the future, and I must plan it well. He is white, and if he is influential, as you say, it might be difficult. The killing of a white man is not ever an easy deed to accomplish, for one's actions will often revert back against one's people. I will have to consider how to do this thing in detail. I know only that it will be done."

She shook her head, as if her slight disagreement might have him changing his mind.

She might have said something more, but he was continuing to speak. "There is one other matter between us that we must discuss."

"Oh? What is that?"

"By our actions today, we may have conceived a child."

"I doubt it. In all those times when Mr. Rathburn forced himself into my life, I did not conceive."

"I am not Rathburn."

"Yes, thank goodness. But I'm thinking that my lack of conception might hint at the fact it may be hard for me to become pregnant. This is sometimes the case with certain women. Perhaps I am one of them."

"Perhaps," he said, as if in agreement. But there was enough doubt in his voice that it rebutted at once any such understanding. "I suspect the fault wasn't yours. It would most likely be his, for the seed of such men, due to their own acts of violence, is often impotent."

"Hmm. That's an interesting observation. Do you suppose it's really true?"

He shrugged. "It matters little. The important reason for us to speak of this is to agree that if you are with child, you will stay with me, regardless of whether I have found Wild Mint's murderer or not."

A note in his tone of voice had Sarah bristling, and she backed away from him slightly, enough to take her body out of his arms. "I am flattered by your attention on my behalf. I see you are trying to protect me, and I thank you. But you must see I cannot stay with you. It was one matter to speak of marriage, as I did, when I had no memory of my past. But now that my mind has healed, I fear there are many reasons to keep us apart."

"And these reasons are?"

She glanced away. "We have spoken of some already, but some are obvious. We have dissimilar values because we've been raised differently, and in two separate worlds. There is the matter of my servitude, as we have discussed, and the fact I have pledged my word of honor to employ myself for the benefit of another for a certain amount of years. Surely, you understand."

He stared at her. "You will not go back to that man."

"You fail to understand. Whether I like it or not, I must go back. I have no choice."

"You always have a choice. The Creator made it so. Now, certainly, I grasp you have been tricked into believing you are not free to determine your own destiny and fate. But to tell me with all sincerity that another has the right to tell you what you can and cannot do in your own personal life, I will never understand, nor will I ever agree that such things are binding. If there is a child created from our actions, all will have to change, and whatever is left of your servitude will have to be forgotten. Instead, you will live with me in my village as my woman."

When she made to speak, he held up his hand. "There is no need to argue with me, for that is the way it will be."

His words had the effect of causing her to draw back farther from him. As she did so, she asked, "And who suddenly made you my master?"

His look at her was surprised, but he said nothing.

She went on to say, "I beg to differ, sir."

He exhaled slowly. "Differ all you would like without consequence—as long as you are not pregnant. If that happens, we will marry."

She shook her head and frowned. "You are a contradiction. You speak of freedom, yet you attempt to tell me what I can and can't do in the same breath?"

"Because you must think of the child. I cannot fathom you would presume that taking responsibility for our child would endanger you or weigh upon your conscience."

"You now put words in my mouth that I have not spoken."

Anger had her sitting up, moving even farther away from him. "You go too far with your demands. I am trying to take responsibility, not only for a child that you and I don't even know has been conceived, but for myself and my bond to others whom I have promised to serve. But there is more that weighs upon my mind. There is you, your injuries and your problems, and my desire to help you. All this I must consider, in addition to the gaps in my memory. I am doing the best I can in a situation with which I am unfamiliar, so do not judge me, for there is much here to be pondered, not simply one aspect of my life."

His look at her was one of thoughtful recollection, and he was nodding faintly, as though he might be deliberating over the delicate points of contract negotiation. "You speak well and you speak wisely, for I had not taken all that you say into consideration. I forget, too, that you have been raised differently than I, and, as you say, with different values, because to a Seneca, there is nothing more important than a child. And no agreement between two human beings, regardless of its legitimacy, would supplant the necessity to put all aside and to concentrate on the rearing of a child. But I see what is in your mind, and I respect all you have told me, and I respect you." He breathed out slowly, casting his glance up toward the stone roof. "If you are pregnant, how would you attempt to raise that child?"

"I little know, sir, for I have not had the reason to reflect upon such a thing."

"If you were to return to the English settlement with a child, would the English put that child into servitude because you are its mother?"

"No. Service to another is, indeed, a different matter than slavery in that the child I would bear would have no pledge or bond of servitude, which must be given before servitude can commence. Thus, he or she would not be bound by the same oath that I am."

White Thunder appeared reflective for a moment. "This would be true, even if you failed to finish the last five years of your servitude? A child of yours would not be forced to answer in your place?"

"I think not," she said, although strangely, she had a bad feeling about this. Illogically and all at once, her eyes felt misty, and her temples started to pound.

"Is something wrong?" he asked after she began rubbing her forehead.

"No, 'tis only that I have a strange foreboding, as though there is an important memory I can't quite grasp." She tossed her head. "Or perhaps it's a feeling that I have done this before in some manner...."

"And have you?"

"I little know. Although, I begin to think that perhaps I may have. Do you suppose, that my parents had something to do with my own servitude?"

He quirked an eyebrow at her. "I have no method by which I can answer that. Already, I find my wits challenged to understand your viewpoint, let alone that of the English slave master."

"Yes, I can see 'tis true. But 'tis also curious, don't you think, that I can now remember so much, yet nothing of my parents or how I came to be placed into the position that I hold? But I was young when it happened. I was only fourteen...."

"And you are twenty-and-nine now?"

"Yes, that's right."

"It is strange."

"What is strange?"

"Fifteen summers ago, about the time when you were being forced into servitude, I lost Wild Mint."

"Indeed." She looked down and away from him. "It seems it was a bad year."

"*Nyoh.*"

Silence fell upon them then, until Sarah took note that he could barely keep his eyes open. Sitting forward, she straightened the boughs and the blanket around him. "Rest, now. I assure you I'm fully capable of fixing our supper, and when you awaken, we shall eat."

He yawned, then smiled at her. "It's a good plan. A very good plan."

There it was again, she thought as she stared down into his eyes. His smile could be likened to a shaft of light descending into a forest of gloom, and, despite herself, Sarah found it difficult to pull her gaze away from his. "I thank you for all you've done for me, and I pray you will be able to rest well, and long before—"

"I would sleep better if you were here beside me." He patted the space next to him.

Sarah cast him a surprised look. "Better perhaps, but not for as long, I think. No, you rest, while I cook."

"Very well," he agreed, "but when I awaken..."

He never finished the sentence. No sooner had the words left his lips, than he fell into an abrupt sleep.

Sarah, watching him, smiled.

Chapter Thirteen

Her touch was as cold as a blizzard in the dead of winter. He reached out for her, but she giggled and moved out of his grasp.

He followed her. "Wait for me," he called, but she had the advantage of floating over the grasses and tree trunks.

She stopped suddenly, allowing him to catch up to her. She gazed up at him and smiled, her round and pretty face mirroring her delight. Then, she pointed to the plant that grew directly beneath her feet.

He recognized that plant. It was one his grandmother had often collected. Its root was used for…

He awoke suddenly. Where was he?

Glancing around him, he realized he had never left the cave. It had been a dream, of course. Looking up, he took note of Little Autumn in the foreground, working over the fire, and he sighed.

Ah, she was beautiful.

She was stoking the flames in an effort to cook something, which smelled very much like a stew. The aroma of it was intoxicating and rich with the scents of bone broth, wild spices, and fresh herbs, and, as he inhaled deeply, his stomach growled.

Narrowing his gaze on her, he studied this woman more closely. Her beauty was, indeed, without comparison, and, remembering all she had told him earlier, he found it singularly odd that, indentured servitude or not, she had never married.

Her hair had escaped the knot she'd used to tie it back, and golden-blonde tendrils fell in loose ringlets around her face. Her dress was simple, a casual affair consisting of a tight-laced structure that made her waist look as if he might span it with his hands. Petticoats that were stiff and hooped on the side brought her a measure of dignity, though the front of her gown was dangerously low at her chest, beneath which her nipples played an enticing game of peek-a-boo with him.

A curl bounced around her face while she worked, and he knew a desire to twirl its softness around his finger so he could study the differences in its color, from pale blonde, to tawny, to daffodil. She was a delicately built woman, small and feminine, and, without consciously willing it, his loins stirred to life as he watched her.

To counter the effect she was having on him, he sat up, yawned and stretched. "I believe I know how to keep you from becoming pregnant."

She clasped her hand to her chest and sent him a surprised look. "You gave me a fright, sir. I didn't know you were awake."

"I have roused myself only recently."

"Yes, you have been asleep for some time. I'm glad you were able to rest easily and long. I have meanwhile made us a soup for our supper. There were many roots and vegetables that you collected, and I have used some of them."

"It smells like a feast, and I am hungry."

She picked up one of the shells that he had fashioned into a bowl and using it, scooped out some soup. "Shall I bring the stew to you?"

"I can come there to you." He struggled to get to his feet. It wasn't as easy as he'd thought it would be, and he had almost collapsed before she rushed to his side to steady him.

"What are you thinking?" she scolded. "You need rest in order to recover. One would suppose, the way you are acting, that you battle with bears daily."

He smiled. "Almost."

She helped him to sit back upon his bed, then straightened the blanket and pine boughs around him. "I'll bring you the soup."

"Good." He shut his eyes. "Good."

She was gone only a moment. "Careful," she said as he made to take the shell full of broth and vegetables out of her hands. "It's hot."

He grinned at her and caressed her fingers as he accepted the shell. When she didn't pull away, he stared straight into the depths of her gentle blue eyes, as though by doing so, he might see into her soul.

He murmured, "I was watching you as you worked."

"Were you?"

"Yes."

"And what did you see?"

"A beautiful woman. A woman I would like to spend the rest of my life with, if only circumstances were different."

She gazed away from him. "But they are not different." She pulled her hand away from his. "Do you like the soup?"

He took a sip. "You spoke true. You are an excellent cook."

She smiled at him, and, as she did so, it was as if the sun shone upon him, even in this dark and dreary cave. It was the sort of grin that made him feel as if he were seventeen again, complete with all the wild impulses of the very young. So lovely was she, he might likely die a happy man to simply look at her.

Upon that thought, he drank the rest of the soup without once dropping his gaze from hers. Indeed, with his eyes, he caressed her. At last, the stew was gone, and he handed the shell back to her.

"Would you like some more?"

"*Nyoh,* yes, please." He watched as she came up to her feet and stepped toward the fire, admiring the feminine sway of her hips as she moved. When she returned, he again caught her hand, only this time he didn't let it go. "I have found a remedy for one of our problems."

"Oh?"

"Yes, I have come to realize there is a root that grows with profusion in these woods, and that, if I prepare it in the correct manner, it might well keep you from becoming pregnant. I used to watch my grandmother make medicine from these roots. Hopefully, it is not too late in the season for me to find this plant and pull it up, roots and all. I will begin a search for it as soon as I'm able."

As he stared at her, he took note of the rosy color flooding her countenance, even as she glanced away from him. But she didn't withdraw her hand from his.

In due time, he said, "In my dreams, Wild Mint showed me this root. I had forgotten it. But I was never apt at learning all that my grandmother knew, though she did try to instruct me."

Sarah frowned at him. "It is a shame your grandmother wasn't able to teach you all of her skills. I'm certain she knew much more about wild roots and herbal remedies than I will ever know. But, sir, I would like to note an observation."

He nodded.

"Has it ever come to your attention that you speak of Wild Mint as if she were a living being?"

"Indeed, I do. That is because she *does* live, but no longer in the flesh."

She paused. "I see. I have said it before, so forgive my repetition, but I am sorry for your loss." She retrieved her hand from his hold and fetched the shell from him. "Would you like more?"

He nodded, and she arose to step toward the fire.

When she returned, she began to speak to him all at once. "I must admit your logic, at times, confuses me."

He slanted a frown at her. "I'm sorry. What have I said now that seems to defy logic?"

"Some of the ideas you spoke of earlier—there are a few of these that are troubling me."

"Tell me."

"One of those notions is that you spoke of marriage and told me without reservation that if I were to become pregnant, I must marry you. On the other hand, if I were not to become pregnant, then you don't wish to marry me at all."

"Yes, I did. But I spoke without understanding you completely. When you told me how it is with you, I changed my mind. This is why I'm happy I've been shown this root. It might prevent the problem of pregnancy from occurring altogether."

"Yes." She sat silently before him, staring at her hands.

Something was wrong.

"Is there another concern on your mind?" he asked.

"Yes, there is. By bringing up this subject of pregnancy, I am urged to think about marriage. Now 'tis not that I'm trying to marry you. On the contrary, 'twould be most implausible to do so. But why were you suddenly demanding I marry you, as though you were a tyrant?"

"This is a good question, and I can see how it might confuse you. Let me explain: A child is a most valuable person to a tribe, and it is agreed upon by my people that a child must be brought into the world in the right way. This requires many sacrifices on the part of the parents, whose duty it is to bring their baby up in a manner that does not destroy his natural curiosity. He must receive training in the ways of the tribe, but mostly, he must be raised with love and devotion. It is our belief that a child prospers best when he has two parents who are deeply in love with each other. It is as though the couple passes on this love to their child."

As he spoke, he watched her closely, for the subject was an important one. She hesitated and frowned before she said, "You speak of marriage, and you speak of love. Tell me, since this is how you see it, do you love me?"

Her question took him aback, for, although he considered himself skilled in the powers of observation, he hadn't seen it coming. Carefully, he schooled his features so his expression wouldn't mirror his surprise.

Did he love her? He certainly wanted to make love to her.

But that wasn't what she was asking, and he knew it.

Was it possible for him to love another woman besides Wild Mint? Unfortunately for him, he had no answer to that.

Therefore, to avoid giving Sarah a direct answer, he asked, "Have we not already made love?"

Her stare at him was more than slightly annoyed. "You are avoiding answering my question."

He took a deep breath. "You are right, so let me say this. There is much passion between us. It is a good foundation for two people."

"But do you love me?"

Feeling trapped, he stared at her, and, despite the fact she was putting pressure on him, he couldn't help but admire the gentle rise and fall of her lashes. Did he love her?

At last, he responded, asking, "Do *you* love *me*?"

She shook her head and bemoaned, "I asked you first, sir."

This was the sort of discussion that a man, regardless of race, would rather avoid. However, that wasn't possible in this situation, simply because she was sitting directly in front of him, and she expected an answer.

In the end, he opted for the truth. "I little know how to answer you, so let me say this. Because of you, my world has grown brighter. Because of you, I look to each new day as a day I might share with you, and it is a good feeling. Do I love you? It is possible, and I wish I could say yes without reservation. However, I cannot. But this I do know, and this I can tell you true. Because of you, I have returned to the land of the living, and I no longer ponder death longingly. Moreover, when I look at you, I admire all that you are. I desire your embrace in the most elemental way a man can, and I would like to see my children growing in your belly. If that be love, then *nyoh*, I love you."

She was silent while her gaze sought out almost anything but him. At last, she asked, "But you are also in love with Wild Mint?"

"I am." Ah, he was beginning to understand where this was all leading. "All that I do is because of my love for her."

"Is there a place then, truly, for *me* in your heart?"

"You are already in my heart. You have been there for many days now."

"But in second place."

He didn't pretend to misunderstand her. He leaned toward her and took her in his arms, bringing her in close and nestling her head against his shoulder. Spotting that lock of hair that had teased him earlier, he grabbed it and twirled it around his finger. He took a deep breath and inhaled the sweet fragrance of her. "I see that we need to speak about this so we understand each other better. Know my intentions toward you are those of marriage. Now that we have shown each other our passion, we should follow that up by making the pledge of devotion to one other. But, even as I know this is how it should be, I cannot do it, unless there is an urgent need to do it. A pregnancy would be such a need." He hesitated briefly as he chose his next words with care. "Otherwise, I can marry no one until my obligation to Wild Mint is brought to a conclusion."

A long pause followed, until she said, "Yes, so you have told me. But I suppose what I little understand is why? I fail to grasp the problem with your marrying another or even falling in love with another, as long as it wouldn't prevent you from scouring the countryside to find Wild Mint's murderer."

He sighed deeply. "I cannot do it because..."

Sarah waited. "Because?"

"Because...she is still with me."

Her body started. "I beg your pardon?"

"She is still with me."

"But she is dead, is she not?"

"Yes."

"Then you mean she is still with you in spirit?"

"Yes, and also in body...sometimes."

"In body? I fear I fail to understand."

"Neither did my family. It is why I left my village and ventured out on my own to find her killer. To those who loved me, I became a brooder, a loner, for I spent all my days with her, a ghost—and ignored my family. They feared my influence over others in my clan, for they thought that at her death, I had lost my wits. But I had not lost my sanity. She was truly with me.

"Often, I would return home from a hunt and find a fire lit for me," he continued. "My meals were fixed as she had done when she was alive, and my living space within the longhouse was cleaned. On inquiry, I discovered that no one had been in my quarters. Over time, she began to appear before me. She would share my meal, and we would talk."

Sarah sat back to look into his face. That she was disturbed by his confession was evident. "How bizarre. How long did this continue?"

"To this day."

"To this day?" she repeated, her astonishment almost tangible. "And how long were you married?"

"A very short time, although we had been in love all through our youth, almost since the time we could walk. But our marriage was no more than a few seasons old—perhaps two or three seasons."

"About nine months?"

He nodded. "Sometimes, she would appear before me, a misty image of how she had looked in the flesh. She would merely talk to me. We walked together. We laughed together, as of old. And though her touch upon me was and still is as cold as the ice on a winter river, still, she comforted me in my grief. She comforts me, even to this day."

"You are still in love with her." It was no question. "Tell me, is she with you now?"

"Sometimes."

"At this very minute?"

"No. She is not here now."

"And so the truth, as I understand it, is that you can't marry anyone because you are still married…to her?"

"*Nyoh*, that is true."

His confession rocked her back on her heels. "Is that why you said that I have brought you back from the dead? Because you were slipping more and more into her world?"

"*Nyoh.* Yes."

"You wished to be with her."

"I did."

She glanced away from him, then back. "What will happen if you find this murderer and kill him? How will that affect the two of you?"

"Wild Mint will be freed from her grief, and so will I. I had once thought that when that happy moment occurs, I might join her and bring about my own death through battle. But now, I think not. Life itself holds much for me. Indeed, I find I have changed my mind about death."

Sarah nodded, but when she remained silent, White Thunder went on to say, "You say I saved your life, and I see how this is so. But if I am to be honest, I would admit that you have saved mine, also."

"Truly?" She sank in against his embrace.

He tightened his arms around her. "It is true. And so I will do my duty to Wild Mint, who has been with me all these years and to whom I gave my devotion so long ago. But when I am done with my duty, and the murderer found and justice served, I would like to have a new life, one that includes you, and if you will have me…as my woman."

Sarah was silent.

After a time, he asked, "Tell me, what do you think? Have I been touched by the sun?"

"No, you have not. Indeed, if your sanity is to be in question, then so, too, is mine. However, your story does raise some questions with me, and I wonder…does Wild Mint know about you and me?"

"She does."

"And does she hate me? Women can be jealous of each other."

"*Neh.* She is happy I have found you."

"Happy? Are you certain?"

"She is joyous to see that I have begun to smile again. For most of these years, I have been like a dead soul, existing but not really living, except by my desire to exact revenge. But as bad as it was for me, Wild Mint was more tormented than I."

"She was?"

He nodded. "She not only lost her life, which is most precious, but she lost her unborn child, as well as me and our marriage. This loss also came at a time when she was to be honored by her clan for her charm and her assistance to the clan mothers."

"It came at the height of her success," Sarah commented.

"*Nyoh,* yes. She is suffering still, and will continue to be tormented until I can find this man and kill him. Only then will she be free to move on to the next world."

Sarah was quiet for so long he was astonished when he heard her say, "I will help you."

"Help me?"

"Yes. I am not without feelings for you, White Thunder. Twice, I would be missing from this world, were it not for you—and I…I care for you. So, yes, I will help you…and Wild Mint."

"I would welcome your assistance." He drew her in closer to him until it seemed she might melt into him. Then, he proceeded to massage her spine, his body reacting with all the renewed strength of a young man who is easily aroused.

He closed his eyes, doing nothing more than glorying in the emotional clamoring of feelings. He wasn't expecting it, but from out of nowhere came a feminine voice that said, "*Nyah- weh.*"

White Thunder knew well who was speaking, but Sarah pulled back to gaze up into his face. "Did you say something?"

"Not I. But if you listen closely, I think you will hear Wild Mint saying thank you to you. She is grateful to you, as I am."

Chapter Fourteen

Two days had come and gone. But it was unnerving to speculate that a ghostly presence might be watching your every move. Indeed, it did much to curtail one's activities and romance.

It also caused Sarah to feel more than a little reserved toward White Thunder, and, as she sat beside him, checking over his wounds and bandages, she avoided his gaze. Happily, she noted that despite the lack of stitches to his arm where the cuts were deepest, he was healing well.

"It appears that your suggestion on wrapping the wound is working." She sat forward to tightly rewrap the bandage.

He nodded, his gaze intent on her. "Yes. It would accomplish much the same."

Silence stretched between them until at last he declared, "There is something weighing on your mind." It wasn't a question.

Because Sarah was becoming accustomed to this man's unusual perception of her moods, she didn't take the pains to contradict him. "I...I wonder how much longer you plan to stay here, and if, when we go, you will help me to discover the whereabouts of Miss Marisa."

The intensity of his gaze hadn't changed, although he responded to her softly. "We will remain here to make dry meat and pound roots and berries so that we may take these foods with us. In this way, we won't require a fire or the necessity to go on the hunt each day in order to survive. And yes, we will attempt to find the tracks of your friend, Miss Marisa, though those prints will likely be gone now. It has rained considerably."

"Yes, I know, but I must try...so I thank you." She tied the bandage in place on his arm. "As I've said, I'm uneasy about her. It seems to me she might be in trouble, and I don't think I'll rest easily until I find her."

"That is to be expected, since she was in your care and you are friends. But I fear this is not what is really bothering you. Is it?"

"No, 'tis not."

He waited in silence, and Sarah found it hard to force her vision up to meet his. Rather, she gathered the rag she was using to wash his wounds and set it over the gashes on his chest.

He caught her hand, and, placing a finger beneath her chin, he raised her head until she was looking directly into his eyes. He said nothing, but then, he didn't have to.

At last, she said simply, "I'm afraid."

"Afraid?"

"Perhaps *afraid* isn't the correct word. Mayhap, a more apt expression might be *concerned*. Since you told me about Wild Mint, I worry that she might be here looking over my shoulder. 'Tis not a good feeling to think someone might be watching me from afar."

"There is always someone watching." He shrugged.

"What?"

He brought her hand to his lips, where he kissed her fingers. "This is well known to the Iroquois. Is it unknown to you?"

"Yes, it is unknown to me. Of what are you speaking?"

He frowned. "Consider all the people who have come and gone before you. Some have moved along to the next world, but some have not. That's why there is always someone watching."

"As in God looking over you?"

He nodded. "But for your peace of mind, let me assure you that Wild Mint is not here, not now."

"How do you know this?"

He turned aside. "I simply know. I'm sorry this has bothered you."

"'Tis an odd situation, is it not?"

"Perhaps. But not to me. I have lived with it these past fifteen years."

They stared at one another, and she was certain a moment of empathy sprang up between them, for she realized if she were troubled, so, too, was he. Circumstance had forced him to live amid distress all these years, as he had tried to appease a woman he had once loved, and loved still to this day.

He opened his arms wide to Sarah. "Come here."

She didn't pretend to be coy, not when she'd been yearning for his touch. Rather, she fell in against him as though he were a magnet and she were made of iron.

He closed his arms around her and nestled in against her. It was a delicious feeling.

He said, "I thought there might be difficulties troubling you, but I had little understanding of how to unburden you. I missed you last night. I had expected you to sleep next to me."

"Yes, I know, but I couldn't. I'm doing the best I can in a difficult situation. We are not married and are not likely to ever be—"

"A condition we should remedy in the future, after we are both free."

"No, you know we cannot. We are from two different worlds, worlds that do not see eye to eye. Once we are away from here, we will share nothing in common, and we will both have to return to our own people—and those people don't marry well, and—"

"Shhh." He laid a finger over her lips. "Most anything can be done if one wishes it."

"But, I—"

"Shhh." This time he placed his lips over hers. Slowly, his mouth ravished hers, and, with a sigh, Sarah capitulated, putting aside for the moment what it was she'd been about to protest.

He cupped her face as his tongue stroked hers. His fingers grazed her cheeks, her eyes, her ears, her neck. It was enchantment pure and simple, and Sarah settled in closer to him.

He exhaled heavily, his breathing hard and fast. "Do you know what you do to me?"

"I little know unless what you feel is similar to what happens to me. 'Tis soul-stirring."

As she spoke, White Thunder began to press kiss upon kiss against her neck, and, with a high-pitched groan, she succumbed to the magic of his skill, falling in completely toward him. She arched her back, that she might partake of his ardor more fully, and he was quick on the uptake, his fingers caressing her every sensitive spot, while he worked his way down to her breasts, where he kneaded each gentle mound.

She sucked in her breath, and, as she did so, his brisk, musky scent filled her lungs, while the hard yet smooth feel of his skin next to hers acted like an aphrodisiac. It was as if this man belonged to her, as though he were hers to explore. Perhaps she, too, belonged to him.

But it could never be, she reminded herself. Still, being here with him like this was akin to ecstasy, and, opening her eyes, she made a mental note of the time and place, and what was happening to her and to him, anything she might be able to commit to memory. Never would she forget him. Never.

"White Thunder, has it occurred to you that perhaps we are not meant—and have never been meant—to marry? Maybe we have been thrust together for one single purpose, which is for you to save me, and for me to help you with the burden of your responsibility."

He paused, his attention riveted on her, although she could have sworn he was deep in thought. It wasn't long before he shook his head, obviously disagreeing with her.

However, there was more she needed to say. "Perhaps we are here to do nothing more than help each other and make memories—memories that will comfort us in our old age, memories that, when we think of them, will bring a smile to us both."

"I already have too many memories." He grimaced. "Rather, I

would like a flesh-and-blood woman in my arms for the rest of my life, however long or short that is. But if it is memories you wish, I will make memories with you."

She frowned. "Perhaps we could even pretend."

"Pretend?"

"Yes, as in make believe. Maybe, for only a little while, we could imagine that the rest of the world doesn't exist, that there is only you and me, no duty to bind us, no social order to pass judgment on us. Just us. For as long as we're in this cave, perhaps we could pretend we're married."

His expression went grim. "Until?"

"Until we are forced to leave here and go back to our own worlds."

His look at her was brooding. "What you suggest is to love without responsibility." His eyes narrowed. "What man could possibly walk away from such a proposal?"

Was he being sarcastic?

She didn't answer him, and, when it was evident she had nothing more to say on the matter, he continued speaking. "I would be foolish if I didn't bring to your attention that there is a danger in what you ask."

"A danger?"

"You might truly fall in love with me, as I might with you also, and yet, our marriage would be based on a lie."

"But if we did fall in love, the memories would be all the more precious."

"Memories." He snorted. "There is a saying amongst the Seneca that goes: To love a woman without a lifelong commitment is either the action of great youth or one of stupidity." He paused. "I am not that young."

She swallowed hard. "Then...your answer is no?"

"It is not. My answer is yes. Let's do it. Let's pretend. But beware, I fear you play with fire."

She was still frowning. "Your warning is well taken, sir. But still, I would like to chance it."

He nodded. "When the time comes, you will remember that I warned you?"

She stared deeply into his eyes. "I will."

What had happened to her? Indeed, it was with a great deal of shock that she realized she had changed. She was not the same person she had been before she met White Thunder.

For one thing, his viewpoints about life and the dignity of man were having an effect upon her thought process. Not that she would let her servitude go unfulfilled. Rather, she would treasure this time with him, these moments of complete freedom, away from the chains of her bondage.

Bondage. It was fast becoming a naughty word in her vocabulary, and she wondered, was a person meant to be fettered to another by reason of debt?

Maybe. But perhaps not. There was much to be said for living off the land and being beholden to none. Though there was no money to be made here and no toil to be done for another in exchange for coin, she and White Thunder yet had all they needed, provided by Nature. In many ways, the experience was proving to be more than a little uplifting.

White Thunder shifted their positions so he could rub his palms up and down her spine, and, the hard feel of his muscles next to her, the pressure of his touch, the way their bodies fit together flawlessly, seemed somehow perfect.

He came up over her, and, smoothing one of his hands over her face, he caressed her cheeks, her lips, her nose, her eyes. "Do not think because I warn you of the dangers of what you propose that I am against what you ask. I would be honored to make memories with you. Let us start now. Let us remember this moment, always."

"Yes," she said. "Yes."

With a gentle touch, he trailed his fingertips over her ears, down her throat and around to the back of her neck. Everywhere he touched, her body responded as if it had never known such joy. She shut her eyes and moaned, and, as each new wave of passion consumed her, she swooned in against him.

He kissed her, his lips paying respect to her everywhere, while his tongue traced each delicate feature. He whispered, "You possess the bluest eyes I have ever seen. But it is not only their color that holds me spellbound to you. It is the fact that when I look into your eyes, I am presented with the glimpse of a spirit as gentle as it is true. You are an unusual woman, Little Autumn. You are also a good woman. Every day of your life, you should be told what a treasure you are."

He lay back and brought her onto her side against him while his fingers massaged her back. "I have never been able to fathom the dress of the English," he whispered against her ear, and it became evident he was trying to untie the strings that held her stays together.

"'Tis not so different from the way you dress. But, what is it you intend? We have never had to remove my corset before."

He grinned at her. "What do you think, Miss Sarah? We have made love, but I have yet to see you naked."

"Naked?"

He nodded.

"What you are suggesting is unseemly."

"It is not unseemly," he argued. "It is beauty, and it is my wish to view you—all of you."

"But…not even a married woman will allow her husband to behold her in the altogether. Dignity alone would ensure she would at least wear her chemise, even to bed."

He shook his head. "The English are, indeed, a strange people. What man would not like to see his wife naked?"

"Perhaps there are many." She smiled at him.

"I would still like to undress you completely."

"But…I cannot allow it."

"Not even if I beg? Or do this?" His hand slipped down to caress her breasts. "Or this?" He bent to suck on each of her breasts.

It was meant to be pure seduction, and it was. She drew in her breath. "You cheat, sir." Even as she said it, she was already moaning and settling herself in closer to him.

"Of course I cheat, as have all men throughout history. And any man who is a man would cheat against such vulgar rules."

"They are not vulgar. The opposite is true."

"Not to me. If we are to be man and wife while we are here in this cave, then I would seek to have all the privileges that are due to a husband. When it comes to making love to my wife, I wish to do it right."

"Hmm… I like the way you say that, your wife, even though it's not really true."

"But it is true." He cast a seductive grin at her. "While we are here, we are what we say we are. Little Autumn, I am but a man, and I have dreamed of seeing you with nothing between us but the sweat of our exertions."

Again, she moaned.

"Please," he said. "Show me how to remove this."

She found herself weakening, and why not? She was fighting a losing battle, anyway. Even now, his hands were all over her, and it felt good.

Perhaps he was right. Maybe it was natural for married couples to make love naked.

At last, she said, "Very well, but we'll take off the stays and no more."

He didn't disagree, but then, he didn't agree, either. She sat slightly away from him, presenting her back to him. "The laces of my stays are here and tie here. Do you see?" She guided his hands to the laces. "If you pull the string here, the entire knot comes out—and they loosen."

He did as she suggested.

"You will have to free them completely up and down before the garment can be removed."

He did so, and the corset relaxed, allowing him to tug it away from her. But there was yet another set of clothing beneath this, her chemise, and he seemed as perplexed to find it as she was overjoyed to be without the tight restriction of her stays, even if only for a few moments.

He commented, "You have on more clothes."

"Yes, sir, I do." She grinned, and he immediately took advantage and kissed her open mouth. It was utterly erotic, utterly seductive, and melting in against him, she kissed him back, one for one.

"What do I take off next?"

She pretended to misunderstand. "Your shirt."

Almost as quickly as she'd said it, he discarded his shirt, then he returned to her. "And now, what of *yours* do I remove next?"

"Oh, did you mean *my* clothes?"

"Exactly."

"Perhaps that would be my petticoats, then. They tie around the waist here." She took his hands and guided them to the garment's knot.

He was a quick learner and had untied her petticoats without difficulty. In barely a moment, the garment was off.

"And now what?" he asked.

"My chemise is the only item left, as you can see. But I would advise you against taking it off. I am naked enough, just like this. I feel I must stress that proper women undress no more than this, even to bathe."

"I think you are a proper woman, but this is still not naked enough for me." So saying, he pulled the garment up slowly. Once it had been raised over her knees, he bent down to trail kisses along its path. As the chemise gradually rose higher and higher over her body, he followed its progress with his lips, lingering at the junction of her legs. He parted her legs and kissed her…*there.*

Sarah immediately raised her hips. Dear Lord, what was this man doing to her? The feelings he provoked were extraordinary. Though embarrassment might have consumed her, it simply wasn't possible to feel guilty and pleasured all at the same time.

As he pulled the garment farther upward, his kisses traced over the trail of her clothes until at last he found her breasts. First, he kissed one, then, the other. Curiously, although he was raising himself over her, one of his hands had never left the delicacy between her legs.

"Open for me," he said between kisses.

She spread her legs, never thinking to disobey him. Then, with his fingers taking possession of her femininity, he loved her. She gazed at him as a tempest took hold of her, and she rocked with the rhythm of his fingers. She felt as though she were a one-woman exhibition, a show played only for him, and no matter how long he looked, it appeared to her that he couldn't seem to see enough.

She had never felt more adored.

In due time, with his fingers still creating magic at the apex of her legs, he moved over her chest until he had come up to her bosom. First he kissed one of her breasts, his tongue encircling her nipple erotically, then, he shifted to the other. It was as though she were a delicate instrument, and he were the musician.

The feelings he was arousing in her were so finely luxurious, Sarah began to wonder how she had lived without this all her life. But he wasn't done. With one hand, he pulled her chemise over her head, while his kisses ranged over the garment's path, to her neck, her cheeks and on upward, to the top of her head.

And then, it was done. She was fully exposed. She lay before him in nothing more than the manner in which she had come into this world. However, there between her legs, White Thunder's fingers were still loving her, even more urgently than before. Momentarily, he rose over her so he could gaze at her in full. Her legs were spread, his hand was upon her, and still it seemed he couldn't get enough of her.

At last, he whispered, "Your beauty should be the subject of art."

Even as he said it, he stroked her, encouraging her to raise to heights that, prior to this, she had only imagined. She couldn't lie still. She was wet, wild with desire, and she cried out, "Please make love to me. I can hardly wait another moment."

His first response was to groan. "I would be pleasured, Little Autumn. Deeply pleasured."

He laid himself beside her, and his fingers created so great a stir, there where he played with her, she thought she might burst. As he watched her, his groans grew more labored.

She was more than aware that she was struggling toward that ultra-fine release, and, as feeling took over thinking, her joy crescendoed so that she could hardly hold back the pleasure. Indeed, the ultimate in satisfaction was coming in on her so fast that when the rapture burst over her, an exquisite kind of euphoria flooded her system, literally rocking her physically. It needed outlet, and, as she cried out, he echoed the beauty of their lovemaking with a moan of his own. She gazed up at him, finding him looking at her as though he were witnessing spiritual revival.

When she settled down, he whispered, "I have great feeling for you, Little Autumn. All the days of my life, I will remember this moment. This, I promise you."

She smiled at him and reached up to grab hold of a lock of his hair, flicking the long strand behind his shoulders. Then, he brought himself up over her, and without delay, joined their bodies together.

Briefly, she remembered that the first time she had made love with him, there had been pain. She expected it now.

But it didn't materialize. Not this time. There was nothing but enchantment. She welcomed him, fully, completely.

They began to move as one. One thrust from him followed another,

her bliss heightening as she tightened her muscles around him. When he pushed against her, she met him. When he withdrew, so, too, did she.

It was an erotic sort of dance. On and on they swayed as they drew closer and closer together. But it seemed as if it weren't close enough, at least, not for her.

Breaking away from her, he came up onto his knees before her. Taking hold of her legs, he placed them around his neck. At once Sarah found the position most erotic, sensuous and utterly stimulating. She closed her eyes, to better bask in the sensual pleasure of the moment. But soon, he opened her eyes with a gentle finger, whispering, "Do not close your eyes. I would know your spirit."

She gazed up, then, into his dark, almost black eyes, and she smiled at him. It seemed her simple action was his undoing. In response, he thrust again and again within her.

As their bodies came together in the act of love, so, too, did she meet him on a different plane of existence. She held that look in his eyes, she wanted that look, even as the dance between them became fast, then faster.

Never had she seen a man so magnificent. His groans were pure music to her ears, inspiring her, bringing her up again so she was spiraling to that same pinnacle she'd met earlier. Faster and faster, deeper and deeper, they swayed, until finally with one last cherished thrust, he gifted her with his seed. And she met him all the way. When he burst, so, too, did she.

Not once during the entire deed had they dropped their heated gazes from one another. It was as though she'd been presented with a glimpse into his soul. Perhaps, he, too, had looked into hers, because for a moment, if a moment only, she knew exactly who he was, and she found him spectacular.

As he collapsed against her, she rubbed her hands along his spine, savoring the feel of his hard muscles against the cushion of her touch. Despite all the logical reasons why she shouldn't fall in love with him, she knew it was useless to consider them.

She had changed. He had changed her perspective. Never again would she look at the world in the same way. This man was hers, and yes, it was true. She loved him.

Chapter Fifteen

Days passed. Days that were filled with lovemaking, with mounting respect for one another, and for Sarah, with the pleasure of falling deeper and deeper in love.

Of course, there was always work to be done, too. White Thunder had produced a warm bear robe that now cushioned their bed. He had also instructed Sarah in the best ways to prepare a food made especially for travel. It was a dry meat pounded into a powdery substance and spiced with fat and berries. Apparently, a handful of this mixture could sustain a warrior throughout an entire day.

They made plenty of it. They made plenty of love, too. So idyllic were their days, Sarah began to wonder if it were possible to remain here in this cave for her whole life through. To her, it had become home.

Meanwhile, the weather outside the cave had turned cold. But it hardly mattered. Inside their little haven, Sarah and White Thunder were scarcely aware of the change in temperature. They seldom ventured far from the cave. There simply was no need.

There was only one problem, and that was due to their activities. Sarah had become sore, and in the worst of all places. Once she made White Thunder aware of the difficulty, he treated her to mud and clay baths, administered lovingly by him. Amazingly, the pain went away.

Days turned into a week, then another. Though White Thunder's strength had returned—as had Sarah's—still they lingered, with good reason.

Here, they were spared the wagging tongues of spiteful gossips. Here, they had no need to fear the damning looks from prejudiced eyes, nor the scornful opinions of others. Here they were free...they were married—at least, within their own eyes…for a time.

As the days plodded forward, Sarah's worry about Marisa increased. What had happened to her? Would the young warrior who was so smitten with her protect her from harm? Sarah assumed he would do most anything to keep his love safe.

What if Marisa needed her? What if there were problems and she had no one to turn to? Much as she hated to admit it, Sarah realized it was time to leave this haven.

She and White Thunder were cuddled up in front of the fire when White Thunder said, as though he were reading her mind, "Are you prepared to go?"

"I think so, but do we have to?"

"You know we do. You have mentioned on more than one occasion that you worry about your friend. And I have a duty to perform, which cannot be accomplished here."

Sarah shot him a sad smile. "Surely there must be something else we need to do to ready us to go. Is there anything we missed?"

He smiled at her before he bent to rub the side of his face against hers. "We have smoked and dried all the meat, pounded it into meal and mixed it with berries and fat. We have no more food here to prepare. It is all stored in the bags we will carry."

"Yes, but you could hunt for more food, and we could prepare that."

"I could, but it is unnecessary. We have all the food we will need."

"Oh." Her voice sounded as disappointed as she felt. "But, 'tis cold. Don't we need warmer clothing?"

"We have already made two warm shirts and extra moccasins for us both from the deer kill and from the bear skin. It will be enough."

"Then, how about the root that is needed to keep me from conceiving?"

"I have dried much of it. It, too, is packed."

"Yes, that's true," she said. Then again, "Yes."

"If we linger here too long, the snows will come, and we will have much difficulty finding your friend."

Sarah frowned. "Do you think we'll encounter trouble?"

"I little know. I have seen enemy tracks in my travels to find food. War rages across this land, making traveling, even upon the lakes and rivers, dangerous. I have given this much thought, and we will do best to make our path through the forest. Although an enemy can hide there easily, so, too, can we."

Sarah stared at him grimly. "Now that you speak of it, I remember this war. I recall that the whole world seemed afire."

"And so it has been since the English and others have come to our borders. It has been a series of one war after another. Once, many years ago, the Iroquois were at peace with themselves and with their neighbors."

"I have heard that this was so. Tell me about it."

"With pleasure. In the long-ago time, hundreds of years before the white man ever arrived on this land, there was the Great Peace. It was started by two men and a woman, who took the idea of ending war from tribe to tribe. It was not easy to do, for not everyone desired harmony, and some were great, but evil magicians. Eventually, these three accomplished it, and they united six heroic nations together under one branch and offered to bring all other Indian nations under its branches. It was what united the Iroquois. It is this that has made us strong."

"And you have a government, I believe. Is that not right?"

"We do, but it is not like the English, who are subject to a king. Our towns are ruled by the people and he who has power, but who would govern for himself and his family alone, is quickly warned, and if he still doesn't behave, he is removed from the council."

"Fascinating. And there is no confusion?"

"Confusion? Not about government or who we are or how we make our laws. We council together, and when all agree to a law or to a suggestion, only then is it passed by the council. But even then, if the people don't like it, they don't have to follow it. One is always left to make up his own mind."

"And this unites you? It doesn't pull you apart?"

"It unites us, yes."

They were both silent, until Sarah asked, "When do we leave?"

"Tomorrow."

"'Tis quite soon."

He nodded.

"I will miss it here. I've been happy, and I've even started to think of this cave as mine."

"I, too."

"But I suppose we can't stay here forever."

"So it is. We both have duties that weigh upon us."

"Yes," she said. "I've had you to myself for all these days, and I have become used to thinking of you as my husband. But when we leave here, that's all behind us, is it not?"

"That was our agreement, yes. It will soon be at an end. However, we still have tonight. For a little while longer, let us pretend we are a married couple, with no other responsibilities except to bring pleasure to one another."

She nodded. "I would like that."

He sighed and tightened his arms around her. "On this night, I would like to think of nothing but the many different ways to love you."

"Yes, White Thunder, please." She smiled at him, but she feared that even her smile reflected her loss. However, when she spoke, she didn't speak of sadness. "Let us make beautiful memories."

He, too, seemed grim, but as he turned her toward him and proceeded to do as she suggested, their lovemaking transformed them both. Once again, there was only him. There was only her.

***

The extreme darkness before dawn ushered in a new day. They had made love through the night, as though, only in this way, could they keep the morning from coming. But here it was already. She was tired. He was tired, also, but White Thunder had already assured her they would rest throughout their journey.

Amazingly, she wasn't sleepy. Just tired.

They had swept away all traces of their stay in the cave—a necessary procedure, according to White Thunder, so their time here might be invisible to the eye of anyone who should be looking for them. He had recently stepped from the cave to say his morning prayers while Sarah had stayed behind to attend to her toiletries.

She was settling her open gown over her petticoats and straightening its bodice when White Thunder came back into the cave. Almost perfectly still, he stared at her as though he had never seen her until this moment.

"You are ready?" he asked.

"Almost." It was the first time she had worn her gown since before she'd awakened to find herself in a cave and in the presence of a man she didn't remember.

The gown had once been one of her best. But traveling over open ground and practically drowning in it had done irreparable damage.

Long ago, it had been beautiful, made of a rich, gold- colored silk brocade. Her petticoats were a quilted cream color, almost matching the gold of the dress, and, as was the fashion, they were displayed in front of the gown. Somewhere in her adventures, she had lost her white muslin apron, although her white neck handkerchief had survived. She wore it now, covering her chest, up to her neck.

On her feet were moccasins, since her own slippers were flimsy and wouldn't provide her with the needed protection against the cold. Sarah had also managed to tie her long hair back, although she hadn't been able to contain the blonde ringlets that fell forward against her face.

"You look very English," he said.

"Thank you, I think." She smiled at him. "Was that a compliment?"

"Perhaps."

She looked toward their luggage, which consisted of several buckskin bags, as well as her own hand-carved cane. "What is it that I'll be carrying?"

"Our bags."

She frowned at him. "All of them?"

"No, I will carry some, but my hands and arms must remain free so that if we come upon enemies, I will be able to protect us. That this requires you to bear the brunt of carting most of our food is to be regretted, for I know this is not the English way."

"Yes, that's true. But your point is well taken. Where shall we go to pick up Miss Marisa's trail?"

"I have given the matter some thought, and I believe we'll start at the beginning, where I found you, by the side of the Lake-That-Turns-to-Rapids. We will backtrack to the falls, since I think that is where your accident occurred. When I found you, you were almost drowned."

"So you have said. I do wish I could remember."

"It matters little. What I have explained is the only conclusion that makes sense. So, I believe if we begin at the falls, we may yet find some trace of your friend."

Sarah smiled. "I will be happy to see her."

"Come here. I would begin our journey with an embrace, if you would humor me."

Happily, she went into his arms, where he buried himself in the folds of her hair. He murmured, "Although I would like nothing better than to make love to you here and now, I cannot, for the strength it would consume might cause me to be vulnerable should we have need to confront an enemy."

She nodded. "But could we not at least kiss?"

He grinned at her, and, bending toward her, he brought his lips to hers, his tongue sweeping her mouth as though the kiss might substitute for actual lovemaking.

She groaned, as did he, until at last he straightened, although he held her closely to him. In due time, he whispered, "We must go now, or I fear we might never leave. As you know, there is a war raging across this country. Stay close to me. We will move fast, but not so swiftly I cannot go back on our trail and erase our prints from the ground. Are you ready?"

She nodded, and, with the both of them bidding *adieu* to the cave, they set off into the woods. Perhaps it was her imagination, but for a moment, she thought that a certain squirrel had come out of his winter hideaway to say goodbye.

***

It was cold, it had rained, and the ground was both hard and wet. There was a scent in the air of decaying, wet leaves, as well as the earthy smell of dirt. The trees were naked of their leaves and looked to be little more than skeletons waving their branches against the gray beginnings of the day. Sarah's toes protested the chilly weather, but as long as she kept moving, her feet cooperated.

They had been gone for no longer than an hour when Sarah began to wish for the relative comfort of their cave. But she knew it was not to be. They had to move on forward; there was no turning back.

Their progress through the forest was slower than what Sarah had imagined it would be, if only because she was weighted down with their supplies, thus their stops were frequent. Although Sarah realized that each day the burden would become less—if only because they would be consuming the food—here at the start of their journey, the bags were still cumbersome and bulky.

White Thunder never strayed too far ahead of her, even though she was certain she was holding him back. While they were on the move, his rifle was always held in a ready position. He was well armed. Attached to his belt were tomahawk, war clubs and knives. Strapped across his shoulders were bags, a powder horn and balls. Within the folds of his leggings, there at his calf, were two more knives. He looked like a walking arsenal.

It made her glad. He appeared fully capable of protecting them.

She took a moment to admire his look, for it was different from what she had become accustomed to. For one thing, he was dressed for the weather with a white linen shirt worn inside a buckskin coat. On his legs were buckskin leggings and moccasins. His blanket, which also was used for warmth, was thrown over one of his shoulders and belted at his waist. Quite incidentally, his leggings didn't reach all the way up to his shirt, which left her with an alluring view of his thighs. And, indeed, she did look. Truth be told, she found her gaze lingering there more often than perhaps it should.

His moccasins—and hers—were winter-proofed as well as waterproof, having been carefully smoked and sewn with the fur turned inside. She knew this because she had helped sew them.

He had insisted that her clothing also be winterized, and she wore a blanket over her shoulders in a style much like a cape. Also, there had been enough deerskin to fashion herself an outer buckskin petticoat, made and worn for warmth. She had long ago lost her hat, a shame, for it would have been a good addition to protect her against this weather.

White Thunder came to a complete stop. She almost ran into him. Quickly, he glanced to his right and left, surveying the lay of the land. He pointed toward a stand of trees, then, gazing at her, brought up a single finger to lie across his lips.

Trouble. Her stomach churned and adrenaline pumped at once through her system.

As noiselessly, yet as speedily as they could, they fled toward the stand of distant trees he had indicated, scurrying over the wet mosses and ferns littering the forest floor. What was it—or rather, *who* was it?

Her questions were hastily answered when she witnessed a war party of perhaps twenty-five young men come around a hill. At the same moment the war party came into view, she and White Thunder reached the stand of trees. Immediately, they ducked beneath the weight of a pine tree's branches.

He settled her up close to the trunk of the tree so she was almost completely hidden by its long and extending boughs. Then, he left. What was he doing?

Why, she wondered, in outfitting her gear for the trip, hadn't she considered a weapon? In a land torn by war, one needed some manner of self-defense.

Soon, White Thunder returned and crouched beside her in a position that afforded him a view of the enemy's approach. He held his rifle in a ready position and gazed toward the path the warriors were making.

Perhaps they were lucky this day, or mayhap this particular group of men was overconfident because their numbers were great, or maybe they were returning from a battle and thus were unaware of their environment. Whatever the cause, they missed seeing the tracks of the two people who had been on that path minutes before them.

Still, it seemed to take the war party forever to pass by—and when, at last, their rear guard was no more than a distant speck, White Thunder continued to wait, his body and his gun held in a position to do immediate battle.

How many minutes passed, Sarah could not estimate, but it must have been at least a half-hour. At last, with his weapon still held in a primed position, he whispered, "Huron war party. We will no longer travel over known paths. They are dangerous. Our way from here on will be hard, but safer, because we will travel through untouched land."

"Untouched?"

He nodded. "Land through which there are no known paths. It will be hard for you, but it must be done, since it appears the Iroquois Trail is no longer safe for travel. Be that as it may, we will, of necessity, go where few wish to travel. Have you a weapon?"

"No. And it is a terrible oversight on my part."

"Do you at least have a knife?"

"Yes."

"Keep it ready to use. I little know what to expect. Wait here while I go back and erase our most recent tracks, but then we must leave quickly before they see our earlier prints and backtrack to find us."

"That could happen?"

He nodded. "Easily." Rising, he left to erase their passage as thoroughly and quickly as possible.

Chapter Sixteen

"In the days before the European came to our country, a person could walk the Iroquois Trail from one end of it to the other and never meet with any danger, at least not from a human source."

"Truly?" she asked, her voice barely louder than a whisper. "And what exactly is the Iroquois Trail?"

She scooted closer to White Thunder as he took his time answering her question. They were sitting within a temporary shelter that White Thunder had fashioned from tree branches, leaves and dirt. Since it was made from materials gleaned from the environment, it blended into its surroundings, disappearing to all but the most discerning eye.

The night was cold. They had no fire, nor did they dare to light one, since, as White Thunder had said, "The smoke from a fire travels farther and faster than a man can easily flee."

They sat close together, not only because they wished to remain near to one another, but for warmth, as well. They were huddled together on one of their blankets, while he used another blanket to wrap around her. Even still, she shivered.

"The Iroquois Trail," he explained, "is a path forged through the forest long ago that links all the villages of the Iroquois Confederation, one to the other. It stretches between the land of the Mohawks in the east to the far western tribe of the Confederation—my tribe, the Seneca. Always in the past, the trail was kept clear and free of branches or other debris so that a runner or anyone, even a child, could easily travel upon it.

"In the old days, no enemy dared to use it or molest anyone upon it, because the Iroquois were strong and could defend what was theirs. But all this has changed since the English and French have come here to stay. Now, we see war parties of enemy tribes traveling upon our trail, where never they used to go."

"I'm sorry. It sounds as if it had once been ideal. But I still don't understand. We've talked of this before, about how the coming of the English and French changed your people. But weren't the Indians at war long before the Europeans arrived?"

"The change took place over a long period of time, a few hundreds of years. Before the English arrived, the Iroquois were a powerful nation, a peaceful nation. But it wasn't always so. In the very long ago, perhaps as long as seven hundred years ago, there were revenge killings, and the people were often crying, for there seemed no end to it. But two great men, Hiawatha and the Peacemaker, brought about a better way to settle grief and to appease the spirits of the departed. They sought to end all war, because at that time, most wars were started due to the need to avenge one's dearly departed.

"They set up a system of government that, with certain ceremonies, would pacify the grief of their loved one, and it would ensure prosperity and peace. When this was done, a great calm fell upon the land.

"This was how it was when the Europeans first came to this country. But we soon learned that the Europeans quarreled among themselves—not out of revenge, as we had, but due to a thirst for wealth. They had, themselves, no great peace. It wasn't long before we also realized that not only did they bicker with each other, but they sought to incite the Indians to their different sides in their disputes. Witlessly, Indians took sides. Thus, the great peace ended, and all with the coming of the Europeans, for soon there was one war after another on this land."

"But...this is fantastic. You must know that the English tell the story of their coming entirely differently. According to our history, it was the Indian who was treacherous, the Indian who was always at war, while our own English ancestors tried to restore peace among them."

He looked at her askance. "It has long been noted that when a man has no defense against the truth, his only option is to accuse another of those things he does himself."

She frowned. "This, you have mentioned to me before, and it is a bit of wisdom I have never heard."

"Simple observation will show you this is true. Now, there are many of my brothers within the Iroquois Nation who have made friends with the English, although I think they are unwise to do so. They fight his wars. They take up his arms. They think they must, for they have become dependent on the beads and metal pots that the English can give them. But not all the Iroquois have been bought by the English or the French. Not all of the Iroquois experience the greed the trade has caused among our people."

Sarah sat silently for a moment. "Then you must very much dislike the society that is springing up all around you."

"Dislike is not the right word. What is more correct is that I think it is unwise to become dependent on a people who do not know you or need you. Do you think we of the Seneca have blind eyes, and have not seen how the English and French treat the white black man who escapes into our country? Do you think we have not noticed the white black man killed or enslaved when the English can get their hands on him? And what about people like you, his own kind, whom he enslaves by means of money and rules? Do you believe we do not realize that if he could, the English, the French too, would do the same to us? But he cannot enslave us—at least not now—because our Confederacy is too strong. We are united."

Her lips parted as though she might respond, but upon further consideration, she closed her mouth. In due time, however, she said, "I truly don't know what to say. If this is your honest viewpoint of my people, it is not a complimentary one."

"So it is not."

She shivered.

He drew her into his arms. "Too much talk and not enough lovemaking."

Sarah smiled. "Surely you're not thinking of making love here? Here beneath a ceiling of tree branches and leaves?"

"I am. Besides its obvious pleasures, it will keep us warm, if you are willing."

"'Tis not a point I can argue..." She smiled.

He grinned back. "What? You do not disagree?"

"Am I that bad?"

"Bad? You are good. Very good." As he took her in his arms, he brought her into a position up and over him in a straddle-like pose. "You are very good indeed."

***

Sarah had never made love in this manner, nor conceived that such could be. He had pushed his breechcloth aside, and, bringing up her skirts and all its layers of petticoats, there was little between herself and his instrument of love. This style of lovemaking was sensuous, yes, and perhaps a little naughty, but oh, so delicious. Because of this position, she found that she was to be the cause of their pleasure, and, despite her fear of losing all dignity, she delighted in the sense of the power she held.

He groaned as she took him within her, and, as she moved her hips over him, he growled so deeply in his throat, she found herself answering him with more of the same kind of action.

Up to her neck, down to her waist, his hands caressed her backside as he gazed up at her. So taken was she with the ultimate sensation, she gazed away from him, closing her eyes to experience the feeling more deeply. At once, he brought a gentle finger under her chin, to turn her face back to him, and he whispered, "I would have us look at one another. Not only so that I might gaze into the soul of the woman I choose to love, but so that the past does not intervene between us, and perhaps cause us pain. I would have you make love to *me*, and not some horror of the past."

She immediately opened her eyes, surveying his dark, dark eyes. Without willing it, her heart expanded with so much love for him, she felt she could barely contain it. She murmured, "I am not unclear about that. I know well whose lap I am sitting on."

He chuckled, and brought his hands around to fondle her breasts. She inhaled swiftly as pleasure washed through her.

In response, she moved more erotically over him, while her eyes never left off looking at him, and what she saw within the deepness of his gaze made her pause, if only very minutely. Had she witnessed the very depths of his soul? What she saw there was beautiful. He was a good man. He was also the man she would love…always. Despite their future, no matter their societies' ultimate censure and what difficulties that might cause, she would always love him.

On that thought, she found herself reaching that flawless pleasure she was coming to recognize so well. She struggled toward it, but it took little, and, as she came closer and closer to that precipice, he took over the manner of their lovemaking, and reaching up to hug her and bringing her face down to kiss him, he met his pleasure at almost the same moment as she. The wondrous sensation, the closeness of their being, the depth of their devotion to one another was an unspoken reality.

She thought she might tell him of her admiration, but words seemed inadequate, and she thought better than to disturb the simple beauty of the moment. Oddly, she fell asleep there on his lap, with him still entrenched within her, and she wasn't certain if it were fact or fiction, but so very much later, she thought she heard him say, "I will never stop my devotion to you. Never…"

***

They traveled through thickets and brambles with stickers that stuck to her dress and petticoats. They stepped through streams that froze her moccasins to her feet, requiring the two of them to stop while White Thunder rubbed her toes and feet back to life. Always, it was cold.

"Why do you not warm your own feet?" Sarah asked once, after observing White Thunder never attended to his own needs. Indeed, were it not for her, he might not have stopped at all, but would have continued on their path, acting as though nothing untoward had happened.

"My body does not require attention. I have bathed in cold and icy water all my life. Even in the dead of winter, the wintry swim is a necessary part of life."

Sarah shivered. "I can't imagine anything worse."

"It is not bad. Over time, the body craves it."

She shook her head at him. "If you say so."

Soon they were back on the trail, even though it had begun to rain and drizzle. In the distance, the roar of a waterfall was becoming more distinct, for this, according to White Thunder, was where he'd found her.

At last, they reached the area of the falls. Though Sarah witnessed them only from afar, their roar drowned out all other sound.

I fell down those? As she watched the utter power of this natural wonder, a shudder rippled through her.

But she soon came to realize that it wasn't White Thunder's intention to stop and admire the marvel of the falls. He plodded on ahead and was so far distant from her that it required her to run to catch up with him. Perhaps she was making too much noise in her mad dash toward him. Whatever the cause, at last, White Thunder turned and stopped, waiting for her to draw even with him.

"Is there a reason you usually travel so far ahead of me?" she asked as she came to stand beside him.

"There is." He pointed forward. "The danger is in front of us, not behind us. I must stay well in advance should there be peril, either from man or animal. In this way, you might escape while I fight the menace."

"Oh," she murmured. "It is interesting, because it is much different in my society. Men in English society are considered mannerly only when they follow the woman."

"I know. But I would not be doing my duty were I to lag behind you. It could cause you to meet the danger head-on, while I am in safety at the rear."

"I see. Thank you."

He nodded.

The rain had started in earnest now, and, in her haste, she slipped over the wet leaves and fell to her knees. Immediately, White Thunder was at her side, helping her up.

"White Thunder," she said, coming up to her feet, "is it really possible that I fell down those falls and survived?"

His arms spanned her waist as he set her back on her feet. "It is my belief that this is so."

Sarah shook her head. "'Tis a shock I wasn't killed."

He brought her into his embrace. "Almost, you were. Almost."

As the rain fell in torrents around them, they stood in the middle of the forest, clinging to one another. He said, "We will begin our search for your friend here."

"...And the young man who was attending her, that man being a Mohawk Indian. I believe he is probably still with her."

"She had a Mohawk man with her?"

"Yes. He was leading us through the forest."

"And he was smitten with her?"

"Yes, I believe he was. In truth, they were quite attached to each other."

"Good," he said. "If he were with her, they could have well survived the falls, and, if so, they would have stayed here to mend themselves and their equipment, since no warrior of any merit would dare the forest without an adequate defense. And if they stopped here, there will be a shelter somewhere in this vicinity. I am happy that you have told me about him. Now, I know what we will be looking for."

"I see." She raised her face to his, a perfect invitation for a kiss. Happily, he accommodated her.

There was something erotic and magical about kissing her lover in the middle of a rainstorm, if only because the downpour seemed to magnify the fire inside of her. It was another moment of pure heaven, and Sarah cherished it, committing this, too, to memory.

Wonderful though it was, they couldn't long stand in the middle of a forest, in the midst of a curtain of rain. Soon, they were heading out again on the trail.

Along the way, Sarah asked, "Aren't you afraid the rain might freeze our tracks to the ground so anyone could follow us?"

"I might be concerned if it stopped raining, but because it continues, there is little danger of that happening."

"Oh."

Onward they traveled, slowly now, searching for clues. One day turned to the next, and still, they found nothing definite.

For Sarah, these days of constant wandering had begun to blur. In truth, because their path required her to traverse a muddy, cold, gray and wet land, the days were beginning to take on the color of utter misery. It wasn't that she didn't appreciate the landscape or what White Thunder was doing. More to the point, it simply was not the sort of journey a woman might enjoy. Indeed, the land they traveled over was the kind of terrain even a rabbit wouldn't have dared navigate at this time of year.

Always, the ground seemed to be moist and littered with the sight and scent of decaying leaves, bushes and undergrowth. The trees were brittle and hosted so many branches that they often scratched Sarah as she passed them by, and her clothes were torn by thorns and stickers. Her hair had long since escaped its knot to hang in curls down her back, which, due to the drizzle, had taken to springing into waves and ringlets.

If the days were wretched, the nights were enchanting, perhaps making up for her daily travails. Each night, White Thunder fashioned a temporary shelter, one built from whatever was at hand. Each night, after making love, they slept in one another's arms. In the morning, they bathed, she in the relative comfort of their refuge, and he in some nearby stream. Always, the feel and scent of nature was all around her, the dirt, the leaves and the freshest air she'd ever breathed.

On a beautiful, sunny day, they came upon the body of a man, months decayed. He had certainly been a huge man, Sarah thought as she turned away from the sight.

Carefully, White Thunder bent to examine the ground around the body.

"There was a struggle here," he told her, "but most of the prints that would tell the complete story of what happened are long gone."

"Is the man a Mohawk, sir?"

"No, Ottawa."

Sarah breathed out a sigh of relief. "Thank the dear Lord. I was afraid it might have been the young man who was so besotted with Miss Marisa. You are certain this corpse of a man is Ottawa?"

He nodded. "Ottawa."

"How can you tell that? Without a doubt?"

White Thunder pointed toward the man's feet. "Do you see the cut of his moccasins?"

"No. I...I don't want to look."

"The pattern of beadwork, the cut. His style of breechcloth, clothes, weapons. He was Ottawa. He was struck several times, the blow to the head the fatal blow. The man who did this was protecting something."

"How do you know that?"

"It was unnecessary to beat this dead man so many times. Whoever it was that fought him was ensuring the Ottawa's death. One has to ask why."

Sarah shook her head.

"Loved ones or a loved one was near, perhaps endangered. Only then does a man become so savage."

"Oh, I see," said Sarah.

"Besides, clamped in the Ottawa's hand is some red hair. Was your friend's hair red?"

"Yes."

He nodded. "It is possible they camped close to here."

"They?"

"By these clues, I think we have found the trail of your friend and her Mohawk protector." Reaching into one of the bags he carried around his shoulder, White Thunder withdrew what looked to Sarah to be a dried herb. Carefully, he crumbled the herb, then sprinkled it around the body of the dead Ottawa. After some moments, he said some words in his own language over the body before he at last came up onto his feet.

Turning toward Sarah, he gestured. "Come, let us search for the place where they built their shelter. If I am right, I believe we will find it close to here."

***

In the end, it took White Thunder several more days of hunting and inspecting the forest around him to locate the shelter, which was nestled in a deeply wooded valley. Constructed as it was, alongside a fallen tree, it first looked to be nothing more than the loose branches of an old, dead tree. But as he pulled back one branch after another aside, the inside of the structure became revealed.

Whoever built this, thought White Thunder, was a good man. Smart.

"This is where they stayed," he told Sarah. "Come, let's see what clues they left us."

"Then, she's alive?"

"I cannot say how she is now, but when this was built, she was alive. Do you see over there?" He pointed into the shelter.

"No, what?"

"Look closely."

"I see nothing, sir, but branches and grass."

He picked up a small piece of white lace. "Unless our Mohawk warrior has taken to wearing a lady's decoration, I think we can assume your friend stayed here."

"Let me see that."

White Thunder handed her the material.

"Yes. I recognize the design of this. 'Tis Marisa's." She brought her gaze up to meet White Thunder's, and he found himself yearning to take this woman in his arms and make love to her here, now, under the broad light of day.

He might have done it too, were it not a dangerous undertaking, given where they were and the circumstances of war surrounding them. He had always been attracted to Little Autumn, thus he'd felt no qualms in agreeing to their pretense at being man and wife.

Since they had started out on the trail, each day brought a new facet of her personality to the fore, and he found himself becoming more and more besotted with her. Her gentle ways, her kind encouragement to him, her courage in the face of so much adversity, was acting as a balm to his heart.

Plus, her beauty continued to enchant him. He knew the harshness of their travels was not a woman's favorite abode. While on the move, she couldn't treat herself to the niceties women tended to favor. She couldn't always manage the condition of her hair, her body or her clothes. Yet, oddly, he couldn't remember ever desiring a woman's companionship more...not even Wild Mint's. Certainly, he had loved Wild Mint. He loved her still.

But he nursed a fascination for Little Autumn that was quickly becoming a deep and abiding devotion. It was the sort of affection that was new to him. Indeed, he didn't quite understand it. In truth, he never grew tired of looking at her, and he couldn't ever seem to get close enough to her. Always, he found himself inventing little reasons to touch her. But there was more. Over these past few days, he had seen deeply into her soul, and what he had witnessed there was the gentle spirit of a woman whom he admired greatly.

"What do we do now?" Sarah asked him, bringing him back to the present moment.

"We will stay here tonight. This shelter can be easily rebuilt and made comfortable. The structure is Iroquois-built."

"Is it?"

"Yes. Do you see how the builder uses the bark against the frame of the structure? The way the poles are positioned? This is the way we construct our longhouses—Mohawk, specifically. Your friend's sweetheart was taking no chances with her being accidently found. I can only imagine that the Ottawa somehow discovered your friend and was taking her away when she was rescued by her Mohawk protector."

"I still don't understand, White Thunder. How do you know these things?"

"I don't. Not completely. But it's what I believe happened. We saw the remains of a man who was killed viciously. His attacker was protecting something. Whatever or whomever that was must have been close by for the attack to be so gruesome. Therefore, one must assume the Ottawa found your friend and she was rescued by her Mohawk sweetheart."

"Oh. It seems simple when you say it, but I didn't see it."

"Only because you do not know what to look for and are not trained to look."

"Perhaps."

"They probably left here immediately, thinking the shelter was no longer invisible to an enemy eye. Where they would go from here, I can only speculate."

"But you must have some idea of where they might have gone."

While she spoke, White Thunder began to reconstruct the shelter, filling in its gaps with bark and logs. It took him several moments before he answered. "You know your friend. Tell me, would she have taken her Mohawk friend back to her village?"

"You mean Albany?"

"If that is her village, yes."

Sarah looked away from him and frowned. "I don't think so. Her uncle was against the two of them even talking to each other, let alone returning there, where it would be seen that they were deeply in love. Their acquaintance was troubled from the start, because of Marisa's position as John Rathburn's niece. She was expected to marry a man of Mr. Rathburn's choosing. This, she knew; this, she expected to do. But she rebelled at the last minute, although I do believe she meant her rebellion to be small—a one-night affair, only. So she escaped one evening to make love with this young man. She never expected to fall in love with him, I think. Rather, I recall her saying to me that she wished to make some memories to last all her life."

"So this evil one, this Rathburn, not only forced himself on you, but he felt himself so superior to others that he could dictate to your friend how she should live her own life? That he, and he alone, should pick her husband?"

"'Tis the way of the English aristocracy. Is it different with the Seneca?"

"*Nyoh*, yes. A Seneca maiden picks her own husband, not the other way around."

"That is often the way of the English too, for someone who is not of the aristocracy."

As White Thunder set the last of the branches onto their shelter, he said, "The more I learn of the English, the more I like the Seneca way. Do you know the name of your friend's Mohawk protector?"

"Yes, his name is Black Eagle."

"Black Eagle." White Thunder shook his head. "I know of him, and I believe now that I will be able to find your friend, for I am fairly certain he would have taken your friend to his village. Perhaps he might feel it is the only place where they would be safe."

"Why, this is wonderful!"

She smiled at him, and staring down into her lovely face, he melted a little. He reached out to run a hand over her hair and bent down to kiss the top of her head. "Stay here. Prepare the shelter as we have done every night while I backtrack to erase our trail. I should return soon."

"Yes, I will."

He returned her smile, and it occurred to him that he was a lucky man to have come upon this woman as he had. Very lucky, indeed.

Chapter Seventeen

Across the Lake-That-Turns-to-Rapids, a party of five men slid their canoe silently to shore. Three of the men in the party were Ottawa, the other two were French. Though they were *en route* to the French fort at Niagara, the Indians had a stop to make here. They had left a man, Dirty Hands, at this place almost two months earlier. Because Dirty Hands had not been in his right mind at the time, no one had desired to accompany him as he went about a self-appointed mission to find his son's killers.

But Dirty Hands had not returned to the Ottawa village, and his wife and relatives were asking about him. These few men had promised to discover his fate, and possibly to send him home, if he were still alive.

Because they were a party of five well-trained men, they were not long in locating Dirty Hands' remains. It took them little time to discover that Dirty Hands had been brutally killed. Quickly, they assessed that the murder had been committed a few months ago.

But what was this? Here were fresh tracks, perhaps only a few days old. Here, also, were the remains of dried sage, which had been crumpled and scattered over the body.

Was it his murderer returned to this place to propitiate the spirit of the departed?

They scoured the area further, looking for more footprints. Those they found were Seneca made, two different prints—that of a man and a woman.

Carefully, the five men took up the trail, if only to solve the mystery of what had happened to Dirty Hands. Moving in single file, they made a path, and like silent shadows, they slid into the forest.

***

At last, Sarah and White Thunder had found Marisa's trail. Sarah smiled as she set to work within the shelter, unpacking their bags and setting out a meal of pemmican and water for herself and White Thunder. It was comforting knowing this was the refuge Marisa and Black Eagle had used, and that they had somehow survived the falls.

As Sarah settled in to begin her work, quite unexpectedly the memory of that fateful day slid into view. Again, like once before when her recall had suddenly returned, it came instantly, easily, and without effort.

It had been a day much like this, sunny and bright, when the Ottawa and the French had attacked herself, Marisa and Black Eagle. The three of them had escaped in a canoe. But what they hadn't been able to avoid were the falls of the Lake-That-Turns-to-Rapids. At least, *she* hadn't.

There was another aspect about that day. Thompson, who was supposed to have been their guide, was a traitor. All those months ago on the trail, there had been accident after accident. It hadn't been completely apparent who was creating those mishaps, or indeed if they were even accidents. Not until Thompson had floundered into the canoe that day and had tried to kill Marisa had he finally showed himself for what he was.

But why had he done it?

Why would Thompson— All at once, Sarah understood. It was John Rathburn. Rathburn had hired Thompson. For some reason that Sarah couldn't fathom, Rathburn had wanted his niece dead. It had to be. But why?

Sarah strained to remember... There was something there that was important—something just out of reach—something that made this all make sense, *if she could but remember.*

As often happened, however, her head began to ache, and soon,

Sarah realized it was useless to try to recollect what couldn't be remembered easily. It would seem that her mind was determined to remain blank. At least there was one detail that was now apparent. She had to find Marisa and warn her not to go home. Until her doubts about John Rathburn were put to rest, Albany was not safe. What if she had already returned home? Sarah's stomach churned at the idea, and urgency rose within her as her mind refused to let her fears go.

As might be expected, Sarah could barely contain her need to leave here and find Marisa. But she couldn't go. Not yet. Not until White Thunder indicated it was safe.

In the end, Sarah busied herself with straightening their bags and placing the blankets on the ground in preparation for the evening. She was careful to be quiet. White Thunder had warned her to make no noise and no jerky movements. War parties, he had said, were out in force upon the trail.

However, what she had missed, and White Thunder also, was that a skunk had found this place long before they had. Its home apparently was within one of the hollowed-out logs that created one of the walls of the shelter.

Alas, one moment she was by herself, the next she was confronting the skunk eye-to-eye. She should have done nothing. She should have controlled herself and frozen all movement.

But she was female, and she was untrained in the ways of the woods. Her first reaction was involuntary, and she let out a shriek. The skunk left in haste, but Sarah was overwhelmed at what she'd done.

Immediately, she clasped a hand over her mouth and shut her eyes.

If a war party were anywhere near, she had very nicely given away her location. Hopefully, her mistake would go unnoticed.

Crunch!

Her eyes flew open. It was a footfall outside the shelter. She recognized the sound at once. Worse, it was close by.

Silently, she chided herself for her foolishness.

There were cracks in the branches that held the shelter together. Staring through them, she saw the figures of two men coming toward her cautiously. They were French.

Were Indian scouts with them?

She swallowed the lump in her throat. Dear Lord, where was White Thunder?

Presently, three Indians joined those French, and Sarah watched as the party approached her shelter, watched also as a red, white and black painted face stared into the cracks of the structure. All it would take was one of them to pull back a few of those branches and they would discover her.

Sarah's heart began to pump blood furiously through her body, while her mind was swamped with thoughts of regret. It was her own fault. Why hadn't she controlled her reaction?

One of the Frenchmen took up his rifle and fired a shot into the shelter. It missed her, the ball whizzing by her harmlessly, landing in the dead log behind her with a *thunk*. But it didn't matter. She screamed.

They were upon her in an instant, dragging her from the shelter. But Sarah was not going willingly. She screamed until her voice was ragged. She kicked out at them.

One of the Indians placed a hand over her mouth, while another picked her up and threw her over his shoulder.

This was it, then. After surviving the falls and the attack of a bear, was her death to be as easily accomplished as this?

Where was White Thunder? Surely, if he were alive, he would be here... Surely, he would.

On that thought, she gasped. *"...if he were alive..."*

She shut her eyes. "Please, dear Lord," she prayed silently, "let him be alive. Please, let him be alive...."

***

White Thunder heard Little Autumn's screams as if from outside

himself. The desperation in her voice was unmistakable, and he knew at once that there was trouble…enemies.
Silently, he cursed in the white man's language.

He'd made two mistakes, he figured. The first was that he'd gone off the trail to look for roots. He'd seen the plants on his trek through the woods, and he'd thought there was plenty of time to dig them and get back to the shelter before any possible adversity might befall them. But his second and major error was being unaware of the environment around him. He'd been so engrossed in hunting for the roots, he hadn't felt the presence of someone else close by in these woods.

He shook his head, more than a little upset with himself, and with what might prove to be a deadly blunder.

With all the strength he possessed, he shot forward, sprinting toward the shelter. As he ran, he checked his gun for readiness. He felt for his other weapons, which were on his belt, awaiting only his hand to use them. Satisfied, he practically flew over the forest floor.

As he came within sight of the valley where the shelter lay, he sighted five of the enemy. Three Ottawa, two French. He watched as two of the Ottawa pulled Little Autumn out of the shelter, looked on as one of them slung her over his shoulder. The two Ottawa then hurried off into the woods, dragging her with them.

Instinct made him long to cry out and attack at once, but he held himself back. Not yet. They were five and were ready for a fight, their guns were primed. He wasn't going to be of any use to Little Autumn if he were killed immediately.

If he were going down, he thought, and there was every likelihood that he might, he could at least prepare to take the Frenchmen and the one remaining Ottawa down with him.

Was there anything he could use to his advantage? He could think of only one circumstance that might be in his favor—the element of surprise. Even that might not be helpful, however, for these warriors were wise enough to know that a white woman wouldn't be in the woods alone.

Watching the three of them, and devising a plan, he crept from place to place in the environment surrounding the shelter. He waited until he had a good shot. He delayed, checking his front sight. He fired. The one Ottawa who had remained behind, dropped.

Because the musket he held had only the one shot, White Thunder threw it to the ground and leapt down into the enemy's midst, his hatchet and war club drawn and ready. The Frenchmen saw him coming and one of them aimed a swing at White Thunder, but White Thunder ducked, and with a backhand, sent a fatal blow into the man's middle section.

There was one Frenchman left, but this one was ready for him and had his rifle pointed straight at White Thunder. He fired. White Thunder ducked.

The shot flew by, and White Thunder instantly sprang up and met the man with his hatchet, but the Frenchman dodged, and White Thunder had to spin around in a split second to avoid a fatal backhand. He aimed his tomahawk straight at the Frenchman's head, but again the man parried, and the steel of their weapons clanged.

White Thunder knew he had to do damage quickly, before the Frenchman did irreparable harm to him. Slamming his hatchet straight at the Frenchman's shooting arm, White Thunder plunged his weapon unswervingly into the man's elbow. It cracked, and the arm hung useless.

That did it. The Frenchman was hurt beyond repair, but he was big and predatory, and he aimed a fatal blow at White Thunder with his left arm. It lacked strength. White Thunder easily ducked, then with another pitch of his hatchet, he struck the mortal blow. White Thunder stood for a moment, breathing heavily. All three men were down.

But there were two more Ottawa, and they had fled with Sarah. Worse, they were long since gone.

Picking up the two Frenchmen's guns and ammunition, White Thunder rushed back to pluck up his own gun, then darted forward to hit upon the Ottawa's trail.

As he sped over the ground, following their unmistakable prints, White Thunder only hoped he wouldn't be too late.

***

Evening came at a much faster pace than Sarah would have liked. At present, she and her two captors had stopped and set up camp. Sarah was sitting upright against a tree, tied to it with a rope around her waist; also, there was hemp twining that bound her hands, which were positioned in front of her. That twine chafed and cut into her skin, and blood oozed from the sores.

Luckily, her clothing prevented the rope at her waist from doing much damage, except discomfort. She despaired at the state of her skirts and her bodice, which were both torn and frayed, and her petticoats, which had been soiled beyond repair. Plus, to her shame, these men hadn't granted her the courtesy to allow her to relieve herself along the trail. Somewhere in their trek this day, nature had had its way.

She'd never felt so wretched, nor so dirty.

What had happened to White Thunder? Even as she had been forced to flee the scene, she had heard his war cry, had listened to the clanging sound of hand-to-hand combat, while a sickening sensation had settled over her stomach. Too soon, she had heard a man's death cry, and as tears had filled her eyes, she couldn't help but despair that it might have been White Thunder's.

She had tried to look back, but she had lost her footing, and she'd been hauled a good distance over briars and bramble before she had at last been able to struggle to her feet. Then, had come the agony of another manly cry, a sob that had crushed her.

She wanted to be there with him. But she was helpless. As tears streamed down her face, her captors raced onward, fleeing deeper and deeper into the forest. And now, here she sat, despairing that she might never see White Thunder again in the flesh.

As though from a distance, she saw that the two Indians were busying themselves with a fire, and it was a big one. They said nothing to her—not that she would have been able to understand them had they tried. But human decency would have thought they'd have at least ventured to attempt it.

What were they planning for her? The question was one that was likely to drive her mad if she didn't gain an answer to it, and soon. If her death was fated to be this night, knowing about it seemed more preferable than being caught unaware.

She'd never been more frightened. Nor had she ever felt more alone. Death awaited. She knew it. It was in the way those men looked at her and how they treated her.

But how were they going to go about it? Was it going to be painful?

There was every indication that it would be so. Even now, they sharpened their knives and tomahawks. They were even priming their weapons.

Was White Thunder still alive?

Many hours had passed since her capture. Hours that had been spent retreating along an obvious trail, her feet flying over ground covered with moss, slime and dead leaves. At times, she'd been dragged when she'd fallen and couldn't keep up with the pace. During those times, it had been a struggle to get back to her feet. Sometimes she'd managed it; sometimes they had simply dragged her.

Surely they had left tracks White Thunder could follow, if he were still alive. A single tear fell down her face.

Presently, one of the Indians rose up and stepped toward her. Realizing his intention toward her was hardly social, she gathered her courage. Without warning, he flew at her and grabbed a handful of her hair. He pulled, practically plucking it out by its roots. He spit upon it. Then he did the same to her in her face.

He said, "Your…husband dead. No sign…him."

Sarah looked away from him, but the warrior forced her face back toward him.

"Our brother…killed. English kill…my father. You pay. Will die in fire."

Though the Indian held her face so she couldn't glance away, Sarah refused to meet his eyes, her gaze centered downward. Tears slipped over her cheeks.

"You cry now…cry more later. Torture first…before fire. You feel…much pain." He untied her from the tree. "You…stand."

He put some effort into making her rise, but Sarah refused to obey. If she were to be tortured, then die by the fire, why make it easy for him by cooperating? If the only defiance she had left was to sit while he wanted her to stand, then that was exactly what she would do.

He pulled her roughly to her feet, but she immediately sank to the ground. The warrior repeated the same process twice.

Had it not been so serious, the situation might have appeared humorous. It was, however, anything but amusing.

Eventually, because the warrior couldn't force her to stand, he let her sit. He came down onto his haunches before her and stuck his face in hers, smiling. His image was a horrible sight to behold, for his entire countenance was painted black, and the stark contrast to the white of his teeth made him resemble a walking skeleton.

All at once, he sliced away the bodice of her gown, as well as the sleeves of her chemise, leaving a large, red cut across her chest and exposing her entire upper body to the cold night air. Involuntarily, her cry shot through the night.

He tried to tear away her skirt also, but she wore so many petticoats, her outer one being made of buckskin, it became impossible. Eventually, he gave up.

"No matter. Soon you…feel manhood." He ripped away his breechcloth, exposing his partially aroused member.

Sarah was sickened by the sight, by his smell, and by the idea of what he intended to do to her. Indeed, what food she had left in her stomach, she lost.

But there was no mercy to be found in this Ottawa warrior's manner. He laughed and squatted again.

Sarah gasped as he took out his knife and once more brandished it. He brought it toward her, slowly, slowly, watching her reaction like a wolf cornering a rabbit. He sliced off a portion of her hair, grinning at her all the while. "We do this…all over…body."

Exposed, vulnerable, Sarah wondered if part of the torture were pure fright. If so, he was being very successful.

Again, he waved that knife as he once more cut off a portion of her hair. This time, instead of her stomach losing its dinner, she lost what was left in her small intestines at the other end of her.

It was degrading, and perhaps that was what decided her. If this were her fate—then, so be it. The least she could do was stop cowering in fear. Since that was exactly what he wanted, then she'd go to blazes before she would give it to him.

Thus, when next he came close, she took action, doing the first thing she could think of. After all, what did it matter? They were going to kill her in the most horrible way possible.

She spit in his face.

Immediately, he slapped her. Though the hit stung, it felt good. It was all she had, defiance, and so long as she was sane, she would resist him to the end.

She hadn't counted on what happened next, however. He picked her up by her hair, brought a knife to her scalp and began to cut.

She screamed. And he laughed, the wickedness of his smile the last thing she beheld before she fell forward into a dead faint.

Chapter Eighteen

The Ottawa were moving fast, but they were also covering their tracks. The warriors were smart. They'd known White Thunder would come after them if he survived the fight with their three cohorts.

Their trail was difficult to follow. Several times White Thunder had been led off on false footprints and had been forced to go back and start afresh. It was slow work at a time when speed was crucial.

But there was one fact he knew that the Ottawa didn't.

He had survived. If he lingered here on their trail, if he pretended he'd been taken down by the French and that no one was following them, perhaps waiting until the last minute to attack, White Thunder might gain an advantage.

Finally, after grueling hours spent tracking, he found them. Luckily for him, his ploy had worked, and they must have assumed he'd been killed, because no one was standing guard, a very unwise move.

White Thunder smiled.

He spotted Little Autumn, and what he saw made his blood boil. Tied to a tree, she was bare-chested and exposed. Plus, there was a gash over her breasts. Even now, she was bleeding. Had he been a younger man, he might have rushed in upon them now, spoiling whatever edge he might have.

Older and wiser, he positioned himself into a good shooting posture. When he saw his own Little Autumn spit in one of the Ottawa's eyes, he smiled again. Not only did she possess a gentle nature—one he had witnessed on more than one occasion—if pressed, she could be as dangerous as a she-cat.

But the Ottawa went too far. He slapped her. Older he might be, but even still, White Thunder could barely contain himself from taking immediate action. He knew, however, that he must control his anger. One single, sure shot was better than taking a chance at wrestling—and losing.

The Ottawa pulled her up by the hair and brought a knife to her scalp. She fainted, but the Ottawa was having none of that, and he shook her awake.

White Thunder couldn't remember a time he had felt more enraged, but in this instance, revenge would be his. He took very careful aim, for the Ottawa was too close to Little Autumn, and White Thunder was well aware that he dare not miss.

He had the Ottawa in his front sight. It would be a fatal shot to the head. White Thunder pulled the trigger. Sarah screamed, and the Ottawa jerked sideways from the strength of the blast. He didn't move.

His friend, the other Ottawa, sprang to his feet, and crouching low, peered in every direction. There was one other fine point these two hadn't realized.

White Thunder possessed another rifle, taken from the Frenchmen. He leveled a clear shot, aiming for the Ottawa's head. He pulled the trigger, heard Little Autumn scream yet again, then watched to see the result. The last Ottawa crumpled over, dead.

White Thunder waited only a moment to determine if either of the two Indians would get up. Carefully, slowly, he rose up and rushed forward to inspect the men before he turned his attention to Little Autumn.

What he saw then wrenched at his heart. Her face was wet with tears, she was naked from her shoulders down to her waist, and her skirts were ripped into rags.

"White Thunder," she sobbed, falling forward onto her knees. "I fear that I thought...you were dead."

He rushed to her, knelt in front of her and reached down to cut the bonds holding her hands. "Not yet," he said gently. "Not yet."

Once she was free, he took her into his arms, where she cried until he thought his heart might likely break.

"It's all my fault," she said. "If I hadn't cried out, they—"

"Shhh." He massaged her head, glorying in the feel of her silky locks beneath his fingers, thankful she was alive and in his arms again. "I share the fault, if there is any to be found. Had I been more aware of my surroundings, I would have been able to avoid this. Come, let's leave here and fast, before more Ottawa come to find their friends."

"Yes," she sobbed. "Yes."

After taking off his shirt, he slipped it over her head. Helping her to her feet, he grasped her hand in his, and they fled into the forest.

***

They shot through the woods as if demons were after them. Perhaps they were. Still, it was a different speed of travel than that of their earlier wanderings. Whereas, before they had traversed slowly, taking one delayed step at a time—which had allowed White Thunder the opportunity to examine every piece of ground—now they sprinted over what was clearly a trail. They dashed up forest-covered hills, down into lush valleys and skirted every bend. They splashed through icy-cold streams, not paying any attention to their depths, and sometimes, they had to swim. Always, they pressed forward at a maddening pace.

Luckily, there was a full moon this night. It lit their path, but it didn't allow Sarah to see the changes in the elevations ahead of time, and she found herself stumbling more often than not. There was nothing for it but to pick herself up and match her pace as well as she was able to with White Thunder's. She couldn't see as well as she ought in the dim, silvery light cast here and there by the moon, and the stark tree branches caught at the sleeves of the shirt that White Thunder had loaned her. To add to her discomfort, Sarah's own petticoats snagged on the stickers, further tearing her underclothes.

Above her, the sky was black, with contrasting light from the moon and stars, but so fast was their haste, Sarah didn't dare spare more than a quick glance upward. Instead, she concentrated on placing one foot in front of the other and keeping herself upright and close behind White Thunder.

The atmosphere of the forest was oxygen-filled at this time of night, its fragrance uplifting to her spirits. It was as though the forest itself were lending the two of them a helping hand. Even the wind conspired to aid in their escape, for it was at their back.

But what circumstance were they escaping? Or who? And why were they hurrying? Weren't the Ottawa dead?

The question, though an urgent one in her opinion, went unasked, simply for lack of the opportunity of posing it.

Sarah was out of breath when White Thunder at last broke his pace and settled into a trot. Simply because she couldn't run as fast as he, Sarah had drawn a ways back from him. With his slowdown, she had a chance to catch up with him.

As soon as she came into view of him, however, they pressed forward yet again. Though the trot was more to her liking, she still lagged far behind.

At last, they came to an open meadow, and White Thunder stopped at the edge. He was gazing out at it, looking as though he had been frozen in his tracks.

Sarah was breathing hard and fast as she drew level with him, and now that she had come to a standstill, she observed her breath was mirrored on the air. Interestingly, the cold, usually intolerable to her, felt good this night.

As soon as she caught her breath, she asked, "Why are we running?"

He brought a finger to his lips.

Immediately, she ceased not only all talk, but all movement, too. She couldn't help wondering what was wrong. Were there other enemies about? She hadn't seen any.

But then, she might not be aware of them. For good or for bad, Sarah was more than sadly conscious of the fact that her experience in the woods left much room for improvement.

Without saying a word to her, White Thunder indicated she was to follow him. They crept low, skirting the woods on the edge of the meadow. They stopped at each moonlit shadow and darkened silhouette.

At last, he seemed satisfied, and he signaled to her that she was to do as he did; that he then came down onto his belly and forearms was almost asking too much of her. However, he was already crawling across the meadow. She was supposed to do the same? In petticoats?

Sighing deeply, Sarah realized she had no option. Not if she wished to keep up with White Thunder. Coming down onto all fours, she fell onto her belly, her elbows taking the brunt of the weight of her body.

The fresh scent of grass, dirt and the nightly dew that covered the meadow felt lightweight on her lungs as she inhaled several deep breaths. Although they were long since ruined, Sarah realized her petticoats would be forever grass-stained.

It was slow going, but at long last they had crossed the meadow. Once they reached the other side and were again within the shadowy midst of the forest, White Thunder came to his feet and struck out, again at a maddening pace. Sarah followed. Tired though she was, her legs still kept sending her forward. Somehow, she made them obey her desire to hurry.

It was practically dawn by the time they stopped. Exhausted, Sarah fell to the ground and probably would have slept right where she had dropped had White Thunder been of a mind to let her.

Indeed, at first it seemed he might. He let her rest while he constructed another one of his temporary shelters made from logs, branches and leaves that were strewn on the forest floor. Sarah watched him with tired eyes as he landscaped around the shelter, fixing a log here, a branch there, so that to the untrained eye, their abode would be unseen. Then, coming for her, he bent to pick her up, straightening her hair away from her face as he brought her into his arms.

He said naught as he laid her down on their bed within the shelter. It was a bed he had fashioned from little more than fresh pine boughs and the grasses of the forest, with a blanket thrown atop it. To Sarah, the bed felt as if she had sunk into the most comfortable featherbed she'd ever known.

He kissed her. She smiled, and no sooner had she rested her head against the blanket than she fell to sleep.

Amazingly, her rest was dream free. If not for the warm arms that held her securely all the morning through, she might have thought she was back in Albany, alone in her bed, and that none of this had ever happened.

***

They slept from morning 'til dusk that first day. Then after a snack of dried meat, water and a few shared kisses, they again slept through the night and on into the next day. Indeed, when Sarah at last awoke, the sun was in the western sky showing off its artistry in pinks, blues and oranges. Scents of moss, pine, twigs and dead wood assured her she was still on the run, not back in Albany in her lonely, yet safe, bed.

Had she and White Thunder escaped into safety? Were there still enemies hunting them? Looking up, she stared straight into the rafters of twigs, and branches of maple, oak and birch. Nothing unusual there. These were the common ceilings of the temporary shelters.

Why this sense of turbulence? Was it because of Marisa? With all the turmoil going on around her, Sarah had forgotten, and she groaned aloud. So much had happened, that Marisa's fate had faded into the distance. And it could not be. It was Sarah's duty that called to her, and she knew she couldn't rest until she found Marisa, and, if possible, warn her of the danger awaiting her in Albany.

Her stomach dropped. The memory of an Ottawa warrior, with black-painted face, white teeth and an evil smile, threatening to murder her in the worst possible way, stirred in front of her, as though he were here haunting her. She almost screamed, but she curbed the instinct. Never again would she cry out without knowing who or what was around her.

She lay perfectly still, afraid to move. Eventually, when nothing untoward happened, she chanced to stretch. It became apparent to her that something else was very wrong: She was completely naked beneath this covering.

She didn't remember having gone to bed in the nude. Tired, she most definitely had been, but she was certain she would have remembered removing all of her clothes.

Where was White Thunder?

Most likely, he was the one responsible for her state of undress. But why? Sitting up as quietly as possible—for there wasn't room to stand—she brought the blanket up with her, wrapped it around her, and sat forward to peer through the cracks in their shelter. Was it safe to leave?

While she sat debating the pros and cons of stay or go, she caught sight of White Thunder climbing up from a ridge below. Were they camped on a hill or mountaintop? Now that she thought of it, she had noticed as they had fled over hill and dale last night that the terrain had sloped gradually upward.

He was shirtless, and, despite her anxiety, she took several moments to admire this handsome man. His chest was broad and muscular, as though he were used to the hard work of carrying game for miles on his shoulders. His chest was also wet. Indeed, he was wet all over, and she wondered where the stream was that he had used for bathing. Sniffing the air around her, she was well aware that she needed to visit that stream also.

Beneath the pale rays of the setting sun, his figure took on the appearance of being engulfed in a mystical kind of haze, and she spent several moments watching him, her spirit full of silent admiration. He wore skintight leggings, which accentuated the muscular beauty of his legs. Those leggings were also thigh- high, exposing the upper part of his thigh and the outline of his buttocks to the fancy of her feminine eye.

Those leggings were tied at the knee with strips of red-fringed cloth, and those strips covered a good portion of his moccasins. A breechcloth of navy-and-red cloth draped down in front of him and in back, and it served two purposes that she could see—support and masculine modesty.

He exuded male beauty, despite the fact that his chest and arms displayed several red, blue and black tattoos in designs of circles and straight lines. His stomach was flat, and tied around his waist was his belt where hung his tomahawk, ax, war club and several knives. In his hand was his ever-present rifle, and strung around his shoulders crisscross over his chest were belts and bags for his powder horn and ammunition. His arms were muscular, and except for two bands that spanned his forearms, they were bare.

His hair was clipped close to his head, with a longer strip of black locks that ran down from his crown to the center of his back. The style was much like that which the Mohawk men wore, except that White Thunder wasn't bald in strategic places.

He looked incredibly dear, sexy, and handsome, and something very warm stirred within her. This was the man who had saved her life three times now, the same and only man to whom she had ever given her complete devotion. She wouldn't have been quite human had she not wished to give him everything that was in her to share.

He demanded so little of her.

At present, he appeared to be at his ease, which prompted her to think that perhaps they were in a safe place. On the chance that this might be so, she poked her head out through the entry flap.

"Hello."

He looked up at her and smiled. "Hello," he responded warmly as he climbed the rest of the way to the summit where he had set up their camp.

"White Thunder, do you know what has happened to my clothes?"

"I washed them. They are drying."

"*You* washed them?"

"*Nyoh,* that is so."

Sarah was taken aback. Having spent most of her life as a maid attending to others' needs, she tried to recall if anyone had ever washed her clothes for her. If it were so, she couldn't remember it.

"I also mended your blouse."

This startled her. What sort of a man was this, who not only rescued a maid from certain death, but then mended the clothing that had been torn in the process?

She said, "Thank you. That was kind of you. But unnecessary. I could have taken care of it myself."

"True, but you were sleeping, and I didn't wish to disturb you. Your clothing, however, needed attention."

Remembering the fact that her captors hadn't allowed her the decency to relieve herself privately, she was well aware of this fact. For a moment, embarrassment consumed her, realizing he was probably understating his case.

But she had a question. "How did you accomplish mending my bodice? Did you bring needle and thread with you?"

"*Neh.* However, I always carry sinew and a sharpened tooth for poking holes. It is a necessity, since one often needs to repair or make new moccasins when traveling."

An emotion, similar to gratitude but all mixed up with respect and love, gripped her, threatening to engulf her. For a moment, she felt overwhelmed. Indeed, tears filled her eyes, and a knot seemed to have developed in her throat. Immediately, she was seized by the realization of how kind this man was. Yes, he was a toughened man, a warrior, and he had shown his ability against great odds. But she thought this one trait outshone them all. He was kind.

"Come here." He squatted in front of their entrance and pushed back the pine boughs they were using as an entry flap. "I have something to show you."

"Is it safe, sir?"

"It is."

"But I think I should stay here. You see, I have no clothes on."

He grinned. "Is that an invitation?"

She looked down, then up and smiled back at him. "Perhaps, but only after I have bathed."

"Come." He held out his hand to her. "If you need a bath, I will take you to where you may have one."

She hesitated only a moment longer before she reached forward and placed her hand in his. He helped her to crawl out of their temporary refuge, for she had hold of her only covering, their blanket.

He asked, "Are you still wearing your moccasins?"

She glanced down. It felt like she was, but… "Yes, I believe I am. During our travels, they have begun to feel as if they are a part of my feet. Will I need them?"

"You will. The way is strewn with sharp rocks. Come."

He led her down the steep, rocky bluff he had recently climbed, lending her his support when she slipped, which was often. Trees, deciduous and pine alike, had taken root on this otherwise slippery slope, their branches and roots creating footfalls and handholds. In the distance, she heard the babble of a fast-moving stream. Interestingly, the sound was soothing.

At last, he brought her to a ledge that looked out over a narrow valley that sat between two peaks. In the middle and at the bottom of these peaks ran the crystal-clear stream she'd been hearing, and on each side of it were lush areas of grasses, now brown, and trees, bushes and shrubs.

Here were willow trees, birch, maple and oak trees, as well as berry bushes and red sumac guarding the water. The colors of brown and gold dominated the landscape, and though the trees were barren at this time of year, this stretch of land looked cared for, as though it were a park.

Off in the distance, branches from the willow trees dipped in and out of the water lazily, as though they moved in time to the music of a cool wind.

Above them, the sky was a deep blue, with white, fluffy clouds spotting the heavens. A dragon fly seemed interested in their goings-on, and it flitted in and around them in its quest to find a sweet treat. Sarah sighed. It would appear they were safe here.

"'Tis beautiful," she said at last. "Where are we?"

"We are deep in the Adirondack Mountains."

"The Adirondacks. Tell me, I had heard that these mountains are named for an Indian tribe. Is that true?"

"It is, and the word itself is from our language and means 'eaters of bark'. This is what we called these people when the Seneca first came to this country. Our elders tell us that they flavored their food with bark—thus, their name."

"When your people first came here? Then your people are not originally from this place?"

"*Neh*, no. The old stories tell us that long ago, perhaps as long as a thousand or more years in our past, we lived in the west, near what the people say was a big river. But my people left that place and came east."

"I didn't know that. I had assumed you had always been here."

"Perhaps all people come from somewhere. Did you know it is because of the Adirondack tribe that we of the Iroquois value freedom as much as we do? Would you like to hear how that came about?"

"Indeed."

He nodded and placed his arm around her. "The Adirondack people were very different from us, and we fought many battles with them. They were good warriors, and they defeated us in battle after battle, and a dark period hung over our people. We were forced to pay the Adirondacks a tribute of skins and meat, as well as much of our crops.

"But my people remembered how it was to be free, and they longed to be unfettered again—as free as the eagle. So they planned to escape. They schemed for years. When, at last, the people had a good store of food and were prepared, they stole away, sending out their canoes upon the river that the English call the St. Lawrence."

"Were they successful?"

"Not at first, for the Adirondacks had much to lose if my people escaped, and so they came after them. My people were heavily burdened with women and children, and the Adirondack men were not. A great battle commenced, and the Iroquois were almost annihilated. But the Creator heard the people's cries and took pity on them, for He believes that all His children should be free. He sent a storm so forceful that day that the Adirondacks were almost wiped out. After that, they returned to their villages, never to bother us again. So it is that we owe ourselves, our crops, our meat and food to no one. We will always be free."

"Yes, may it always be so. If there is one idea that you have impressed upon me, it is that a people should be free."

"*Nyoh*, yes," he said simply. "Now come, there is much privacy here. The creek is but a short distance from our camp, and we are alone, I believe. You can bathe in the stream if you wish and wash your wounds, for this is a special place. I'll help you to the water, and if you will allow me, I'll assist you to bathe."

"*You* would help me bathe?"

He grinned at her, his look more than a little seductive. "I would. Your wounds need to be tended, and it's best if I do that. Besides, I think you might like the manner in which I clean you."

Sarah shook her head, but she smiled back at him all the same. For a moment, the nightmare faded. If only it would go away for good.

Chapter Nineteen

"Why is it warm here, when it's been so cold elsewhere?" Little Autumn asked. "Aren't we higher in the mountains? Should it not be colder here?"

White Thunder grinned as he helped her to negotiate—one slow step at a time—the grassy slope to the stream's shoreline. "I think the English call it Indian Summer."

"Oh, yes, of course." She cast him a tender look, and he felt encouraged by it. "I'm glad that it's warm today. I have great need of a bath, but unlike you, my body does not crave an icy swim."

"Careful," he warned as she negotiated a steep passage. "Now, do not be deceived. The water is cold, but the air is warm. Here." He stooped down to pick some goldenrod growing close to hand and offered it to her. "This makes a good soap for hair and body."

"It does? Just the plant all by itself? I don't have to do anything with it?"

"You have never used this?"

She shook her head.

"Then it truly is best that I wash you."

Delicate color came quickly to her countenance and spread slowly over her cheeks. White Thunder found that he was much fascinated. It wasn't that he was intentionally trying to cause her distress, it was simply that these little details endeared her to him.

"We have been intimate for many weeks now," he said. "And still I embarrass you?"

"Yes." She gazed away from him. "Don't you see? There's a

difference. I have always been fully dressed when we make love, except a few times recently. But to undress here in the light of day, fully upright and in complete view of you…"

"You will come to love it, and I will, also," he replied quite honestly, "because I won't give you a chance to be embarrassed. Besides, soon the evening will be spreading its dim shadows around us, and it will give you some protection from my leering."

Again, she smiled, but he saw that she still hesitated. "I don't know."

He bent and kissed her long and hard, his lips and tongue seeking out the sweet recess of hers. While it wasn't his intention to make love to her here and now, the caress caused such an instantaneous response from her that his body reacted in a way that promised much pleasure, were he to follow up on it.

But he was not in such a mind. She needed time to recover. After her ordeal, she required peace, and he would see that she had it.

But that didn't mean he couldn't tease her.

As they kissed, he rocked the lower part of his body against hers and reached down to her buttocks to pull her in close. He even fought her for hold over the blanket. But she won, clutching it firmly to her bosom.

Breaking off the kiss, she asked, "Why did we have to run so hard, and for so long last night?"

"Bad spirits there. Not a place to linger. It was also in Abenaki Territory, enemy of the Iroquois. In rescuing you, we made much noise, and the Abenaki will investigate it. When they do, they will see that a Seneca was there, and they will try to find me. But this place where we are now has long been a symbol of peace for all tribes. It is on the border of Abenaki Territory, but they do not control it. All tribes come here because here one can more easily talk to the Creator. This is His safe haven. But to arrive here without harm, we had to hurry."

"Ah, now I understand. And that meadow—why did we have to

crawl across it?"

"Abenaki were in those woods last night. Did you not see their signs?"

"I little know what to look for."

He nodded. "Their prints were on the trail, and they were fresh, meaning they were crawling in those woods. If we had crossed that place upright, we would have been easily seen, especially because there was a full moon."

"Oh." Her gaze settled on something over his shoulder. "There are my clothes, drying on those tree branches." She pointed. "Thank you again for your kind attention to my needs. Do you think they're ready for me to wear yet?"

"*Neh,* I have only just washed them. But come, I still see fear in your eyes from your recent experience, and there is a sadness that I sense in your spirit. Let us bathe you in the fresh water here and see if this might help to cleanse the body...and perhaps even more." Bending to kiss her again, he loosened her grip on the blanket then let it fall to the ground. He stepped back to admire her breasts, her rounded buttocks and the splattering of hair between her legs. It was obvious she was uncomfortable under his scrutiny, and not wishing to cause any awkward emotions, he picked her up in his arms and stepped to the water.

The shoreline was rocky, and long grasses grew close to the bubbling water, which swirled over the rocks in its path. There was nothing unusual in this—it was all as it should be—and he strode through the grass and waded into the fast-moving stream.

To him, the water was refreshing, but he feared she would find it too cold. Luckily, this rivulet wasn't deep, and it would be possible to gradually acquaint her with its temperature. At this part of the stream, the water came only to mid-calf level, which allowed him to kneel, come down on his haunches, then position her over his lap.

To say he was not sexually excited by her because of holding her naked form in his arms would have been a terrible lie. Given a chance, he would have liked nothing better than to lock their bodies in the dance of love. It was simply that he knew what she needed most at present was comfort.

"Place your arms around my neck," he said, "so that if you slip, you won't be subjected to a cold dunking."

She did as he asked, and, bending over her, he removed each of her moccasins, throwing them to shore. He washed her feet, massaging them in the process. She sighed and melted against him as though she might likely go to sleep.

However, the feel of her skin, silky and smooth against his fingertips, was having a purely carnal effect on him. Indeed, touching her was as potent an aphrodisiac as if she had asked for his lovemaking, and, despite the cold water, his body was more than ready for her.

He reminded himself it was not his intention to make love to her now. She was fearful. She was hurting. He could see it in her demeanor, could feel it in the slight jerks and shivers of her body.

His arms tightened around her. If he could, he would keep her with him always.

Keep her with him always. It was a potent thought, and, as he hid his face in the silky tresses of her hair, he realized it was time to come face-to-face with a truth.

He loved her. Moreover, he loved her more than he'd ever loved another.

He'd denied it silently, telling himself that what he felt for her was little more than an intense admiration. Certainly, he had offered her marriage, especially when it seemed likely they might have created a child. But love?

It had come at a time when he hadn't wanted to love anyone again, had even promised himself it would never happen. Love could hurt.

But it could also be healing, he amended. Hadn't she proved that to him? Wasn't he a living result?

Because his thoughts were profound, he swallowed hard and kissed the side of her face. He rubbed his cheek against hers. In time, he murmured, "After we wash your body of its nightmare experience, I have an item of importance to give you that I think will help to heal your fear and grief."

"Oh? What is it?"

He reached into one of the bags draped over his shoulders and pulled out a string of white-and-purple-beaded wampum.

"Wampum?" she asked and she sat up, crossing her arms over her chest. She looked surprised, and amazingly, she also seemed suddenly upset.

"*Nyoh*, yes, it is wampum."

"I don't understand. After all we've been through, I—"

This was not the response he had expected. "Is something wrong?"

"Sir, what is it you are saying to me? Is this meant to be an insult?"

He frowned at her. "*Neh*, the opposite is true. I am showing you great respect."

"Then, why have you decided to give me Indian money? Perhaps it's not like this in your society, but in mine, when a man gives a woman money after they've made love..."

At last he understood her meaning. "Wampum is not money. Is that what you think?"

"I do, sir."

He shook his head. "I fear some trader has stuck you with a great misunderstanding. Wampum is not used as money. It never has been. The English, with his gold and silver coins, has assigned a value to wampum that is in error."

"But I have heard that people will trade fortunes for it. So, if not money, then what is it?"

"Its use is to cure the mind of the madness of grief, to open the throat so a person may speak openly and at free will, and it is given to take away the heartache of losing someone close to you. Come here." He sat forward to gather her into his arms and bring her back in close to him. "It is my desire to help ease the fear and grief that your experience has brought you. This is the correct use of wampum."

She sat silently for the space of a moment. "I understand, I think. You were trying to help me, and I misunderstood. I apologize, and I thank you for your consideration."

He nodded.

"But now you have excited my curiosity. What exactly is wampum?"

"That will take some explaining. If you will settle back here in my arms, I'll finish washing you, and I'll tell you about it."

She did as he asked, and he rubbed her legs with water and the sand from the bottom of the stream. "There are three words that are used to banish what we of the Iroquois call the insanity of grief. Long ago, the two men who founded the Iroquois Confederacy sought to console a person who was consumed with grief." While he spoke, his touch explored higher and higher up on her thigh.

"Hmm…that feels good. But tell me more. What are the three words?" Meanwhile, she shifted position so his hand was captured between her legs, there at their junction.

He swallowed. "They are called the Three Bare Words, and they are the first few words that the Peacemaker spoke to Hiawatha in founding our Confederation. It is our Condolence Ceremony, which is performed with the intent of wiping away the craziness caused by grief, for it is this misery of loss which we believe causes endless fighting and war."

She had parted her legs slightly, and he was not slow on the uptake. He placed his hand on her where he knew she ached to be rubbed, and he gave her what she appeared to need. In response, she moved her hips against the pressure he was exerting, and with the magic of his fingers he began to love her.

"We can talk about this later," he said.

As she wiggled her body against his hand, she murmured, "Yes."

He sighed, and keeping his voice low and his fingers intent at their task, he said, "It has not been my intention to make love to you while you are still recovering from your fear. But if you want it..."

She didn't answer all at one time, though her legs parted wider and she danced in time with the rhythm of his fingers. She had relaxed against him, with nothing hidden from him, and not only did look his fill at her, but by his touch alone, he was bringing her to a release.

"Don't you believe, White Thunder, that making love is part of the healing process?"

Though they were speaking all around it, the truth was he was becoming very excited. Apparently, she was also.

"I believe it might be," he answered, "if one is willing."

Her hips were gyrating faster now against his fingers, and when she moaned, then whispered, "I'm willing," he thought he might likely be the luckiest man alive. He groaned.

Her lips were still parted, and the invitation she provided would have required a saint to resist. He was hardly that. Slowly, his head descended toward hers, and when his lips took possession of hers, she moaned while she squirmed against him.

It was a long, slow kiss, during which he repositioned her, settling her in front of him, with her legs wrapped around his waist. Then he came up onto his knees, and, holding her up by her buttocks, he settled her over his shaft. Slowly, he entered her.

She was hot, she was wet, and, so aroused was she, he sensed she was already close to her peak. It was an erotic position, and they made love as if their lives depended on it.

As he thrust into her, he whispered, "I think I died a thousand deaths when that Ottawa warrior slapped you."

"I have never been so frightened."

"Shhh. I know."

They were working themselves into a frenzy of sexual tension, and his thrusts had become fast, jerky and driven. He knew she was close to her pinnacle. When she rose to fully experience that pleasure, he met her with his own need, spilling his seed into her.

On and on the pleasure lengthened, extending far beyond the physical deed. As he drifted back to earth, he came to realize that his life from this point forward would be different. He was not the same man he had been before he met her. She was now as much a part of him as was his own identity. With her, he was whole.

As they continued to move against each other in the aftermath of love, he sat back on his heels, bringing her with him. He murmured to her, his voice husky, "I would do most anything for you."

With her arms around his neck and her body intimately connected to his, she responded, saying, "I, too."

Chapter Twenty

The love they created between them was pure, good and a little like magic. Perhaps, as she'd said, it was what was needed to help her to heal. He hoped it was so, for it was not within him to purposely bring her more heartache.

At present, she was wrapped around him, and he had little desire to unsettle her. So, with himself still firmly encased within her warmth, he finished the task of washing her body, starting with her legs and thighs.

In time, his manhood returned to its more usual state, and, when it did, he lifted her above him slightly so as to wash her there, too. Then, he rinsed the dirt from her arms, her breasts and her back. But when he came to her chest, he hesitated.

Setting her slightly away from him, he traced the slash that had been made by the Ottawa warrior. "Does this hurt?"

"A bit." She nodded.

He left off touching it to splash fresh water on the wound, then sneaked in a few massages of her breasts before he reached into the water, his hand seeking the mud in the river's bed. Grabbing a handful of it, he dabbed it onto the cut.

She jerked a little, then settled back into his arms, her own arms hugging him firmly around his neck.

Interestingly, she didn't object to the movement of the cold water over her body or to the mud he had spread over her chest. Rather, it seemed as if she'd fallen asleep. But he wasn't done yet.

Because he had made himself her protector, he felt responsible for her capture, as well as the real and threatened tortures forced upon her; it was his intention now to wash away her fear and grief as best he could . He only wished it were as easy as cleansing the body.

He said, his voice no louder than a whisper, "Are you ready for me to wash your hair?"

Her answer was a sigh. "Will it be cold?"

"I fear it will be, for I'll have to submerge the length of it and your head into the stream."

"Must we?" She gritted her teeth. "Truly, you needn't continue to wash me. I'm a big girl now, and I can do the job myself."

"You would deny me the fantasy of my dream come true?"

She laughed, and the sound of it was as pretty as she was.

"Besides," he continued, "if I hold you crossways over my lap, it might not be too cold."

She sighed. "I think that I am little more than clay in your hands for the moment. Do with me as you will."

He growled. When an answering moan escaped her lips, he almost lost himself to her. But then, with trusting eyes, she stared up at him innocently, and said, "White Thunder, I think I should confess a bit of truth to you."

He raised an eyebrow in response, an encouragement for her to continue.

"It may or may not matter to you. But..." She hesitated. "I...I've fallen in love with you."

Every nerve ending within his body suddenly screamed at him to do something, anything. For answer, he pulled her hard and fast against him, practically crushing her.

So lost was he for words, he swallowed several times before he was at last able to utter, "I, too."

She backed up slightly from him. "Did I hear that right? Did you say that—"

"You did. I love you."

She shifted until she was so close to him he could feel the imprint of her breasts against his chest, then she spoke, asking, "But what about Wild Mint and your promise—"

"I love you," he repeated more firmly. "I have for many days, perhaps weeks, but until I saw you with those Ottawa warriors and realized I could lose you, I hadn't had the courage to admit it, even to myself."

Sarah sat up, and was only inches away from him, presenting him with the glorious picture of a nude woman. Ah, what a fortunate man he was.

"And Wild Mint?"

"She will always have a place in my heart, and my duty remains as it has been for years. But it's been fifteen years and…I have changed. No longer do I wish to join her in death. Indeed, I have come to know what life is, and it is a life I would like to share with you."

"I, too, feel this way." She hugged him tightly. "But we must face the fact that we are from two different worlds. You know this. When we're here, separated from the rest of society, it seems it would be a matter of simplicity to create our lives with each other. But the prejudice of others might sometimes get in the way. And I am still an indentured servant, with five years left to serve. Surely, you understand, for we have discussed this at length. After five years, I will be free, and will be without the worry of owing my work to someone else. If I tried to escape before then, I could be forced into service for the rest of my life."

"Shhh." He pulled her face in toward his until her head fit into the crook of his neck. "I know, but we have come here to wash away your grief, not add to it. Someday, we will have to face this together. But for now, we are still married, if only because we have not yet had to part. And if we never part…"

He felt her smile, heard her slight chuckle.

"We cannot fight all the battles that lie before us on this one day. It's true that the moment may yet come when it appears we will have to go our separate ways, but it is not here now. We have time to prepare. Meanwhile, let us have this one evening without worry."

She nodded.

"Now, it was not in my thoughts," he admitted, "to make love to you here, now, in this stream. I think the shore would be a more comfortable place. But first, we should wash your hair."

"I am honored, sir, that you are thinking of my comfort." She changed her position yet again, so that instead of straddling him, she was merely sitting in his lap. "You have my best interests at heart, and I thank you. But, White Thunder, if I am to wash my hair, then I should swim, and so should you. And forgive me, but I believe you have on too many clothes."

He closed his eyes and smiled. What had he done to deserve such pleasure? He said, "That is easily remedied."

He accommodated her at once, shifting position so he could come to his feet. He still held her firmly in his arms, but since he was now ambulant, he waded to the shoreline.

Once there, he let her down so she was standing on her own, and, as quickly as he could, he removed his leggings and the belts and straps he wore over his chest and shoulders. But he left on his breechcloth, as well as several of his weapons.

"You are not naked, as I am."

"I am as naked as I can get. Until I am within the safety of a Seneca village, I cannot relax and leave my weapons behind me. This may be the Creator's own valley, but there are those who do not respect even the Creator of all things. Therefore my tomahawk, my knives and my war club will remain with me."

"If that be the case, then I shall swim as I usually do—in my chemise."

He nodded. "Perhaps I should tell you that it is not much protection, for it is so flimsy that I can see beyond its threads to the treasure beneath. But if you desire it, I'll get it for you."

"That would be most kind of you."

The tree where he had laid out her clothes to dry was not far, and he was back in an instant. He held the chemise out at arm's length. "Is this what you need?"

"It is." She reached for it, but he withdrew it before she could take hold of it.

She gave him a puzzled glance.

His response was a smile. "Come and get it."

"Sir?"

With his hand, he urged her to come forward. Again, he held the garment out toward her.

She took a step toward him, another, then she lunged at him, grabbing for the chemise.

He sidestepped her easily and caught her so she didn't fall. He tickled her a little too, and quite expectedly, she giggled. "You have to learn to be quicker. Would you like to have another try at it?"

She gave him a wild leer. "I little know if I wish to play this game with you. I seem to be the loser of it."

"Loser?" He shook his head and smiled. "I think you are the winner of all my attention."

That caused her to laugh again, and it was a delight for him to hear it. "White Thunder, I would like my chemise now."

"And so you shall have it." He held it out to her. "Little Autumn, you simply need to be faster."

She shook her head, and he knew she was suppressing a smile. He taunted her with the chemise, holding it at arm's length.

"You have to hold it still," she demanded, "and you can't jerk it back when I reach for it."

"Ah, do you see, I am holding it still."

"Yes, you are now. But you have to continue to hold it still. Those are the rules."

He grinned at her. "And so I am holding it still for you."

She made to reach for it, but he quickly moved it out of range.

"I said you had to hold it still."

"I was. I am. It was the fault of the wind, which moved my arm."

She sighed. "I fear the chemise is not to be seen on my body while I swim with you, is it?"

"I have no say over that, Little Autumn. You have only to reach for it...and beat me."

She laughed. "It doesn't appear this is going to happen, and I think I should take that swim while my body is still used to the temperature of the water and while we still have light to see by. Already, the sun is disappearing in the western sky."

"Then, come. Let's swim before you get too cold, and while I can still look at you to my fill." He rushed toward her and took hold of her hand with his own—the hand that was holding the chemise. Quickly, she grabbed it from him and slipped it over her head, letting it fall to its full length, which came to mid-calf on her.

She said, "Thank you, sir."

"You are welcome. But come, let's take that swim."

***

As he'd promised, he washed her hair with the goldenrod flowers, which he rubbed in his hands with water until they made a paste that could be spread through the hair.

"It's best to dry the plant first and then make the soap from that. But this will work," he said.

They washed each other's hair, and Sarah curiously asked about the common Indian hairstyle of the Iroquois, the one known to most as the Mohawk.

He ran his hand over the top of his head. "This is called the scalp lock, and it is a dare to the enemy. Most tribes take scalps to prove the accuracy of their war deeds. They are like the Englishman's medals, and they are honored in the same way."

"However, one is bloody, and the other is not."

"Yet, they are obtained in the same manner, Little Autumn, and for the same reason—war. And war is not without blood. Perhaps the Indian way is better, because it is a reminder that the token is taken by sacrificing the life of another."

Sarah didn't have an instant reply to that, and so they fell back into their animated romp in the water, mostly playing tag and splashing one another, for the water was only deep in particular places, which didn't allow for actual swimming. But it didn't matter. It was a perfect end to a memorable afternoon.

Indeed, she'd had so much fun, she'd almost forgotten about the torture. Almost.

The evening shadows finally chased the two of them from the water—that and the cold wind that arrived with the night air. By the time they were ready to leave, Sarah had discovered that her clothes were dry, and she hurriedly slipped them on before White Thunder had the opportunity to get at them and tease her with them. At last, she was fully dressed. It felt good.

"I'm hungry," she said as they began climbing the slope that led to the summit, where they had set up camp. "What's for supper?"

"I fear we are still eating a diet of dried meat and berries. Perhaps tomorrow I might hunt, and we will fix some fresh meat."

"I think dried meat and berries sound delicious." She followed him, placing her feet in the same footholds he'd made.

Before they reached the top, he turned to her and signaled her to silence and to remain where she was. *Oh no. Now what? Were they never to escape the enemy?*

Her heart picked up enough speed that she could hear its beating in her ears. Her stomach twisted as White Thunder crawled up the remaining incline of the slope and quietly, carefully took out his tomahawk and took aim.

He let the projectile go, and she heard a dull thump and the cry of whatever life he'd hit.

White Thunder signaled her to follow him on up the slope. Perhaps it wasn't as bad as she'd thought. She did as requested, dreading what she might find, but knowing it had to be done.

White Thunder grinned as she caught up to him, and he held out his hand to her. "The Creator must have heard us speaking of our dull supper. Do you see what He put here, awaiting us?"

It was a deer, a buck.

"We will have fresh meat tonight."

To Sarah, whose duties in the household had never included kitchen activities, the idea of skinning and preparing the meat was neither appealing nor appetizing. Even that first time when he'd brought a deer to the cave, she hadn't helped him. She had watched. But that was past, and she'd be darned now if she'd let him know that the task was hardly pleasant.

She smiled as though he might have presented her with a jeweled ring. "It's wonderful. We can make more dry meat."

"We can, but first there are parts of the animal that have to be eaten fresh after it is killed. The liver is one of those. We'll eat that tonight and make dry meat tomorrow."

"Yes, yes." Sarah hoped she was feigning the same sort of enthusiasm for the work as White Thunder.

They set to work over the deer, and, to Sarah's amazement, she discovered it wasn't as gruesome as she had thought.

Indeed, with White Thunder at her side, she enjoyed the evening very much.

Chapter Twenty-One

The black-painted face of the Ottawa hung in midair in front of her. It had arms that reached out to grab her and sharp teeth to bite her. Inch by slow inch, it cut her skin, taking part of it off as though the Indian were skinning a deer.

It said, "I will make this into a robe for John Rathburn, who will enjoy it because it is made from your skin. He will like it because he owns you, body and soul."

"You shall not do this."

Now, it was Marisa speaking, who had suddenly appeared in the middle of the Ottawa camp. "Miss Sarah's parents are guarding her, and they will not let you do this to her. Come this way, Mr. and Mrs. Strong."

And then, there Sarah's parents were, staring at her with such loving expressions, they might have been alive. But they weren't alive. They'd been dead since...

Suddenly they were gone, and in their place came the Ottawa warrior once more, knife in hand. Closer and closer he advanced, and always he smiled, though the look of it was wicked. He brandished his weapon in front of her face. He cut off part of her hair, then plunged the knife into—

Sarah screamed and screamed and kept on screaming.

White Thunder, now awake, sat up and pulled her into his embrace. He said nothing. He simply held her close, pushing back her hair to caress her.

"It was so real," she cried. "It was as though he were here again, as though he had come for me."

White Thunder didn't reply. Nor did he ask who *he* was.

Perhaps he knew.

Gradually, White Thunder began to rock back and forth with her still in his arms. "It is possible your body is not in harmony with itself, and it might need some food and water to bring back its accord. Come, we have food here, and water. Eat. Drink. Then let us sleep again—only I think you should remain within my arms for the rest of the night."

She nodded.

Because all their needs were close to hand, her requirements were satisfied quickly. But Sarah was far from ready to go back to sleep. She was too frightened. Still, she settled back down, hoping against hope that because White Thunder's arms were around her, she would simply drift off to sleep again.

However, it wasn't to be.

White Thunder must have realized this also, for in due time, he spoke to her. "Do you want to tell me about it?"

"I... Yes. It was the Ottawa, but it was only his head and his arms that threatened me. However, this time, he didn't stop at simply cutting my hair. This time..."

White Thunder's arms increased their pressure around her. "That time is not now. Though it is possible his spirit might haunt you, the danger from him doing you physical harm is gone."

"*Yes.* Because of you, I am still here to speak of this. Again, White Thunder, I thank you."

He nodded. "Does the Ottawa's spirit haunt you?"

"Perhaps. I'm uncertain how to judge that. But something else happened. I dreamed of my parents, and when I did, something good occurred. My memory of them returned, and..." She fell silent.

"And?" he prompted.

"My full recall has returned to me, sir. I remembered how my parents died, how I came to be an indentured servant, and what those two separate experiences have to do with one another. I recalled that Miss Marisa and I were fleeing from Albany, and I remembered why."

With his arms wrapped securely around her, he nodded. "Go on."

"It is complex, I fear. My parents were Dutch. They'd owned a farm, a house, and had much to live for. They were happy, successful. My father was investing in raising tobacco as a crop, and had borrowed the needed finance for this from John Rathburn. All seemed good until they were raided by 'Indians' who set the farm, the house, the barn and the fields afire. My parents died in those fires. In the end, there was nothing left with which to pay the debt to John Rathburn. No crops, no house, no barn. So…Mr. Rathburn took my family's farm, he took their land, and he took me into servitude for twenty years."

"He is an evil man."

"Yes, sir, I think you're right. But the terrible part is that through Marisa, I came to learn it was most likely not Indians who started the fires that night, but Mr. Rathburn himself, or people he had hired to do the deed for him. In other words, it was never his intention to help my father. Mr. Rathburn financed my father simply to bankrupt him and take from him what he had."

"If this be true, then your services to him were obtained through lies."

"That, they were. Unfortunately, it changes nothing in the eyes of the law. I'm still duty-bound to honor my bond, no matter how ill-gotten it was obtained."

"How can this be, if he gained what he did through dishonesty?"

Sarah tossed her head. "Because it is hard for poor people to fight rich people in court."

"Then it is a bad system."

"Perhaps."

"How is it, then, that you came to be in the woods, so far from your home?"

"That's another story altogether. Through a series of incidents, Miss Marisa found out what Mr. Rathburn had done, and when she did, she arranged to get me out of John Rathburn's reach. She was taking me to some friends who live far away from Albany. I think it was her intention that I should serve out the rest of my debt there."

"And now she, too, is gone from you."

"Yes."

He sat silently, as though lost in thought. After a few moments, he said, "All those years ago, when your house was set afire, did you try to stop your mother from going to the aid of your father?"

"That, I did. How did you know?"

"Because when you were delirious with fever, you called out to your mother. I knew, then, that there was a memory that haunted you. Now, I understand it is their deaths that possess you even to this day."

"Yes, that is true. It is a terrible incident from which I have never recovered."

He dipped his head in agreement. "Perhaps it is time that I speak the Three Bare Words to console you in your grief, no matter how long ago that sorrow occurred. If I do this, it has the power to relieve the dead, who might surround you, so that they too may go on their journey. Would you like that?"

"Very much, I think."

"Good. Come and sit up. Though it is dark, we can climb down to the nearby stream, where I will speak these Three Words to you."

She nodded. "Very well."

"I only ask that you forgive me if I make mistakes, for I have long been gone from my village, and my memory of the ceremonies may be at fault."

"I would forgive you most anything. Know, however, that you don't have to do this. I've managed to make my way in life so far, and I dare say I'll continue to do so."

"But why should it be difficult for you? *Neh*, you are important to me. So come, it's late, but though night has taken over the evening sky, let us set a path to the water, where I can conduct the Condolence Ceremony as best I am able."

Grasping hold of his bags, his weapons and his rifle, he threw the straps over his shoulders, situated all his weapons on his person, then crawled out through the entry flap. Turning, he held it open for her.

As she crawled out through the flap, she froze. Not from fear. Rather because it was an unusually beautiful night, dark, cool, and still. The air was crisp and scented with pure oxygen, as well as the fragrance of pine. Without the warmth of the sun, the cold bit right through her skin, and she was thankful White Thunder had taken the time to fix her dress.

Above her, the moon was almost full—though, at present, it was half-hidden behind a cloud. A million or more stars glimmered above her, some twinkling more brilliantly than others, and the Milky Way stood distinct and clear in a sky that seemed broader than eternity.

Had she ever seen so many stars?

There was a fragrance about the atmosphere this high up that gave her a feeling of gaining room, and as she gazed around the moonlit summit, her thoughts seemed to spread out, away from her. Interestingly, it brought her a feeling of relief.

There was little time to spend in admiration of the surroundings, for White Thunder was quickly pacing toward the edge of the slope. She hurried to catch up with him, and once again, she followed him down the steep incline, clinging to him more often than not when she lost her footing.

At last, they traversed the level ground that led to the shoreline of the stream. She watched as White Thunder looked around their surroundings, took note as he started for a large maple tree, and followed him toward it.

After spreading his blanket over the ground, he indicated they would sit. She followed his lead, taking her position opposite him.

"Please forgive me if I err in the performance," he stated again.

"Of course. But, I wouldn't know if you made an error."

"Although that is true, it's still important that I do it right. We will begin." He pulled out eight different strings of wampum from his bag. Holding them in his hand, he began. "Tears, throat, heart. These are the words that were first spoken by the Peacemaker to Chief Hiawatha, to comfort Hiawatha in his grief."

White Thunder took a string of wampum and leaned forward to wipe it over Sarah's face and eyes. "With this string, I brush away the tears from your eyes so that henceforth you may see more clearly and not be blinded by the madness that true grief can bring." White Thunder handed her the string of white-and-purple wampum.

Sarah accepted the gift and sat before him silently. As the moon cast down its misty beams to the earth below, the light caught White Thunder in its glow. Under its silvery effect, his profile looked more like an artist's depiction of male beauty than that of a flesh-and-blood man. Though she had always found White Thunder to be handsome, to describe him as merely attractive wouldn't have done him justice. He looked warm, approachable, magnificent.

White Thunder took hold of another string of wampum and brushed it over her throat. "With this string of wampum, I take away any hindrance that would keep you from speaking freely." Again, he handed her the string of wampum.

Slowly, and with great deliberation, he repeated the ceremony with the other strings of wampum. With these, he wiped away the blood that had been spilled due to her parents' death; he covered her parents' grave, that they would bring her no grief; he collected up the bones of all her relatives and buried them deep so that not even they could cause her grief; he made the sky beautiful again; and he expelled the insanity of grief. With each step, he handed her another string of wampum.

When White Thunder had only one string left in his hand, he said,

"With this last string of wampum, I banish the weighty thoughts that encircle you. From this moment forward, light and sunshine shall again be a part of your life." As before, he handed her the string. Then, he came to his feet and held out his hand to her. "Come."

She followed his lead, standing to her full stature and taking hold of his hand. He led her to the fast-moving creek, where he squatted and gathered water from a pool that had collected there.

"Today," he said, "as we were playing, I saw this part of the stream. Because of all the waterfalls that drain into it, is the clearest and cleanest."

She nodded.

"Now, I'll pour this water, which is the cleanest that I can find, into your body so as to clear your mind of any distress." He guided the water to her lips, and when she had drunk it, he said, "And now, you must return the wampum to me, strand by strand, as I did to you, and give me your reply."

She understood what he meant without having to query him, and one by one, she gave each string back to White Thunder, replying to him in the same manner by which he'd given them to her. When she stumbled on the words, he encouraged her, until the last string of wampum was returned, and with it, she said, "I thank you for banishing the dark thoughts that were troubling me. I can now behold the beauty of the world around me."

He inclined his head. "And now, it is finished."

She smiled up at him. Soft, shimmering moonlight held him in its trance and cast the planes of his face with silvery light. She was already standing so close to him, she could feel his breath upon her. It was beautiful. *He* was beautiful.

Her voice was a mere whisper. "I do see more clearly, and it does seem as if my heart is purer. Thank you, White Thunder. I am trying to remember if anyone has ever performed such a kindness for me.

Outside of Marisa, I think there is no one. Please know I am honored, and deeply touched."

He bent down and kissed her gently. Taking her in his arms, he said, "Grief for a loved one can be a terrible thing. It can cause vengeful war to commence. It can bring about paralysis and nightmares. It is like a poison to the system. This ceremony was established long ago by the Peacemaker to wipe away the grief of the people, and, by doing so, to do away with war. It is my pleasure to do this for you. Just as it was their hope all those hundreds of years ago that by wiping clean a person's grief, they could do away with war forever, so it is my desire to wipe away your fear and anxiety so that you may look upon the world again, not as a place of despair, but as a world of beauty."

She reached up to run her hands through his hair. "My love, I am again deeply touched. Indeed, I bless the day you came into my life. I know little what the future holds for us, but this I do know. I love you." She sighed against his shoulder. "I simply love you."

He backed up, but only minutely. Placing his hands on the sides of her face, he bestowed one soft kiss after another against her lips. Meanwhile, his hands massaged her face, her neck, her cheeks, her hair, her scalp. He whispered, "This is not part of the ceremony—it should never be part of the ceremony—but I want to make love to you."

"Oh, yes," she said. "Please."

Chapter Twenty-Two

Soft, moonlit shadows flickered over the delicate features of Sarah's face, her pert nose, her full lips, the dainty bone structure of her cheeks, the creamy-blonde tendrils of her hair. Even her complexion appeared flawless beneath the flattering rays of the misty moonbeams, though White Thunder knew personally that her skin bore scratches from their journey, as well as her encounter with the Ottawa.

As her clear blue eyes glanced up at him adoringly, and, as he beheld the look of gentleness and trust in her gaze, he knew true happiness.

Oh, to keep her with him. But how? After the many conversations concerning their future together, it always reduced down to the same objections. He had his duty, and she had hers.

In truth, even if there were no obstacles between them, there was still society's considerations that would make their life together difficult. Perhaps they two wouldn't bend to the wagging of tongues, and the dark lies which seemed to spread so easily.

But he knew from experience what the lies could do. Hadn't half-truths and slander driven him away from his own tribe?

True, he and Little Autumn had come together under unusual circumstances, and it was an indisputable truth that their love itself was an uncommon sight. However, it didn't necessarily follow that their love, once realized, shouldn't be sanctioned. Now that the deed was done and love had blossomed between them, there was no going back. Regardless of others' opinions, they were a twosome, united in love. They would always be in love.

Perhaps that was why they were lingering here so long. Because once they had recovered sufficiently—both physically and mentally—he would be obligated, due to his own pledge to her, to take her where she wished to go. Apparently, that was back to her society, back to servitude.

Regardless of their discussions concerning the crime of slavery, she seemed to be of a mind that she still owed her service.

He was no sachem, and he couldn't see into the future, but if there were one detail under his control, it was this: He could give her a love neither would ever forget. Forever, they would share this between them.

Bending down to her, he pressed a kiss against her lips, then another and another. Over and over they caressed, for there was no such thing as quenching their thirst of one another. When she swooned toward him, and, as he caught her and inhaled her fragile scent, it was a stimulant, more potent than a swig of rum. Ah, had he ever loved anyone more? He whispered, "Open your lips to me."

She did, and without pause, his tongue invaded her mouth. She tasted of pure femininity, both sweet and salty, and he explored her mouth with the promise of what was to come.

His hands caressed the contours of her back as she pressed in against him, and he discovered there were certain advantages to having mended her gown earlier this day. Now that he understood how the garment was sewn together, it took no great effort to unfasten the few hooks and pins holding it up. Within a few moments, he had her dress falling down around her ankles.

Still, they kissed. The feel of her curvy figure, now clothed in only her undergarments, sparked his heartbeat to race like liquid fire.

He took those remaining clothes off of her without incident. Then there she was, enchantingly beautiful and naked...and encircled within his arms.

Although they might have made love in the late afternoon, that was then—this was now. As the balmy fragrance of her femininity teased him, and, as the silvery beams of the moon emphasized every bend and arch of her figure, he realized he had never craved the consummation of his passion more than he did at this moment. It was almost his undoing. But he kept himself under control. Slowly, he told himself; one step at a time. In the end, he would give all that he had of himself to her, and fully.

"My love," she whispered against his lips, "again, I fear you wear too many clothes. You have an advantage over me. Thus far, I have never seen you naked. Is it safe enough, do you think, that I might look upon you, too?"

He groaned. What a request for a woman to ask a man. Did she know the impact that her words, though softly spoken, had over him? If not, she was very soon to become aware of their effect.

"Come." He led her back to the blanket he had placed beneath the maple tree. But there wasn't enough privacy there. Casting a quick glance around their surroundings, he said, "I think we will move this over by the trunk of the willow tree, where we will be hidden from any casual view. And there, I promise I'll take off my weapons, my breechcloth and my leggings. Even my moccasins. I give you my word of honor that we will lie together naked."

Still holding her hand, and more than aware of the feminine beauty within his grasp, he reached down to pick up the blanket.

Quickly, they stepped away from the maple tree and fled into the protection of the weeping willow. White Thunder spread the blanket close to the trunk so as to give them maximum privacy, even if it were only privacy from the night itself.

Once there, he turned toward her, let go of her hand and placed his rifle on the blanket, though she noted that he set it with care and within easy reach. Next, off came his tomahawk, his war ax, war club, and several of his knives, many of them hidden in the material that tied at his knees and waist.

She observed, "You are not only well-built with masculine brawn, sir, but you are well-armed, also."

"Is it different in English society?"

"No. Oftentimes, a man is judged by the condition of his pistols alone."

He nodded. "A man's duty is protection, and this can only be done by having a good arsenal of weapons close to hand. All he values is at risk if this is omitted."

Next, he removed his leggings, which tied to his belt, and from across his chest, the straps of his bags, powder horn and ammunition. Then, off came his belt, his shirt, his moccasins, and finally, his breechcloth.

As he let the breechcloth fall, he was well aware that he was ready for her, and there was no hiding the obvious influence she had on him. If the amorous state of his body alarmed her, she didn't show it. Indeed, she took the necessary few steps to bring her body next to him, throwing her arms around his neck and say, "You are as handsome as any Greek god."

The feel of his sex nestled against her stomach was exhilarating. As though she were layering on one sensation after another upon him, she twisted her body up close to his. Once again, he almost lost himself to her, right then and there.

He moaned and pressed his hips to her, cautioning himself again to move slowly, inch by inch. Since it was his intention to love her and give her a love she would never forget, he realized he had best proceed in a manner that would allow him constant stimulation but without him reaching the apex of their love too soon.

Perhaps, if he were very lucky, she would never again consider living her life without him. Truthfully, he held out little hope for that, but a man could always dream.

He brought her to her knees and followed her down, kneeling in front of her, where they swayed with one another as if they danced to a music of their own making. As though in collaboration, the south wind blew gently, the willowy branches of the tree their accompaniment.

She was ready, she was wet, and he realized there was much to be admired about his sex resting on her hot core. For a moment, he joined himself with her. It was not his intention to bring their lovemaking to a peak so soon. He only wished to arouse her passion to a fervent level.

However, he soon found there was danger here. He had to keep himself well-checked. Indeed, he was much too ready to realize the full extent of their lovemaking.

He pulled away from her and laid her into a position on her back, where he leaned over her from the side. From here, he showered her with kisses, as though she were a work in progress. But there was also a method to his endeavors. He was winding his way down to her breasts.

First, he nibbled at one softened mound, while his fingers massaged the other, then over to her other breast. Here, he lingered.

He nestled his head between her breasts. For a moment, he wished he could stay in this position a little longer. But he was completely aware that there were other treasures that awaited him.

Gradually, he slipped farther down her body, his kisses extending slowly downward, over her stomach, until he had at last arrived at the center of her femininity.

With a slight nudge, he pushed her legs apart. She was uncooperative, and, as she brought her legs together, she came up onto her elbows, where she gazed down at him.

"White Thunder?" she queried. "What is it you intend on doing?"

"To love you, my wife."

"There?"

He nodded. "There. But do not concern yourself. You will enjoy it."

She frowned at him. "Perhaps I might wash first."

"There is no need. You are perfect as you are."

She sighed, but at last she relaxed back, and, when he again parted her legs, she acquiesced.

He made love to her, showering her with the full extent of his admiration. At first she lay stiffly beneath him, but as his lips and tongue worked their exquisite magic over her, she settled down. After some moments, as if compelled, she began to move in synchronization with the rhythm of his tongue.

Her breathing caught, then quickened. Her muscles contracted around him. She spread her legs, as though she offered herself to him.

He accepted her gifts, while his tongue, his mouth, his lips, gave her as much erotic pleasure as he was able. He felt the fire building, felt the fiery pressure of her hips, knew she was close to release. She was breathing hard now, and her embarrassment seemed to have been a temporary affair. She moved, twisted and strained until suddenly, magnificently, she tripped over the edge of release.

It was a certain aphrodisiac for him. He might have eased off his lure over her, but instead of withdrawing, he gave her as much of himself as he could, even using his fingers to bring her to the ultimate pinnacle of pleasure.

She exploded with satisfaction, and he reveled in the sounds of her release. As her breathing returned to a more normal pace, he came up onto his knees over her, and from there, he gazed down at her with all the admiration in his heart. And it was plenty.

"White Thunder," she whispered. "I believe that when you said I would simply enjoy it, you belittled your case."

He laughed. "You liked it?"

"I think…that you speak in understatement. If there is a heaven on earth, I judge you have given it to me, if only for a moment."

"You flatter me, but your joy brings me delight, for it is my intention to make memories—as you asked me to do—that you will never forget…me…."

As he positioned himself between her thighs, she reached up to bring him in close to her. "I think you have accomplished your purpose, my love. But I have yet to see that you have met your pleasure."

He sighed. Oh, the complete thrill of her. "Then, you are ready for me?"

"Oh, yes. That, I am."

At long last, he joined himself with her in a passionate embrace. The warmth of her femininity surrounded him, and it occurred to him that this was home. Here, with this woman, was home.

Slowly, he began his dance with her. One thrust led to another, her hips meeting and encouraging his euphoria. He shifted position, because although they were sexually embraced, he wished for more. After coming up onto his knees before her and reaching for her legs, he brought them around his neck. It was a position that offered him a look into the essence of who she was, for there, within the depths of her eyes, was mirrored her spirit.

He caught her glance as he bore against her. He watched with something akin to awe as she once more rose to the heights of lovemaking. He stared as her movements became more and more intense, as she stretched toward her release. He smiled at her. She smiled back. They met, man to woman, spirit to spirit, and his love for her exploded until it consumed him.

Their struggle had become frantic. They strained against each other, they gave to each other. When he at last felt her muscles contract around him, he gave to her every bit of him.

As she toppled over the precipice of her passion, he met her with his own need, flooding her body with his seed. And as their pleasure met its climax, he felt himself become as one with her. As he did so, he was aware that he understood all that she was.

She was pure beauty; she was grace. Whatever the future might hold, he would love her. Always.

***

As he collapsed against her, Sarah wrapped her arms around his body. Tears stung the back of her eyes. *She loved him.* They were bound together, and it didn't matter if they were to be together physically for the rest of their lives or not. Always, she would love him.

Why did the two of them have to be from different worlds? She wanted all those things that women the world over wanted from the man they loved—to stay here with him, to be his woman, to have his children and create her life with him.

Who, in English society, would understand? Her friend, Marisa? Yes. But that was only one against many.

As she ran her hands through White Thunder's thick, dark hair, she knew pleasure, yet loss. They had pretended to be married, and, as he had warned her, she had fallen in love with him.

She'd wanted memories. She had them. But at this moment, all she desired was to be with him for the rest of her life, and even that seemed it might not be enough.

At least she had him with her now. She would savor every minute of their time together. Always.

Chapter Twenty-Three

They were moving fast, and they were traveling by night. Sarah had long ago learned to keep her stride even with White Thunder's. Although he sometimes surpassed her by a large margin, he was never so far ahead of her that she couldn't catch sight of him. Though he adjusted his pace to accommodate her, he still outdistanced her more times than not.

They weren't using the regular pathways through the woods. "Too many war parties on the move," White Thunder had said.

So once again, branches, brambles and burrs caught at her dress. White Thunder had warned her to ensure that nothing was left behind as evidence they had passed this way. It slowed her down, but she checked and rechecked those areas of the trail where her dress had snagged.

They were en route to the Mohawk village of Andagoran, which sat squarely on the Mohawk River. This was the place where Black Eagle resided. It was fortunate that White Thunder knew Black Eagle and was aware of what village he was from. Perhaps this was because they were both part of the Six Nations. Mayhap somewhere in their past, they or their fathers might have counseled together.

Whatever the reason for his knowledge, Sarah was simply glad they wouldn't be required to search from village to village in order to find Marisa and Black Eagle.

Sarah had at first disagreed with White Thunder on journeying to the Mohawk village, if only because her main concern was to warn Marisa against returning to Albany. In her mind, anxiety alone would have sent Marisa to Albany.

But White Thunder was convinced that if Black Eagle cared for Marisa as much as Sarah had believed, he would have taken her to his home. After several conversations on the topic, Sarah had recognized the logic of White Thunder's thoughts, and she had capitulated.

They were already two days on the move. Back in the Adirondack Mountains, they had spent another two days wrapped in each other's arms. Now and again, they had exerted themselves and had applied their talents to the task of drying meat for their journey. But all their work had only been done halfheartedly. It seemed they were both more engrossed with each other than they were with food. There had been no further reason to stay, even though the spot could be compared to a cathedral in the wilderness. Even they had come to realize that, eventually, they would have to rejoin society.

At present, although their quickened pace didn't allow Sarah to study or appreciate the woods, she noted that straight ahead of them there appeared to be a clearing in the trees. Was this it, then? Had they finally arrived at the village of Andagoran?

All at once, the clearing was upon them, and like two deer suddenly frightened, they burst out of the forest. No sooner had they cleared the trees and undergrowth than they were surrounded by large fields. Because it was late autumn, the fields lay barren. Here and there, a few black tree stumps dotted the fields, and occasionally, they passed an empty sentry post, which was a lean-to that had been raised high on poles. Outside of the remnants of these lean-tos, the fields were deserted.

Sarah pointed to one of the outposts. "What is that for?"

White Thunder glanced in its direction. "When the fields are ripening and the crops are growing, the women and children come to those posts to watch for crows and other birds. All must be scared away lest the animals eat all the food. These outposts can also be used to watch for the approach of an enemy. That's why they're built high."

"Oh, I see. And where's the village? All I can bear witness to here are fields."

White Thunder pointed toward a cliff set high and slightly back from the river.

"Ah," said Sarah. "I see it now."

Their pace had slowed but little, and though they no longer traveled at a run, their walking stride was almost as fast as their sprinting had been.

"Guards have spotted us. Come," he said, "we must sit and await their sentries."

"Truly? Why is that?"

"Because it is considered uncivil to enter a village without invitation. Even then, as soon as we are taken into a village, we'll be escorted to the Stranger's House, where we'll remain while the people are told we are there. In this way, the people will have the opportunity to prepare food for us to eat and bring us skins to sit on in order to see to our comfort. Only once we are well-fed and relaxed will we commence conversation. It is at that time we'll be able to ask them about Black Eagle and your friend."

"It sounds very hospitable. And truly, after all of our adventures in the woods, I will be happy to accept any goodwill shown me."

"I think you will find it pleasant."

In due time, two old men approached them. "Brother," one of the men addressed White Thunder. "I see by your clothes and by the tattoo on your arm that you are my Seneca brother. I see also by the state of your clothing that you have traveled a distance to visit us, and have, perhaps, encountered much hardship."

"This is so."

"Then, Brother, come let me escort you into our village, where I will take you to the Stranger's House, while I alert the people that we have a guest." He nodded toward Sarah. "Is the woman a captive?"

"She is not."

The old man nodded once again. "Come, I will show you to the Stranger's House."

***

The view was spectacular. The village was positioned on a cliff overlooking Mohawk fields and the Mohawk River, which flowed and gurgled over rocks and boulders in an ever- continuing cascade of white waves. In the distance, mountains and hills rose both east and west of them. Set against a blue sky, Andagoran was surrounded by breathtaking beauty.

The entrance to the town was unusual, consisting of overlapping logs instead of a gate. At this entrance was yet another outpost. Big, dangerous-looking men stood guard at the entry point. That each of them stared at her, not in greeting, but as though she were an enemy, was intimidating.

Sarah looked away, swallowing hard. She must have lagged behind, because as soon as she glanced forward, she noted that White Thunder was well in the lead. She hurried toward him, following on his heels. As she and White Thunder, along with the two older gentlemen, rounded the corner of the overlapping logs, the village came into view.

Like a scene gradually opening up before her, her first impression of the village was that of colors: the greens and browns of dried grasses; the browns of the trees and longhouses; the oranges, yellows and golds of produce set upon the ground; the multicolored prints of the people's clothing, although there were only a few people in sight. The village was not without beauty.

She heard male voices singing and a drumming noise in the background, but the sound was muffled, as though it were coming from within a building. The scent of smoke hung heavy in the air, as well as the fragrances of farm—rich beans, squash and husks. And somewhere, someone—or perhaps more than one someone—was cooking food.

The flavors filled the atmosphere, and were so numerous and

delicious-smelling that Sarah was reminded that her recent diet of dried meat and berries was not the only food to be had.

She and White Thunder were led to a longhouse, the one that their guide called the Stranger's House.

"Soon," said one of the two elderly men, "one of us or another will return with food and clothing, as well as furs to sit on. Eat, be at your ease, and make yourselves comfortable. After you are refreshed, we will smoke, and then we can begin conversation."

The door to the longhouse remained open, and this was good, for the shelter smelled of dirt, bark and the charred remains of a fire. It was also dark in the interior of the structure, if only because there were no windows. The only light, it seemed, came from smoke holes in the ceiling and from the open door.

A long corridor led from one end of the longhouse to the other. In the center were two hearths, evenly spaced apart. Sarah thought the longhouse might have been forty feet long, twenty to thirty feet wide, and perhaps twenty feet high. On each side of the structure were compartments, where she supposed a guest might berth if he or she were staying the night. Attached to several posts hung corncobs to dry, as well as gourds and other articles needed for cooking.

Both she and White Thunder had been seated only a few minutes when a woman entered, bearing a tray of food. Sarah saw corncobs heaped upon several plates, corn cakes, ribs, and a dish she learned was called succotash—a mixture of corn, beans and squash. To drink, there were bowls of water and a sweetener that might have been maple syrup. To a person from any culture—Indian, English or other—it looked like a feast.

Behind the woman followed another maid, who looked to be a younger version of the elder, and she was bearing furs to sit on, as well as a handful of clothes. There were shirts, a belt, moccasins, a navy-colored breechcloth and leggings for White Thunder. There was also a simple, trade-cloth dress in a light blue color, intricately embroidered with designs of pink, white and blue flowers. The sleeves were puffed at the shoulder and fell down to just below elbow-length. Accompanying the dress were leggings of the same color and embroidery work, as well as moccasins.

Hesitantly, the young girl placed the clothes beside Sarah. Sarah smiled at the girl and said, "Thank you," but the maid was shy, and, outside of a brief nod, did no more than look away.

The two women left, and White Thunder and Sarah were left alone with their meal.

"Are these clothes meant for us?" asked Sarah.

"They are."

"But they're beautiful. Are we to wear them only while we're here?"

"No, they are ours now."

"Ours? That's incredible. Do they expect them to be returned at some future date?"

"*Neh*, no. It is all part of being hospitable. All strangers are given food, furs to sleep on if they are tired, and in our case, clothes, because ours are obviously torn and in disrepair."

"But there must be something required in exchange for this. Money perhaps? Although I think it obvious we are not a man and woman of wealth."

"Nothing is expected in return except perhaps that you will remember that they treated you with kindness and respect when you were in need. It is the hope of the Six Nations and our belief that all people should honor each other in this manner. If it were so, wars would be less, I think."

"Yes. I believe you are right."

Silently, Sarah and White Thunder applied themselves to the food, and once their appetite was satiated, they dressed in their new clothing. What was amazing to Sarah's mind was how well the dress fit her. Even the moccasins were neither too big nor too little.

They were now well-dressed, well-fed, and comfortable. Soon, the two old men and an elderly woman entered. A pipe was offered to White Thunder, which he accepted, and while smoking, the conversation began.

"We see that you are from the Turtle Clan of the Seneca," began one of the elderly men in English. "Is this from whence you came?"

"Indeed, it is not," said White Thunder, whereupon he relayed who he was, where they had come from, and the circumstances surrounding Sarah's rescue.

The conversation continued, and when asked why he had come to their village, he answered with the truth—that they were seeking Black Eagle and his companion, Marisa, who was a friend of Sarah's.

The old man nodded, and, leaning toward the elderly woman, he addressed her in their own language. The woman rose and left the house, while the old man turned back to White Thunder. He said, again in English, and probably for Sarah's benefit, "We know of Black Eagle and his companion, who is now his bride. We call her *Ahweyoh*, Water Lily. Neither is here in the village at present, but I have sent for Black Eagle's mother and *Ahweyoh's* sister, that they can inform you where you might find them."

"*Nyah-wah*, thank you," replied White Thunder. "Do you know how long ago they were here?"

"It was only a moon ago and a day that *Ahweyoh* was captured—"

"Captured?" Sarah bent forward, but White Thunder placed a hand over hers, as if to caution her not to interrupt the speaker.

"*Nyoh*, yes, she was captured by her own people, the English," said the old man. "She did not wish to go, and there was some trouble, for the English assaulted *Ahweyoh's* sister, that they might steal *Ahweyoh*. Her husband, Black Eagle, was away on the hunt, but he has since returned and has gone to save her. But where that place is that he has gone, I know not. However, his mother might have knowledge of this, or if not, *Ahweyoh's* sister might know. Thus, I have asked for them both to come here."

Soon the two women arrived. However, neither of them spoke English, and Sarah had to wait to learn through White Thunder's translation that both women believed the English had taken Marisa to Albany. Although they couldn't be certain, Black Eagle had said this was where he would go to find her.

As soon as Sarah understood what had been related, she murmured to White Thunder, "It is as I feared. She went to Albany. We must go there at once."

White Thunder nodded. He thanked them all for their hospitality, for their kindness and for their information. But, he told them, both he and Sarah would need to leave as quickly as possible, since they possessed urgent information for Black Eagle and his bride.

"And where be your destination?" asked the older gentleman.

"Albany," replied White Thunder. "We go to Albany at once."

Chapter Twenty-Four

Evening shadows were already falling upon the forest when Sarah and White Thunder quit the relative safety of the Mohawk village to again travel through the woods.

Their pace was that of a light run, fast, lively, and quick, which kept Sarah warm, though the air temperature was cold and turning ever colder as evening crept in around them. Again, White Thunder took the lead, and for now, perhaps because they were still close to the Mohawk village, they traveled on the well-worn Iroquois Trail.

Because the trail was kept clean and clear of debris, Sarah's trek through the woods was easier, if only because she didn't have to worry about catching her dress on the brambles and burrs of the trees and bushes.

"Aren't you concerned about war parties?" Sarah asked White Thunder as they slowed their pace to a fast walk.

"Indeed, I am, but not this close to the Mohawk village, which is still patrolled by the warriors and sentries. Tomorrow, we will have to resume our more usual trek through the unkempt places in the woods, those paths where no one travels. But I think we are safe here, for now."

"How long will it take us to arrive at Albany?"

"A day and a bit. Perhaps more, depending on the state of the lesser-used paths."

"Have you ever considered utilizing the river instead of the trails through the woods? Couldn't we simply paddle a canoe to Albany? It would be faster."

"It would be faster if this land were not at war and we were not in danger of being exposed to all eyes on the water, friend or foe. *Neh,* no, better it is that we travel in the woods, concealed."

"Yes, I see. Of course."

They pushed onward through the evening and late into the night, not stopping until dawn was a dim light on the horizon. Only then did White Thunder quit and begin to set up camp.

"Will we arrive in Albany tomorrow?" Sarah asked as she and White Thunder sat beside one another in their temporary shelter, enjoying a meal of dried meat, corn cakes and berries.

"We will."

"I suppose we'll first need to visit the Rathburn estate to determine if Marisa is there and safe. But if not, I assume we'll have to discover where she might have gone and why she left."

White Thunder nodded. "It is a good plan. You forgot one important detail, though. We will go there only in the evening, when there are shadows that might hide us."

Sarah frowned. "Must we? I understand your concern and need for stealth, White Thunder. I, too, am anxious about Marisa's safety. But to have to wait until the evening… I lived there for fifteen years, and it seems to me I might go there and make inquiries without having to sneak about."

"There is every reason to conceal ourselves and wait until evening," White Thunder rebutted. "If we go there and confront Rathburn, and he sees you, he will keep you there as his servant."

"Yes, he could. He has that right by law."

"He does not have that right," protested White Thunder. "Not by any law. No man has the right to own and control another human being for his own profit. And if, as you say, there is a law that states he does, then that law is against the tenets of the Creator, thereby making it no law at all, but rather a crime."

Sarah sighed. "'Tis so logical sounding when you say it to me. However, that is not how the courts will look upon it, I fear. And I am subject to those courts."

"You are subject to no one."

"You are if you're a woman."

"Because you are a woman? What does your gender have to do with being subject to someone?"

"Because, a woman is always subordinate to her husband or to her father or to some other male relative."

"This is English law?"

"It is."

"It is a bad law. Is a woman a life form different from man that she should do nothing but serve him? Does she not hold the welfare of the clan and its prosperity in her hand? Without woman, man is nothing but a pitiful creature. Therefore, she deserves a place of honor, not a position of servitude. You come live with me with the Seneca," he went on to say. "The women in our tribe hold the balance of power, and they are no man's subject."

"Truly? 'Tis much about your society that we could learn, I think. But whether we agree or not, 'tis not the manner in which English law is conducted."

"Law or no law, subject or no subject, do you forget this is the same man whom you suspect killed your parents?"

"Yes, I have not forgotten, and perhaps if I had the finances necessary, I could fight him in the courts and win my freedom, although I still think those courts will favor a man of influence."

"Or you could stay here. Instead of putting yourself in a bad situation, I will go and learn what I can of your friend and then return to you here. Once we discover what has happened to her, or if she requires our help, we can assist her, follow her or go into the west, where we will still find freedom and a people who will not judge our marriage because of who we are."

"It sounds so good… But, do you forget your duty to Wild Mint?"

"I do not."

"Then, what is your plan as regards her?"

"I might have to return to Mohawk Territory from time to time to search for her killer, but I will no longer make this the reason I live. There is another now who is important to me...you. I would live in truth. I would be alive. And if I can, I would live with you."

Sarah glanced away from him. Oh, yes, it sounded so perfect. Except for one thing. "I fear, my love, that it—it wouldn't work. Eventually, you would begin to dislike me because I influenced you to turn your back on a pledge you made to another. And as for me, I would always be looking behind my back to see if someone were coming for me to take me back into servitude. Better it is that we confront our obligations here and now, rather than drag them with us elsewhere."

He sighed and was silent for so long Sarah began to wonder if he had drifted off to sleep. At last, he said, "You are right, and wise. We will both go to Albany, but as I said before, we will use stealth, and we will go in the evening, when the staring eyes of the English villagers will have a difficult time seeing us together. And if you are to go back there, you must first visit these courts that you talk of and tell them the truth of John Rathburn. Only then might I feel that you will be safe. Only then will I take you."

Sarah nodded. "Yes. This is good advice, and I will do it. You have been seeking to help me, and I appreciate your concern. Please bear with me, however, for first I must see about Marisa, and discover if she is safe or not. Then, with my mind at ease, I'll do as you say and visit the constable in Albany, where I will tell him what I suspect of John Rathburn."

"Can you not visit this constable first?"

"Yes, I could. Is this what you wish?"

"It is."

She sighed. "Then, so be it."

***

They camped in the wooden grove of trees on the north side of the Rathburn estate. White Thunder discovered a tree that would make a good base while they were in Albany. It was a tree much like the one Marisa had once described long ago. Perhaps it was the same, for it was a solid oak, and it appeared as though it had been hollowed out by a lightning strike. Here, in that section of the tree, they left their food, extra moccasins and a few other bags. Though Sarah would rather not have to sneak into a village where she had lived for so many years, she could readily understand White Thunder's hesitation. Besides, there would be no harm in visiting the constable before she had to confront John Rathburn.

With this explicit purpose in mind, she and White Thunder visited the offices of Constable Phelps, only to discover he was gone. They even traveled to his home, but when that still produced no result, Sarah insisted it was now time to find Marisa.

At present, both she and White Thunder were safely hidden by the bushes and trees of the woods surrounding the Rathburn estate. Their plan was simple. Sarah would try to solicit the cook's help. If anyone would know what had happened to Marisa, it might be Mrs. Stanton, the cook. Not only was her heart good, but she had always held sympathy for the girl Marisa had once been, and for the young lady she had become.

White Thunder seemed unusually alert, as though his attention were not only here, but scattered over the entirety of the estate, watching for trouble. At last, he indicated they should approach the kitchen door.

They crept up to it. Sarah knocked. White Thunder stepped to the side, out of the light.

No one answered. Sarah knocked again.

This time, they were in luck. A kitchen maid answered. Immediately, Sarah asked, "May I see Mrs. Stanton, please?"

The maid gave Sarah a confused, searching glance, trying to discern exactly who Sarah was.

To ease the kitchen maid's unspoken questions, Sarah said, "Cook knows me. I used to work here, too. My name is Sarah. Please, would you find Mrs. Stanton and tell her that Miss Sarah Strong is here to see her?"

The maid nodded, closed the door and turned away. Sarah waited, trying to frame in her mind what she would say.

Without delay, Mrs. Stanton appeared and opened the door a crack. She peeped out. "Miss Sarah? Be it true that ye are here?"

"'Tis I, Mrs. Stanton. And I have had quite the adventure getting here."

"Why, Miss Sarah, it *is* ye. Enter, please." She opened the entryway to its widest width.

"I have someone with me, Mrs. Stanton—an Indian. May we both come in?"

"Aye, child. I could've gathered from yer dress that ye've been rescued by the Indians. Miss Marisa was the same."

"Miss Marisa? Is she here, then?"

"Nay, Miss Sarah, she is not." Cook's glance skipped off her to stare at something at Sarah's back, and Sarah assumed White Thunder had stepped out of the shadows to stand behind her. "But she was here fer a time. Locked in her room, she was, while that evil man tried ta marry her off to an ugly old good- fer-nothin'. Now, get ye in here. Would ye like some stew? I've only jest made it."

"We would be delighted." Both Sarah and White Thunder entered into the inner sanctum of the kitchen. "But what happened? Did Marisa marry the man her uncle had selected for her and then leave?"

"I daresay not. She escaped, and in doin' so, she forced that evil man John Rathburn to write out his own confession. He did it, too, had little option."

"He had little option? Why? What happened?"

"He tried to kill her."

Sarah gasped and almost swooned. For a moment, she could hardly speak, and she grabbed hold of a chair to steady herself. "*Miss Marisa*?"

Cook nodded.

Eyes wide, Sarah asked, "But he didn't accomplish it?"

"Indeed not."

Sarah let out her breath. Gingerly, she laid a hand on Mrs. Stanton's arm. "How did it happen?"

"Him and that giant Thompson tried to kill her—happened in his study, it did. That Indian lad of hers saved her—kilt Thompson dead."

"Thompson is dead? Can't say that I'm sorry. But, Mrs. Stanton, what did Mr. Rathburn confess to?"

"I wouldn't be knowing exactly, but rumor has it he had business with a Dutch settlement, and he destroyed it and murdered all those people, and—"

Sarah's hold upon the chair was convulsive now, her fingers almost white from the strain.

"Miss Sarah, are ye all right?"

"Yes, I am fine. I think. But please, don't stop. Please continue with your story, Mrs. Stanton."

"Are ye certain?"

Sarah nodded.

"Though it happened long ago, long before ye came to live here, Miss Sarah, Miss Marisa forced John Rathburn's hand at a confession of that Dutch settlement."

"Then, he truly *was* responsible for my parents' deaths..." Sarah placed her hand over her heart.

"What was that?"

"It was nothing. Please, do continue."

"I be thinkin' that if he done it once, he done it many times. But I guess all we'll ever know about is that poor Dutch colony."

"Yes, you could be right."

"He has been under house arrest since he made that confession, and I daresay he'll remain that way until his trial, and 'tis Albany's own constable who be here with him tonight."

"The constable is here?"

"Aye, that he is."

"But Miss Marisa is not?"

"No. She left with that Indian gent who saved her."

"Is she truly well? She is not harmed?"

"The last time I saw the girl, she was well…and seemed content."

"And Thompson? You say Black Eagle killed him?"

"Aye, lass. He was kilt dead, right here in this very house. He tried to kill Miss Marisa. But her Indian lad took care of Mr. Thompson, and like ye, I say good riddance."

Sarah nodded. "He did deserve it, Mrs. Stanton. He tried to kill Miss Marisa while we were *en route* to New Hampshire. Had it not been for that same Indian gentleman, she might not have survived."

Mrs. Stanton nodded. "'Tis true, what ye say. But come now, ye look like ye've been through the gates of hell and back. Ye and yer friend are welcome here in me kitchen for as long as ye wish to stay. Both of ye, make yerselves at home. Sit. Eat."

Sarah did as ordered. Indeed, she didn't think she could have stood much longer, even had she tried. It was as though she had been delivered one shock after another.

True, she had suspected Rathburn was responsible for the deaths of her parents. But it was one matter to suspect it, another to be confronted with the reality of it.

Still, good manners came to her rescue, and with all the well-said thank-yous, Sarah picked up a spoon and forced herself to eat.

Noticing Mrs. Stanton was hovering near her, Sarah asked, "Did Miss Marisa say where she was going?"

"Nay, lass, she dinna."

"I suppose I'll have to see Mr. Rathburn so as to obtain his approval to go and find her, since she is still in my charge."

"Lass, dinna ye hear?"

"Hear what?"

"When Miss Marisa made that evil man write a confession sayin' how he'd destroyed that Dutch colony, she also forced him to confess that he had no right to keep you in servitude. Before she left, she not only told me so, she showed me the confession."

"She did what?" Sarah came up out of her chair.

"Yer free, lass. Yer free of him and all the evil he planned to force upon ye."

With a clatter, Sarah dropped her spoon onto the floor. She felt dumbfounded. She was free? As easy as that? There would be no court of law to pronounce her a fugitive from justice? No master to appease? It was over?

"You're certain, Mrs. Stanton?"

"I be certain. But don't ye take me own word fer it. Constable Phelps is here. Go and ask him yerself."

"I will. I will. But not tonight. For now, I need to try to assimilate all you've told me. For much has changed since I was last here."

"That, it has, lass. That, it has."

***

Since Marisa wasn't in residence at the Rathburn estate at present, and Sarah was apparently her own free person now, there seemed to be no reason for her and White Thunder to stay. Eventually, they bid Mrs. Stanton farewell and stepped back into the darkness of the night.

Sarah barely knew what to think, what to do with herself. For fifteen years, she had lived under the yoke of servitude. It had become a way of life for her. Now, what was she to do?

She must have asked the question aloud, for White Thunder suggested, "Stay with me. Become my wife."

"Yes," she said, although her attention felt scattered. She simply didn't know how to take it all in.

"Then, you will become my wife? Stay with me? Live with me?"

"Yes," said Sarah, this time with more passion. "I would like that very much."

White Thunder smiled at her before he bent to kiss her. As his lips touched hers, that old feeling of belonging to this man, heart and soul, returned, heartening her.

"I, too, would like that very much." Again, he kissed her before he turned away to take the lead. Happily, they made their way back into the woods.

Chapter Twenty-Five

"He is here."

It had to be Wild Mint who was speaking. She appeared before them in physical form, blocking their path, although Sarah had to admit that Wild Mint's body substance was weak and filmy, as though one could easily put their hand through her, if they dared.

Sarah stood still, momentarily stunned at Wild Mint's beauty. Even though the image was as sheer as a lace curtain, it was clear to see that Wild Mint's long black hair, which was slightly wavy, fell across each of her shoulders. Dark, almost black eyes stared at White Thunder with a look that seemed to be as serious as it was impish. It was apparent, also, that Wild Mint was dressed in all the esteem of a well-do-do Seneca lady, for her dress was impeccable. The material of her outfit was a light blue and appeared to be a rich cotton-looking creation. Full sleeves fell to her wrists, while a dark blue sash was tied around her tiny waist. White embroidered flowers decorated the triangular sash that fell over her shoulders, while a white embroidered purse fell from the tie at her waist. Her feet were nestled inside deer-hide moccasins, highly decorated with white embroidery. She was young, flirty and the look in her eye seemed to boast of a playful nature.

Could there be any wonder, then, thought Sarah, that White Thunder had been living with his loss of her for so long, and that it had held him fast beside her all these fifteen years.

Sarah barely knew what to think, what to do. She had never before had occasion to confront a person who was literally a ghost, and the experience was a little daunting. Perhaps the shock of seeing White

Mint, following so closely upon the surprise at being set free from servitude, might explain the cause. Whatever the reason, this shock was more than Sarah could easily assimilate.

Still, Sarah gazed upon Wild Mint as though Wild Mint were alive in body, and not little more than a sparkling, though vivid image. All at once, Wild Mint spoke again, and the timber of her words echoed the air around them, as though they came from a place that was hollow. However, she delivered her message in a clipped and fast fashion, and she spoke in English. "The man who killed me and our child, is here."

"Who is he?" asked White Thunder without pause, looking and acting as if seeing Wild Mint in this way were a most common and ordinary happening. It probably was for him, Sarah surmised.

"The man is the one known as John Rathburn. I would recognize him anywhere. It is he, the one you have been searching for all these years. I thank you, Little Autumn, for bringing my husband here, and I thank you for all you have done to help him. But understand, now, that until justice is done, he is and never has been yours to take. Now, he must fulfill his duty."

"But...but..." Sarah stumbled over her words as she tried to determine what to say. How could this be happening? Hadn't she and White Thunder been through trouble enough already?

Despite herself, Sarah despaired. There for a while, life had suddenly seemed to be so right, and her world had turned good. But it appeared there was a price for such happiness.

However, neither White Thunder, nor Wild Mint paid Sarah any heed.

"I will kill him," declared White Thunder, and no sooner had he said those words than he spun around toward Sarah, whereupon he took Sarah in his arms and pressed his forehead against hers. He whispered, "I must do this. I must fulfill the purpose for which I have endured these past fifteen years. I ask you please to understand."

"But—"

"It is possible I may not return to you in the flesh, but if that happens, never doubt that I love you more than I love life itself. Remember that. Always."

"No!" She gulped. "Please, you don't have to do this. If Mr. Rathburn is in the hands of the Constable, he will be put to justice without you having to do anything at all."

White Thunder shook his forehead against hers, even while he uttered, "And be branded a coward for the rest of my days?"

"No, it—"

"I must consider, too, my duty, which is and was a matter of honor long before we ever met. Understand, this is something I must do."

"I—"

He cut her off, then, with a kiss, his lips tugging at hers, and his tongue delving deeply into her mouth. It was as though he would show her all the force of his passion in this one single moment.

"I love you more than I have ever loved anyone," he uttered against her lips. "It will always be."

"No, I—"

"You once offered to help me find Wild Mint's killer."

"Yes, I—"

"I ask for your help now. I ask that you understand."

"I fear I don't know how to do as you ask." Tears gathered in her eyes, and her voice shook as she whispered, "Please don't require me to understand. Please…" Sarah stopped speaking as the weight of her own promise echoed within her mind. Swallowing hard on the bitterness in her heart, she at last murmured, "Yes, you are right. I will do what I can to help, even though—"

He placed his forefinger over her lips. "I must go."

She simply nodded. She couldn't speak.

It was only then that White Thunder turned to retrace his steps to the Rathburn residence.

Sarah hung her head, although suddenly and without reason, she felt an icy touch upon her shoulder, and looking around, she saw that Wild Mint's hand rested there.

"Come," said Wild Mint. "Together, we will help him."

Shaking off her temporary distress, Sarah said little more than, "Yes," before she turned around to follow White Thunder. Running hard to catch up with him, she saw that Wild Mint had outdistanced her easily, and that Wild Mint was floating closely upon White Thunder's heels.

Meanwhile, White Thunder was already striding back toward the residence and Cook's door.

He didn't even knock. He simply let himself in easily enough, for Cook hadn't locked the door. Sarah followed along on his steps, sprinting to catch up with him.

As soon as she could, she stopped him by plopping herself in front of his path. Arms held akimbo, she pleaded, "I will help you if I can, but before you do something that might cause your own demise, think about this. If you kill Rathburn now, and in cold blood, the society here will hang you. But if you let justice have its way, Rathburn will be the one hanging at the end of a rope instead of you. You would live to have the pleasure of seeing him dead without having to risk your own life."

White Thunder stopped perfectly still in front of her. "Do not do this. You have twice now tried to encourage me to be fainthearted. Is this what you want? To have me cower like a babe before evil?"

"No, but I would have you be alive, sir."

Mrs. Stanton came hurrying toward them, adding to the confusion. "Be there something wrong?"

"Yes, Mrs. Stanton, there is." Sarah turned to welcome the woman. "Apparently Mr. Rathburn killed another woman, long ago—fifteen years ago. It is this man that White Thunder has sworn to kill because he destroyed the woman, who was his wife, and their unborn babe."

"Oh, no."

"Oh, dear," moaned Sarah. While she and Mrs. Stanton had been carrying on their conversation, White Thunder, along with Wild Mint, had darted away and they were both almost out of sight. Quickly, Sarah spun around to trail after them, along with Mrs. Stanton.

As soon as they reached him, White Thunder turned toward Mrs. Stanton. "Which room is Rathburn in?"

Mrs. Stanton didn't answer. Indeed, Sarah watched as Mrs. Stanton flinched, backing away from White Thunder. When it became evident no answer would be forthcoming, White Thunder addressed Sarah.

"Do you know which room he is in?"

"I…I don't."

"*It is his study,*" said Wild Mint, her voice floating above them. "*This way.*"

Sarah took note that Mrs. Stanton didn't even bother to ask who had spoken. Perhaps Mrs. Stanton couldn't hear Wild Mint. It made sense, because when White Thunder paced forward to follow Wild Mint, with Sarah running after him, Mrs. Stanton still appeared to notice nothing out of the ordinary.

Again, White Thunder and Wild Mint left Sarah to follow in their wake. Sarah shook her head, fearing what was to come. As she turned to say a word to Mrs. Stanton, she suddenly noticed a thing that had escaped her notice. There on the wall, neatly nailed to it, was a musket.

At once, she took it down from its mounting, and a quick study of it revealed it to be primed and ready to shoot. Drawing a deep breath, she realized that this weapon might be the only method by which she could help White Thunder. At least she might provide him cover.

With the contraption firmly held within her grasp, she raced down the hallway. At last, she and Mrs. Stanton caught up to White Thunder, who stood outside the study. They halted when White Thunder indicated they should stop and remain perfectly quiet. Tiptoeing forward, Sarah listened at the door. "I tell ye, she forced me to write the confession at gunpoint."

"She is but a woman, John. Are you telling me you couldn't overpower a woman?"

"Ye saw the Indian with her. He would have kilt me, too, if I hadn't written it. As it was, ye saw that he kilt Thompson."

"It was self-defense, then," Constable Phelps said. "The first moment you stepped into my office, you said this was so, yourself. And it's in the confession."

There was a heavy pause. Somewhere in the room, a log from a fire crackled. "I'll give ye ten thousand pounds if ye'll look the other way."

"Are you trying to bribe me, John?"

"Nay, never a bribe. Just an exchange between businessmen."

Silence. Sarah couldn't hear Mr. Phelps's reply. But it mattered not at all. It seemed that White Thunder had learned enough.

Breaking through the door, he burst into the room with Sarah close on his heels. In a strong, yet steady voice, he said, "You, John Rathburn, I accuse you of being killing my wife, Wild Mint, and our babe."

Whatever Constable Phelps had been about to say came at once to a close. He gaped.

"Who is this Indian, and what is he doing in my home? Guards!"

Slowly, Rathburn backed toward his desk. But he had made a mistake. Clearly, he'd forgotten he was under house arrest. There were no guards to come to his defense.

White Thunder stepped closer to Rathburn. "Many seasons ago, you dressed yourself as a Huron Indian and invaded a Mohawk village of Onnontogen where my wife was visiting relatives. There, you raped her, cut her child from her belly, and then you killed her. For all these seasons, I have searched for you. I have dedicated my life to finding you to kill you. Now, you will die."

"Ye are insane!"

White Thunder held his position and commanded, "Why did you do it?"

"I don't have to answer any questions from a species so low as an Indian."

Both Sarah and Mrs. Stanton gasped.

White Thunder had planted his feet firmly, and he demanded, "Is that why you did it? You think Indians aren't human?"

"I *know* they are not human. What does it matter who lives and who dies? Indians feel nothing. Besides, they had built their home on me own land."

"The Indians who lived there had been on that land for hundreds of years."

"'Tis mine, I tell ye. I wanted it. 'Twas mine. A man must do whatever needs being done to make others fear him and drive the squatters off his land, now, doesn't he? Guards!"

Again, Rathburn seemed to have forgotten the circumstances of his arrest, and sadly, the only guards available were the constable and White Thunder, himself.

White Thunder brought up his weapon.

"Please, White Thunder. Can't you see he's insane?" pleaded Sarah.

"I am not insane!"

Sarah ignored him. "Don't you see, White Thunder? You must let the constable deal with John Rathburn and treat him for the murderer he is. You must understand that if you kill Rathburn now, there are too many witnesses. You will hang. But if you leave it for Mr. Phelps to do, Rathburn will be the one to hang, and you will live."

"Hush, girl!" shouted Rathburn. "It's not your place to talk."

Sarah continued to ignore him. "Please, White Thunder…"

It seemed that all she had accomplished with her entreaty was to give White Thunder time to take aim. But Rathburn was nothing if not clever, and he burst across the room and grabbed hold of Sarah, disarming her of her weapon with a fast, quick motion, and aimed the musket straight at White Thunder. With all the finesse of a bull, he grappled with Sarah until he had pulled her in front of him. Then, all at once, he placed the weapon against her side. "Go ahead and shoot, Indian! Yer shot will go through her to me. Do it, if ye dare."

Sarah struggled in Rathburn's hold, attempting to pull away from that firearm. She bit his arm, gaining a yelp from him. She stomped down hard on Rathburn's foot, but she was wearing only moccasins and the action did little damage beyond making him wince.

Taking aim at her head instead of her waist, Rathburn said, "Be still, girl."

But Sarah was no one's fool. If what Rathburn wanted was for her to be still, that was the last thing she would do. Wiggling again, she bit down on his hand and stomped once again on his foot. Still, he held her firm, with the gun pointed directly at her.

Meanwhile, White Thunder had lowered his weapon.

"If ye don't be still, girl, I promise ye, I'll kill ye along with the Indian."

Even as he said it, Rathburn suddenly changed his aim and pointed his pistol at White Thunder.

BOOM!

Rathburn's aim was quick and sure. Plus, it was a small room and they were standing at close range. However, he had shot without knowledge of Wild Mint's presence. Wild Mint sent a blast of air into the ball's path, sending it slightly off its course. The shot caught White Thunder in the shoulder instead of his head.

For an instant only, Rathburn settled Sarah to one side of him so he could check the accuracy of his shot.

Without warning, White Thunder jumped to the right flank of the room, his motion so swift it looked as if he were in two places at once. *BOOM!* The second shot seemed to come from midair.

There was an instant explosion, and smoke from the two weapons was everywhere. John Rathburn's hold on her tightened, then unexpectedly, he let her go. He fell to the floor. The smoke hadn't even cleared when White Thunder rushed toward her. Pushing Rathburn out of the way, he took her in his arms, and held her so tightly, Sarah's breath caught.

From out the corner of her eye, Sarah saw that Constable Phelps paced toward Rathburn's body, where he nudged it with the toe of his boot. "He's dead."

If White Thunder had heard what was said, he ignored it, and he asked, "Are you all right, Little Autumn?"

Was she all right? Looking down at herself, Sarah saw that she was covered in blood. Plus, the love of her life had just shot a man and would probably hang for it, even though it was in self-defense. And he'd asked if *she* was all right?

Sarah didn't answer. She simply shut her eyes and moaned.

"Miss Sarah. Miss Sarah." Mrs. Stanton came up behind her. "Did ye catch part of the shot, also?"

"No, Mrs. Stanton, I seem to be all right."

"Forgive me, Miss Sarah," Constable Phelps said. "I was aiming for Rathburn only, and it took me a great bit of courage to pull that trigger when he was holding you. But if I shot you too, I'll never forgive myself."

Sarah pushed herself out and away from White Thunder's embrace. Addressing the constable, she said, "You? You shot him?"

Constable Phelps nodded. "I'm afraid I did."

"Then, White Thunder didn't?"

"Check his rifle, Miss Sarah. I think you'll find 'tis cold."

She did as asked. But the musket was far from cold. In fact, it burned her hand, confirming that White Thunder had, indeed, been the one to shoot that deadly shot.

She glanced up at White Thunder, who was shaking his head. Then she looked at the constable, who winked at her. "I'm sorry you had to witness my firing upon your employer, Miss Sarah, but there seemed no other way. I couldn't very well let him kill you, could I? So sorry."

Sarah hardly knew what to say. Although her voice shook, she said, "There is no need to apologize. I…I thank you, Constable Phelps."

Constable Phelps bobbed his head once. "Now, if you don't mind me giving advice, I'd say the two of you should leave here, at once."

Sarah stepped completely out of White Thunder's embrace then, and, coming up to Constable Phelps, she placed a kiss on his cheek.

"We will do that, Mr. Phelps. As soon as I see to Mr. Thunder's wounds. Come," she addressed White Thunder. "Let's go to the kitchen, where I'm certain we'll find plenty of bandages."

White Thunder didn't object.

It was a pleasure to leave that room. It would be an even greater pleasure to leave the house entirely.

But where was Wild Mint? After sending that blast of air at the shot aimed at White Thunder, she had vanished.

It wasn't until they had entered the kitchen, and White Thunder was seated, that Sarah asked, "Where is Wild Mint?" She had picked up a cloth to wash White Thunder's wound, and had placed it against his arm before she continued to speak, saying, "It was she who deflected that musket ball. She saved your life, White Thunder."

"I know. I saw." He gazed away from Sarah as he said, "Perhaps doing as she did caused her great distress. Perhaps she is here with us in spirit even now, but lacks the energy to show herself. Whatever the cause, I will be forever in her gratitude."

"Then you do not believe that she might have already gone on her path to the next world?"

"No. I do not. Not yet. Her relief at Rathburn's death would cause her joy. Perhaps she is taking a moment to relish in her good fortune, and to try to envision what she will do now that fifteen years of hardship are behind her."

Sarah nodded. He didn't speak of his own relief at his sudden freedom from duty, but she was certain he was also experiencing a feeling of satisfaction at the discharge of his obligation. But she didn't mention it. Instead, she washed his wound until it was clean, binding it at last with a bandage.

She couldn't help but think, however, that a reign of malevolence had come to an end. Perhaps, she thought, the old adage that one cannot victimize one's fellows in this life without becoming himself the victim, was true.

One circumstance was apparent, however. In all the days and weeks to come, no one mourned the passing of John Rathburn. Alas, the opposite was true. Perhaps he had, after all, lied to and cheated too many people.

Chapter Twenty-Six

White Thunder and Sarah finally caught up with Black Eagle and Marisa in the Seneca town of Geneseo. Geneseo was another Iroquois village that had been built so the people could live their lives in the beauty of the hills and mountains. Indeed, the entire town had been recently relocated in an area the Iroquois called Neahga.

Sarah had been on edge when she had entered the town, wondering about her welcome, although she need not have worried. No sooner had she and White Thunder entered through the barricades than she was met by a red-headed beauty, who seemed intent on running headlong at her.

"Sarah! It's you! You are alive!"

Sarah laughed until she thought she might cry. "Yes, Marisa, it is I."

"I searched for you everywhere. I mourned your loss, my friend. But with the help of Black Eagle, I somehow thought you might still be alive. Oh, but you *are* alive. And you are here! I don't know when I have felt more happiness than I do now." She cried, and Sarah cried along with her. Indeed, they hugged and hugged until at last their men-folk had to pry them apart. At last, Marisa asked, "Did you know I was here?"

"I had hoped."

"But how?"

"It was my husband, White Thunder, who sent inquiries to all the Iroquois tribes, until at last runners found us to tell us where you were. Black Eagle had sent them to us."

"Is this true?" Marisa turned toward her husband, Black Eagle.

Black Eagle suddenly looked contrite.

"You knew they were coming here?"

"I had hoped," he answered his wife. "I didn't wish to tell you in case they did not arrive here. But it is why I have delayed leaving here to go farther West. If it were possible that the two of you could be reunited, I wished it to be."

"Oh, I thank you, my husband. I thank you. Sarah, I think I died a little when you let go of my hand that day at the falls."

"I, too," agreed Sarah. She sighed. "But it has turned out well, has it not? I was found, and by White Thunder."

"White Thunder, your husband. He is quite handsome now, isn't he? And he seems devoted to you. I'm happy for you."

"And I'm happy for you."

"Come," said White Thunder, "let us walk outside these walls where the two of you might converse in private. Black Eagle and I will watch over you to protect you, for there is some danger here."

"Yes," said both women in unison. Then they smiled at one another.

The two couples left the village, then, to walk through the deserted corn, bean and squash fields.

***

"What are you planning to do?" asked Marisa. "You know that Black Eagle and I would like for you to come west with us. There, I think we'll find comfort in the fact that no one will look with disfavor upon each of our unions. I would like nothing better than to have you come with us. Won't you, please?"

"I would love to do that," said Sarah.

"Oh, I'm so happy."

"But—"

"But?"

"I have discovered that a certain friend of mine—you— ensured that all the rights of her parents' property was transferred to her. In truth, Marisa, White Thunder and I have thought we might like to settle there. It's away from all the other farms—at least it is for now. And we've talked about taking a chance at working the land."

"Oh, yes, of course. I had forgotten. But you know there may come a time when there are too many settlements that surround you, too many prying eyes, too many wagging tongues that carry too many lies. If that ever happens, you must come see us. There will always be a place for you with us."

Tears stung the back of Sarah's eyes, and apparently, Marisa felt much the same, for her eyes were shining as she tried to blink away the wetness there.

"I will miss you, my friend," said Marisa. "My life is good because of you. I will never forget you, in this life or any other. Always, there will be a place for you in my life.

Sarah cried openly now. "And I will miss you, Marisa. Watching you leave will tear at me. But I think I should try to farm the land of my parents. I believe it is what they would have liked. I do have something for you."

"You do?"

"Yes, I do. I do believe that it is important, for it was given to me with strict instructions to give it to you as soon as I had found you." Reaching into her bag, Sarah pulled out a letter, which had been given to her by Constable Phelps.

Marisa frowned. "For me?"

"Yes."

"What is it?" Marisa asked as she broke the seal to read the letter. "Oh, my. Did you know this?"

"I fear I did."

"And you didn't tell me at once?"

"There has been little time to do so. Also, I wanted you to read it for yourself. No one came forward to claim the estate. Therefore, Constable Phelps has ruled that John Rathburn's estate shall become yours."

Marisa wiped a hand over her forehead. "But...I don't want it.

Albany is not a place where Black Eagle and I will thrive. I'm sure you understand why that is."

"That, I do."

Marisa shook her head as she passed a hand over her forehead. "But I think I know someone who would do the property good."

"You do?"

"Yes. Mrs. Stanton, our old cook. Did you know that despite John Rathburn, she helped me?"

"She came to my aid, also."

"Yes. I think I will convey the property to her, or at least I will try to. Sarah, if I write a note to Constable Phelps, would it be too out of the way for you to deliver it to him?"

"It will be mine and White Thunder's pleasure to take it to him in your stead."

Marisa grinned, and Sarah smiled back at her.

"Always," said Sarah, "we will be friends. John Rathburn might have been insane, as well as a scoundrel and all sorts of other bad things, but he did one good deed in his life."

"And what is that?"

"He brought us together."

They fell together and hugged. Tears flowed openly and with joy down both of their cheeks.

"I will always love you, Marisa. I will always treasure our friendship."

"And I, yours. Be well, my friend. Flourish. Do well. But most of all, have many children."

All at once, both women laughed.

***

"Are you certain you'll be happy settling on our farm in Pennsylvania?"

"Wherever you are, my wife, I will be delighted and pleased to be there with you," said White Thunder. "Besides, if we decide we like it very little, we can always pick up our roots and join your friend."

White Thunder and Sarah had packed their belongings that very morning and had left the Seneca town of Geneseo, heading back east. Meanwhile, Black Eagle and Marisa had begun their journey onward into the west. Parting had been difficult for the two women, but at last their men had pulled them apart, and, saying their goodbyes, each couple had set off on their own separate paths.

"Yes, if we don't like it, we can always go farther west. But if we could stay for a while on the land that my parents originally purchased, I think it would honor them."

"And so it will be. I love you so much that I cannot envision my life without you. Always will we love, I think. And so long as I live, I give you all of me that there is to give."

"I love you," Sarah said. "But White Thunder, do you know what has happened to Wild Mint? I wish I could say more to her. I wish to give her my thanks for her saving your life. If she has not gone on yet to whatever fate lies before her, I wish I could speak to her to help her along her journey."

"And so you may." The voice was feminine, was hollow, as if the words came from a distance.

"Wild Mint!"

"It is I."

"Oh, thank you, Wild Mint. Thank you for what you did for White Thunder, and for me."

Wild Mint nodded. "It was my pleasure to help. And now, if you might allow it, I would have a word with my husband."

"Yes." Sarah nodded, and turning her back on the two of them, she paced away.

"Please stay," called Wild Mint before Sarah had gone very far. "You are a part of this, for he is your husband, also."

Sarah turned around. "You are certain?"

"Yes," said Wild Mint. "We must counsel together. I thank you, my husband, for never leaving me. I thank you for loving me all these years and for being true to our purpose." She took a step toward White Thunder. "Always, I will love you. Always, I will love you...and Little Autumn."

White Thunder's voice shook, as he said, "And I love you."

"Thank you. I must go now. Always, the two of you will love. Always, I will remember your kindness, and wish you joy."

White Thunder reached out to take her hand in his. "I will miss you."

"And I, you."

He bent toward her, then, to place a kiss upon her cold, cold lips.

"And now I must go," whispered Wild Mint, her voice fading into the gentle breeze in the air. "Thank you, White Thunder. Thank you, Little Autumn. *Dah-neh hah.* It is finished."

Historical Note

I hope you will bear with me as I take literary license with a bit of history. The Code of Handsome Lake didn't originate until close to the end of the 1700s, which would place it around forty years after our story. Handsome Lake (1735- 1815) was a religious prophet who was born in the town of Caughnawaga on the Genesee River.

When I read of his story of how the white race came to America, a part of Handsome Lake's prophesy, I found it so engaging that I knew it would probably find its way into the story—which, of course, it did.

My thanks to Arthur C. Parker, author of *The Code of Handsome Lake, the Seneca Prophet*, and to Fintan O'Toole, author of *White Savage*, for first bringing my attention to this legend.

Karen Kay writing as Gen Bailey

Remarks from Benjamin Franklin Regarding the American Indian

"Savages we call them, because their Manners differ from ours, which we think the Perfection of Civility. They think the same of theirs."

"The Indian Men when young are Hunters and Warriors; when old, Counsellors; for all their Government is by Counsel of the Sages; there is no Force, there are no Prisons, no Officers to compel Obedience, or inflict Punishment. Hence they generally study Oratory; the best Speaker having the most Influence. The Indian Women till the Ground, dress the Food, nurse and bring up the Children, & preserve & hand down to Posterity the Memory of public Transactions. These Employments of Men and Women are accounted natural & honorable. Having few artificial Wants, they have abundance of Leisure for Improvement by Conversation. Our laborious Manner of Life compar'd with theirs, they esteem slavish & base; and the Learning on which we value ourselves, they regard as frivolous & useless..."

"Having frequent Occasions to hold public Councils, they have acquired great Order and Decency in conducting them. The old Men sit in the foremost Ranks, the Warriors in the next, and the Women & Children in the hindmost. The Business of the Women is to take exact Notice of what passes, imprint it in their Memories, for they have no Writing, and communicate it to their Children. They are the Records of the Councils, and they preserve Traditions of the Stipulations in Treaties 100 Years back, which when we compare with our Writings we always find exact. He that would speak rises. The rest observe a profound Silence. When he has finish'd and sits down; they leave him 5 or 6 Minutes to recollect, that if he has omitted any thing he intended to say, or has any thing to add, he may rise again and deliver it. To interrupt another, even in common Conversation, is reckon'd highly indecent. How different this is, from the Conduct of a polite British House of Commons where scarce every person without some confusion, that makes the Speaker hoarse in calling to Order and how different from the Mode of Conversation in many polite Companies of Europe, where if you do not deliver your Sentence with great Rapidity, you are cut off in the middle of it by the Impatients Loquacity of those you converse with, and never suffer'd to finish it—"

"When any of them come into our Towns, our People are apt to crowd round them, gaze upon them, & incommode them where they desire to be private; this they esteem great Rudeness, the Effect of & Want of Instruction in the Rules of Civility & good Manners. We have, say they, as much Curiosity as you, and when you come into our Towns, we wish for Opportunities of looking at you; but for this purpose we hide our Selves behind Bushes where you are to pass, and never intrude ourselves into your Company—"

"Their Manner of entering one another's villages has likewise its Rules. It is reckon'd uncivil in travelling Strangers to enter a Village abruptly, without giving Notice of their Approach. Therefore as soon as they arrive within Hearing, they stop & hollow, remaining there till invited to enter. Two old Men usually come out to them, and lead them in. There is in every Village a vacant Dwelling called the Strangers House. Here they are plac'd, while the old Men go round from Hut to Hut, acquainting the Inhabitants that Strangers are arriv'd who are probably hungry & weary; and every one sends them what he can spare of Victuals & Skins to repose on. When the Strangers are refresh'd, Pipes & Tobacco are brought, and then, but not before, Conversation begins with Enquiries who they are, whither bound, what News, &c, and it usually ends with Offers of Service if the Strangers have occasions of Guides or any Necessaries for continuing their Journey and nothing is exacted for the Entertainment."

Benjamin Franklin, 1782—1783

Source: www.wampumchronicles.com/benfranklin.html

About the Author

Multi-published author, Karen Kay, has been praised by reviewers and fans alike for bringing the Wild West alive for her readers.

Karen Kay, whose great grandmother was a Choctaw Indian, is honored to be able to write about a way of life so dear to her heart, the American Indian culture.

"With the power of romance, I hope to bring about an awareness of the American Indian's concept of honor, and what it meant to live as free men and free women. There are some things that should never be forgotten."

Find Karen Kay online at www.novels-by-karenkay.com

Stay in touch with Karen Kay by signing up for her newsletter;

https://signup.ymlp.com/xgbqjbebgmgj

Brave Wolf and the Lady

He saved her life, then stole her heart….

To escape an arranged marriage, Mia Carlson, daughter of a U.S. senator, instead elopes with the man she loves. As they are escaping from her Virginia home, heading west, their wagon train is brutally attacked, leaving Mia alone and in grave danger. Rescue comes from a most unlikely source, a passing Lakota scouting party, led by the darkly handsome Indian, Brave Wolf.

Although Brave Wolf has consented to guide Mia to the nearest trading post, he holds himself apart from her, for his commitments lie elsewhere. But long days on the trail lead to a deep connection with the red-haired beauty. Yet, he can't stop wondering why death and danger stalk this beautiful woman, forcing him to rescue her time and again. Who is doing this, and why?

One thing is clear, however: Amid the flurry of dodging assassin bullets, Brave Wolf and Mia come into possession of a powerful love. But is it all for naught? Will Brave Wolf's obligations and Mia's secret enemy from the past finally succeed in the sinister plot to destroy their love forever?

Warning: Sensuous romance and cameo appearances of Tahiska and Kristina from the book, ***Lakota Surrender****, might cause a happily-ever-after to warm your heart.*

ISBN 978-1-09079-0-439

Made in the USA
San Bernardino, CA
12 August 2020